The Sixth Sense

Lawrence W. Gold, M.D.

A Grass Valley Publishing Production
To order additional copies of this book, e-mail
grassvalleypublishing@gmail.com

Cover Art©2012 by Dawne Dominique

ISBN-13: 978-1478267607
ISBN-10: 1478267607
First print edition July 2012

Printed in the United States of America

Dedication

To my wife, Dorlis. Her dedication and support made this work possible.

Acknowledgments

Donna Eastman of Parkeast Literary Agency who helped make this possible.

Joseph Barron, a true renaissance man, my writing buddy. Gone but not forgotten.

Writers groups on both coasts. WOW in Palm Coast, Florida and Sierra Writers Fiction Critique Group in Grass Valley, CA

I want all my senses engaged. Let me absorb the world's variety and uniqueness.

Maya Angelo

Nothing is understood, which was not first perceived by some of the senses.

John Locke

The first condition of understanding a foreign country is to smell it.

Rudyard Kipling

Chapter One

I stared through the bay window as the sun's first rays broke over the east bay hills, scattering the early morning San Francisco haze. I turned and slid my arm under Lois's waist. Her soft breathing hesitated as her body struggled against awakening and then resumed its regular rhythm. Awake or not, she raised her hips to accept my arm, and a moment later rolled over to face me. Lois sensed my mind and other body parts and whispered. "Quiet, Arnie. Please, they're still asleep."The sun angled through pale-yellow curtains and streaked across the foot of our bed. We embraced and all extraneous thoughts surrendered to the intense physical desire of lovers still hungry for each other after twelve years of marriage.

We collapsed in sweaty exhaustion just in time.

The hall toilet flushed, and a moment later tiny feet padded toward our bedroom and Amy, our five-year-old daughter, jumped into bed.

She squirmed her way between us and Lois pulled her close. "Hi, sweetie."

Thirty seconds later, she was asleep.

I turned to the nightstand clock that read 6:10. I leaned past my sleeping daughter to kiss

Lois. "It's about that time. I have a busy morning and better get an early start on hospital rounds."

"Don't make too much noise. If I'm lucky, Becky will sleep for another thirty minutes. Disturbing that girl is like stepping on a nest of fire ants. Give me a few moments before I fuss with her about getting ready for school."

By the time I finished my shower and shaved, both girls were at the kitchen table with their bowls of sugarcoated cereal — our dentist forever grateful.

I kissed my wife and daughters goodbye and drove through light morning ground fog to my Berkeley office near Brier Hospital. I parked in my space with the sign, "Arnold Roth, M.D., Family Practice." I grabbed the morning newspaper and entered the converted Victorian we'd purchased. I shared it with a child psychiatrist and an optician. I threw the paper on my desk, grabbed my white coat and stethoscope, and left for morning rounds.

Brier Hospital grew from the turn of the century Brier Hills Convalescent Home to a private, not for profit community hospital. It sat in the hills, west of the University of California, Berkeley.

For three weeks, the hospital was running near 100 percent occupancy due to an epidemic of viral encephalitis and influenza. Too many patients and not enough beds put the hospital in emergency mode, canceling elective surgery, and admitting only the sickest patients.

I had two patients with encephalitis. One, Henry Cass, had suddenly developed severe headaches after what initially looked like the flu. Henry's recovering. The other, Samantha Goldstein, was another story. The carefree, healthy twenty-year-old Berkeley student hovered near death in a deep coma. I watched her rapid deterioration over thirty-six hours — a child carried out to sea on a cruel riptide, my worst nightmare.

I resisted the elevator's seduction. Its open portals beckoned, but I heeded my own advice for exercise by climbing five flights and then walked the long corridor toward the ICU. The entire west wall was floor-to-ceiling glass windows with an imposing view of Berkeley, the Oakland-San Francisco Bay Bridge, and the Golden Gate to the northwest. The city glowed orange in the distance, the last wisp of fog yielding to the bright morning sunshine.

I approached the ICU's door labeled, AUTHORIZED PERSONNEL ONLY, and pushed the call button.

"Can I help you?" the ward clerk's voice crackled over the loudspeaker.

"It's Dr. Roth."

"Good morning, Arnie. Come on in," she crooned as the door lock clicked open.

The ICU's ambiance was unique. I felt it each time I entered. When peaceful, it had the serenity of a chapel. When turbulent, the staff struggled to preserve the aura of calm control. The unit was silent this morning except for a single ventilator clicking and whirring next to bed five across from the nursing station. Several nurses, having completed the night shift were coming out of morning report while the 7 a.m. to 3 p.m. shift prepared for the day ahead.

The Intensive care unit had twelve beds in the open and three isolation rooms for patients with infectious diseases or for those who needed protection from the bacterial sewer that was our world. We called that reverse isolation. Each open-space bed was on the unit's periphery and paralleled large windows facing to the west and north.

Jack Byrnes was ICU's director. He sat at the nurse's station talking with his wife Beth, the unit's Director of Nursing. Years of working with them as colleagues had moved us from a professional relationship to a close personal one — we were good friends.

Jack and I were polar opposites on medicine's spectrum. After entering practice, I discovered that every physician griped about their work and envied the lives of other practitioners. It was a professional grass-is-greener affliction.

Jack smiled and taunted me. "I don't know how you primary care docs do it, Arnie. How do you keep up with every advance that comes our way in medicine?"

"Obviously, I don't. I do what I can and hopefully I'll know when and who to call for help."

"Sometimes I wish I'd chosen primary care. My life would be simpler. I can't keep up with the information overflow in intensive care medicine."

"Not to worry, Jack. By definition, a specialist is one who knows more and more about less and less. Eventually you won't have to know a thing."

He laughed. "Right. I think I'm there already."

"In my senior year, I had decided to be a specialist. Then I came to my senses and chose family practice. Not an easy decision since General Practitioner had become only slightly more reputable than chiropractor or podiatrist."

"Not anymore," Jack said. "The worm (pardon the expression) has turned and you guys have the power. You decide what tests to order, what specialists your patients see, and which medications to dispense. You've ascended into the highest echelons of medicine's priesthood."

"Right. When they pay me more, I'll believe it."

"Sooner or later, that will change."

"Not in my lifetime. The label, 'Family Practitioner' rather than GP, is more than spin, but most patients don't understand. They still insist on seeing specialists and requesting procedures they don't need. That hardly puts Family Practitioners in the stratosphere of prestige. Insurers embrace us as gatekeepers, but I hate that phrase and its meaning. It puts me between my patients and the medical care they need, costly or not. According to insurers,

I should be a team player. I should go for the greater good, but that only works if you don't have a conscience."

Jack and Beth made an attractive couple. Jack was in his late thirties and about six one, three inches shorter than I am, but he didn't have my husky build. Everyone loved Beth at first sight. She had a beautiful smile and a charismatic personality.

Jack hugged his wife. "I can never get enough of this woman."

Beth smiled and caressed Jack's cheek. "He's good, isn't he? Jack knows how to keep a woman happy." She turned to me. "Good morning, Arnie. How are Lois and the girls?"

"Everyone's fine. I'm finally getting used to living in a woman's world."

I glanced across the room at Samantha Goldstein. "Have you seen her this morning?"

"I just examined her. It's bad. She's still unresponsive."

We gave her Acyclovir, an antiviral medication, though we weren't sure this would attack the virus causing her encephalitis. We hadn't identified the specific virus, and that left us with general supportive measures and cortisone to lower the pressure on her brain. We both understood that this was a pathetic counterattack on a virulent virus intent on destroying Samantha's central nervous system.

When I approached the isolation room, Richard and Marion Goldstein, Samantha's parents, were in gowns and gloves. They were sitting at her bedside. Pleading, tear-filled eyes mirrored their desperation.

I had struggled under the burden of Samantha Goldstein's tragedy each day since I admitted her. Death was death, and tragedy was tragedy, but for me, certain cases were most heartbreaking. Samantha, so young and with so much life ahead, was my toughest case.

When I was a medical student, I spent the summer between my second and third years with Simon Katz, a pediatric hematologist.

Each day, we made rounds at several hospitals. In those days, childhood malignancies and leukemias were uniformly fatal. I still recoil from the image of Simon, a gentle, caring man, struggling to find a way to speak the unspeakable to parent after parent—that their child was going to die. I don't know how he did it. I couldn't.

Life cut short at any age was tragic, but even now, after years in practice, I still cringed at the thought of death in the young. When you lived each day with death and disease and remained healthy, it was easy to believe that it couldn't happen to you or to your loved ones. Yet each time I saw a child die, I knew that these beliefs were nothing but dangerous illusions stretched on the fragile threads of certainty.

Richard turned to me. "What's happening, Arnie?"

"I talked with Dr. Byrnes. Nothing has changed."

I spent ten minutes examining Samantha. The ventilator initiated each breath, an ominous sign as it said that her severely damaged brain was unable to trigger breathing. I performed a detailed neurological examination that revealed abnormal reflexes, but no response to painful stimuli.

Marion grasped Richard's hands. "Tell us what you think."

I signaled them to follow me into the anteroom.

Talking to someone whose face was hidden behind a mask was like concealing a fine work of art, wholly unsatisfying. Speaking in front of a patient thought to be comatose could prove embarrassing when they awakened and recalled details of your bedside conversation.

We pulled off our masks and surgical caps.

Why did I study their faces when I already understood what they were feeling? I've seen about every reaction to medical tragedy from helplessness to waning hope to anger, but impassivity and denial in the last hours of their daughter's life was the least intuitive response and left me uneasy.

Marion stared into my eyes and whispered. "You must do something."

"I can't begin to tell you how sorry I am. We're doing everything possible, but this is an aggressive virus and it's already done extensive damage."

"Extensive damage?" Marion cried collapsing in tears into Richard's arms.

How stupid of me to use such careless, crushing words, I thought.

I hated the next step, but it was unavoidable. I would not allow any oblique phrase to obscure my meaning. "If we don't see signs of improvement soon, we'll need to reassess what we're doing and whether we should continue treatment."

Marion stiffened, and then reeled backward as if someone had slapped her. "What are you talking about? Stopping treatment! Are you out of your mind?"

Today wasn't the time to fight this battle. It would come soon enough. At least I had fired the first volley.

"Nobody's recommending stopping anything, but if Samantha doesn't improve, we should consider what she would want."

"What Samantha would want?" Richard asked. "Do you really think a twenty-year-old has thought that through?"

I softened my voice. "In light of events like the Terri Schiavo case, and the publicity surrounding end of life issues, everybody's been forced to think about that."

Jack Byrnes had told me of a similar case at Brier Hospital. He'd consulted for a plastic surgeon who'd managed to perforate a woman's abdomen during a routine liposuction. For days, the surgeon refused to diagnose the perforation and the subsequent peritonitis, as if denial would make it go away. The patient was in shock when they finally admitted her to ICU. She never regained consciousness and within five days, it became clear that she never would. Her clinical examination and all tests including CT head scans and electroencephalograms, demonstrated brain death.

"I thought we had covered all bases," Jack said. "We had the patient's signed Advanced Directive for Health Care that gave her husband the responsibility to decide what treatment was appropriate and when support should cease. As we got into a discussion about terminating life support, her estranged daughter arrived from out of town and demanded that we do everything."

I shook my head. "How could she force a decision contrary to her mother's wishes and the legal document empowering her father to decide?"

"It's like a lawsuit, Arnie. You can sue although you don't have a chance in hell of prevailing. Everybody, especially hospitals, are risk averse and will try anything to avoid going to court even when they know they'll win. If that wasn't bad enough, the daughter went to the media and to the Evangelical community's fanatic fringe. For a while, we had a mini Terri Schiavo case."

"What happened?"

"I tried my best to convince the daughter that she was doing her mother a disservice, but she refused to hear me. The hospital, smarting from the daily demonstrations at its door and all the media coverage, went into full defensive mode and stopped us from terminating care. Fortunately, nature was more sensible than we were, and had the good grace to stop the patient's heart and resist our obscene and futile efforts to resuscitate her."

"I can understand and forgive the daughter, Jack, and the hospital, but the outsiders piss me off. To paraphrase John Galsworthy — the idealistic beliefs of these meddlers increases in direct proportion to their own distance from the problem."

Jack looked up at me. "I like the Latin proverb best: beware the tyranny of the minority. Those watchwords are more significant today than ever."

Chapter Two

I returned to my office at 8:30, poured coffee, and pushed aside stacks of charts to make room for the morning paper.

My office would have consisted of a large desk and bookcases if they'd left the decorating to me. It's a good thing I had Lois. She knew that understatement and practicality suited me best. I had a large teak desk, bookcases and she'd added a soft leather sofa, end tables, and comfortable upholstered chairs. I'd insisted on a credenza behind my desk chair, but Lois objected. "You're going to stack things on it. It'll look awful."

Of course, she was right. I could tell by her groans each time she entered my office and saw piles of charts, journals, and magazines behind me.

She had my framed diplomas on one wall and several Ken Hornbrook landscape photographs on the other.

Each time I saw Arnie Roth, M.D. Family Practice at the entrance to my office, it amazed me that things had turned out so well. My father died when I was young, and I grew up in the loving embrace of three women, my mother, and two older sisters. I'd worked hard for everything in my life. My sisters were academic stars, straight A's, but I didn't read until the third grade and often confused words and spelling. Teachers and counselors whispered about my learning disability. I felt relieved when I first heard the term dyslexia, a word that sounded a hell of a lot better than retarded.

Despite my "handicap" and the "well-meaning advice" that medicine was a stretch for me, I graduated from St. Georges University School of Medicine on the island of Grenada with honors, aced the foreign medical graduate exam, and completed my training in family medicine at UC Medical Center in San Francisco. I received high praise for my skills and dedication, but I couldn't escape the stigma of having attended a foreign medical school — permanent, second-class citizenship.

Beverly Ramirez, my office nurse, dropped a large bundle of mail into my inbox. "Good morning, Arnie."

Beverly was a second-generation US citizen born to Mexican parents. They had been among the first to benefit from the illegal alien amnesty program in 1985. Her dark hair and eyes reflected the family's indigenous background. The entire family had worked hard. They owned three cars, their own homes, and all were U.S. citizens. Two brothers were doctors, three were nurses, and one was a professor of computer science at Cal State, Hayward.

Beverly had been with me from day one. With Lois, she helped create and grow the practice.

She was smart, reliable, and had a wonderful sense of humor that made our days in the office enjoyable, even in the face of all the annoying problems that came with running a medical practice. Her personality and her fluent Spanish attracted many Spanish-speaking patients.

I suggested early on that she speak with me only in Spanish, as part of my latest attempt to conquer the language. When she remembered to whom she was talking, we communicated well, and my Spanish improved dramatically. When she forgot that I was, after all, a gringo, and flooded my ears with lightning Spanish, I shook my head in frustration.

Although I was far from fluent, Beverly and many of our Spanish-speaking patients appreciated the attempt and the respect for them my attempts implied.

I eyed the stack in my inbox. "Anything interesting?"

"The usual, laboratory and x-ray reports, discharge summaries, and consultation notes. I got rid of the insurance and investment offers, and the free drug company trips to Paris. I know you'd never leave us for Paris."

"Paris. You know I'd sell my soul for Paris."

She smiled and pointed to the phone. "That flashing line is for you."

"Your smile is making me nervous, Bev. Who is it?"

"It's your favorite HMO medical director, Charles Kingston."

"Terrific. What does he want this time?"

Beverly shrugged her shoulders and left.

Charlie's voice boomed. "You did it again. Why in hell send Ernie Clark to Stanford when we have our own cancer specialists."

"Good morning to you, Charlie. I love hearing your voice."

"I'm sorry, Arnie. This is one part of my job I hate."

"Find another job."

"Once they replace me, you'll be telling everyone that working with Charlie Kingston... those were the good-ole-days."

"If you were my patient, Charlie and you had Ernie Clark's problem, I'd send you to Stanford where they've treated hundreds of malignancies like yours and have access to experimental treatments not available elsewhere."

"*Wellcare* can't afford it, and as you know, we don't have a contract with Stanford."

"So you wouldn't go?"

"Sure I'd go, but I'd pay for it myself."

"You can afford it, Charlie, but what about the poor schmuck who can't?"

"Life's unfair, Arnie. Don't blame me or *Wellcare* for that, too."

"We're never going to agree. I can read the financial pages and I don't think we need to take up a collection for *Wellcare* or its overpaid executives."

"Will you at least try to stay in the *Wellcare* system?"

"Of course, Charlie. You can count on me when it's best for my patients."

"Another thing, Arnie."

"Yes."

"Come and do my job for a month."

"No insult intended, Charlie, but I wouldn't do your job."

After Lois and I finished dinner, I helped clear the table and loaded the dishwasher. I stretched out on the great room sofa and patted my forty-inch waist. "I'm heading out for the gym. I'll be back at nine. I'll be nice and sweaty, just the way you like me."

"Right. Why don't you see me after your shower, Big Boy. Maybe you'll get lucky, that is if you have enough energy left."

Practicing medicine doesn't offer much physical activity. Since I hated exercise per se, I played over-thirty basketball one or two evenings each week when possible. My father's premature death had affected me my entire life. If I had the money, the time, and the necessary narcissism, I might spend years on an analyst's couch to understand the effects of his death on me. His massive heart attack at thirty-six was a mind-numbing shock. Afterward, my every twinge and ache was the harbinger of 'The Big One'.

Studying medicine was the perfect prep school for the incipient hypochondriac who caught each disease as it appeared in the medical syllabus. That's understandable, but I concluded long ago that a headache was just a headache, and not a brain tumor. In addition, I learned after heart screening and sophisticated testing of my blood fats and cholesterol, that my risk for coronary heart disease was low. Still, since we only understand about 50 percent of the risk factors for this disease, I played all the odds.

I'd been athletic since childhood when I grew early in height and bulk to six feet four inches tall. I played power forward in college at two hundred forty pounds, but today at a mere two hundred pounds, I was less muscle and more fat. I enjoyed the game and was athletic enough to do well, but I lacked — as my coach freely expressed it — the killer instinct essential to that position. Knocking a player down was okay. Taking someone out deliberately wasn't in me.

Lois found me bear-like, and in private called me her Teddy Bear. We kept terms of endearment to ourselves, but neither of us made excuses for these small intimacies. They simply said that we were still, after all these years of marriage and two kids, crazy about each other and confident enough to let it show. Overt affection was as natural for us as breathing. It was a proud legacy to leave for our daughters.

Chapter Three

Henry Fischer, the President of Horizon Drugs, scanned the red-inked spreadsheet for the third time and shook his head in disgust. He'd worked the numbers repeatedly, but the bottom line remained the same; they were losing money. His desk at corporate headquarters in Emeryville was an enormous cherrywood custom creation. The offices sat before the fourth floor window with a spectacular view. Henry looked out over the San Francisco Bay with a panorama of the Golden Gate Bridge and the San Francisco skyline. He'd had his first good look at the view when he purchased the building and thought how it would impress visitors.

Horizon Drugs had opened its doors thirty years ago as Horizon Pharmacy, a neighborhood drugstore in El Cerrito Plaza, a small East Bay mall. Henry came from a long line of pharmacists, and although he had dreams of going to medical school, his family, especially Theodore (Teddy) Fischer, his father, and tradition, prevailed over ambition. Teddy raised five children with upper-middle-class advantages and conservative Germanic values.

"We're pharmacists," Teddy said, "My father, and his father were pharmacists in Munich. By 1935 with the rise of the Nazis, I decided to leave the country before it was too late."

Although Teddy had considered Henry capable, he remained concerned with his son's extravagance. When Henry took over Horizon Pharmacy, Teddy haunted the place. He still counted each pill, checked daily receipts, and studied the books, fearing that Henry's stewardship would destroy his life's work.

Henry shook his head as Teddy studied the books. "What's the matter, Pop? Don't you trust me?"

Teddy smiled. "Of course I trust you, Henny. If I can't trust family, whom can I trust? It's hard for an old man to break lifelong habits."

"Please, Pop, don't call me Henny, it's Henry."

"Of course. Excuse me," he said smiling as he embraced his son.

Henry Fischer had been one of those kids born with absolute confidence. While most children of his generation were shy and spoke only when spoken to, Henry was outgoing, charming, and completely comfortable with children and adults alike. Friends and relatives would blink with surprise and smile as this precocious child extended his hand to greet them with a warm hello, and engaged them in near-adult conversation.

Henry charmed his way through school. With a bright mind, Henry became each teacher's favorite and won every elective office he sought. He graduated with honors from Berkeley High as class president. He continued to UC Berkeley, and graduated from UC San Francisco School of Pharmacy.

Henry made up for his short stature with elevated shoes and hair combed high. People called him a spark plug for his high energy level and rapid speech pattern. Built like a gymnast, he worked out feverishly especially when his scale drifted above 140 lbs. Henry wore Yves Saint Laurent and Valentino suits. He'd paid over $2000 for a few and drove the tailors crazy until each fit perfectly. He went weekly to the unisex hair salon for a trim.

Only his sister, Joanie knew the real Henry Fischer as a man living a charmed life. She tried to tell Teddy. "Henry lies with such conviction that no one recognizes it. He gives his word and breaks it without giving a shit about the people he hurts and he still sleeps like a baby."

Teddy smiled. "You're jealous of Henry."

Joanie shook her head and left the room.

When Henry heard that Highland Pharmacy was in trouble, he arranged a meeting with Morey Sherman, its owner, and a collegial competitor.

Morey was Teddy's contemporary, but looked much older as the stress of his failing business had taken its toll.

Henry studied the older man. "I'm sorry to hear about your troubles, Morey. Teddy has a special affection for you. Can we do anything to help?"

Morey's eyes filled. "It's my fault. I should have changed with the times. Now it's too late. I'm going to lose everything."

"I've talked it over with Teddy," Henry lied. "We'll buy your entire inventory, but we have our own problems and can only pay you a fraction of its value."

"What choice do I have? Where do I sign?"

"We'll seal this deal with a handshake, like your deals with Teddy."

Three weeks later, a desperate and disheveled Morey Sherman approached Henry. "You haven't paid me yet. I need the money right away."

"Take it easy, Morey. We have problems, too. I'll pay you when I can."

"You promised me half by last week. I need the money. I have obligations and can't pay my bills. Please Henry, this has never happened to me before. My honor is at stake."

"I'd like to give you the money right now, but we have cash flow problems. I'll get it to you when I have it."

Henry kept up the delaying strategy for months, until one morning Morey's wife found him dead in the garage with his car's motor running.

Teddy was livid. "What's the matter with you, Henry? Morey was my friend for twenty-six years. We were amiable competitors and often helped each other. How could you treat him that way?"

Joanie smirked. "Don't say I didn't warn you. You don't know your son, Teddy. Henry will stop at nothing to get his way."

Henry smiled at his father and sister. "Don't blame me. I would have paid, if he'd told me how important it was to him. He should have told me."

Henry married Ruth Carlin, a petite and athletic woman. She was the only daughter of Bertram Carlin, the CEO of Lathrup industries, a major supplier of after-market auto parts.

Bert Carlin was a tough and ruthless businessman, but he left that persona at work. At home, he doted on Ruth, indulging her every whim including dance, piano, art lessons, and gymnastics. She went to the finest summer camps learning to ride, surf, and write fiction and poetry. Her closets bulged with the finest clothes and shoes, many she'd never worn. In Bert's eyes, she could do no wrong. Miraculously, Ruth resisted these corrupting influences and grew into an unpretentious and generous woman. Bert encouraged her into the business administration program at UC Berkeley, hoping that she'd join him in running Lathrup Industries. When she declined, preferring to teach, he embraced her choice at once.

Ruth taught fourth grade in the upscale Lafayette school district in Contra Costa County east of the Oakland-Berkeley hills. She loved teaching, but loved Henry more. After the birth of the first of their three kids, she retired to be a stay at home mom.

Henry was generous with his wife and children, so Ruth overlooked his character flaws, as part of what it took to be successful in business. She'd grown up with her father's small ethical lapses.

One evening as they were preparing for bed, Ruth turned to Henry. "Now that we have our youngest in first grade, I'd love to go back to teaching."

"I don't think that would be such a good idea."

"Why? I loved my work, and with all the kids in school, I can restart my career."

"I don't see what the big deal is all about," he said jerking the bedspread off the bed in anger. "You have everything a wife could want. Moreover, the kids still depend on you."

Ruth sat at her dressing table, head down.

Henry joined her on the cushioned bench and rubbed her shoulders. "Now don't go getting upset. We agreed before we had children that we wanted them to have a full-time mother, not a nanny or tossed into childcare. It's best for them."

"How about what's best for me? I can't be a mother forever. One day they'll be gone and then what do I do?"

"You can do anything you want. Go back to school, work, volunteer, or whatever. Only your energy and imagination limit you."

I've lived my life to support him, Ruth thought. Nobody coerced me, and I enjoyed pleasing him. When is it my time?

"I've talked with the school district. They need me for either third or fifth grade. My hours will coincide with the children's."

Henry reddened. "You've accepted their offer?"

"I told them that I'd let them know in a few days. I want to do this, Henry. Try to understand."

"Do what you please. I don't give a damn!" he said as he stomped from the room.

Chapter Four

I looked up as my office manager, Beverly Ramirez, stuck her head into my office. "Can you speak with *Wellcare*, Arnie?"

"Tell them I died."

As I worked through my busy morning, the image of Samantha Goldstein crept into my mind.

"How many more?" I asked Beverly as the clock approached 10:30.

"Seven."

"Seven more before lunch! I don't believe it. I have a noon meeting at the hospital."

"Relax, Arnie. You'll make it. Most of them will take you minutes, and," she retreated defensively toward the door, "and, we had to squeeze Missy Cabot in this morning."

"Shit! Anyone but her. That woman will take most of the morning. I thought I was off the hook with her for at least three months."

Missy Cabot, age fifty-seven, was a pain in my ass. A bitterly unhappy woman with an uncaring husband and ungrateful kids, Missy chose hypochondriasis for two purposes, one to relieve her largely imagined symptoms, and two, to torture me. When she first came to my office many years ago, I ignored my first impression that the woman was a kook, and put her through an extensive evaluation. The negative test results did little to ease her symptoms, and forced me to do what I hated the most, ignore them.

Beverly handed me Missy's chart. "I tried to hold her off, but she's too good. She knows exactly what to say. When she went to that terrible chest pain moving down her left arm, we were dead meat. You need to examine her. I'd have sent her to the ER, but Wellcare would have refused to allow the ER to see her. She's on our dime, Arnie."

"Do another EKG and let me know when she's ready."

After seeing my sixth patient, I looked for an escape route as only Missy remained. Beverly attached the useless EKG tracing to Missy's three-inch thick office file. I compared it with her most recent cardiogram, one of twenty plus that decorated her chart, and that I'd committed to memory (it's a bad sign when you remember a patient's EKG). It didn't surprise me to find her cardiograms unchanged.

I entered the examination room trying to smile. "How's it going, Missy?"

She was a thin woman with straw-like, shoulder length bleached-blonde hair. Her face showed the coarse wrinkles of a heavy cigarette smoker and ruby-red lipstick feathered her vertically fissured lips.

She rubbed her chest with her palm. "It my ticker. Maybe I got too excited this morning when I had it out with my pain-in-the-ass daughter."

"Is this pain the same as you had before?"

"Yes, Doctor Roth. It's like someone's sticking sharp needles into my chest, and it hurts to breathe," she stabbed her chest with a crimson acrylic fingernail.

"What about the arm pain?"

She rotated her arm. "I think I pulled a muscle yesterday when I tried to clean my windows."

I examined her carefully, and then showed her the EKG. "Missy, your heart tracing is normal. This is nerves or maybe you pulled a muscle."

I reassured her for the umpteenth time, and made my usual fatal error. "Call me if you have more chest pain."

"What about my dizziness, nervousness, headaches, and itchy scalp, Doctor?"

My head swam. "We've been over all this before, Missy. It's nothing."

"Thank you, Doctor," She said and reached into her huge purse to grab a notebook. She thumbed through three pages. "I have a few other things I need to discuss with you, Dr. Roth."

I shook my head and checked my watch. "No time now, Missy, let's keep them for your next visit."

Ignoring symptoms even when they came from a neurotic patient was a potentially deadly game. With my luck, one of these days she'd really have something life-threatening.

I glanced over at the business office and saw Lois. She served as my part-time office-billing manager.

When I finished for the morning, Lois came into my office. "Do we have enough money to put out a contract on Missy Cabot?"

She smiled. "Sure, but you don't look good in stripes. Not to worry, I'll come and visit you in San Quentin...I'll even bake cookies."

"It's justifiable homicide, killing her before she kills me."

"You're done for the morning, honey. How about taking your wife to lunch?"

"I'd love to, but I have a Quality Assurance meeting in five minutes."

"Don't say I didn't ask. I'm off this afternoon. See you tonight."

Lois gave me a hug and a kiss. "Love ya, babe."

Lois was the force that kept me on an even keel. In spite of the declining image of physicians, I found most people were still a little in awe of us. The deference a physician received was seductive. Like politicians, too many of us came to believe our own propaganda.

Early in our relationship, Lois took every opportunity to deflate my ever so slightly overblown ego. She thought it was funny to couch terms of endearment with a little comic sarcasm. "Kiss me, Dr. Roth," then later, "make love to me,

Dr. Roth." The good-natured kidding, however, never discouraged my enthusiasm for her offers.

I met her when I started my residency at UC San Francisco. She worked in the medical education office as an administrator, bookkeeper, and a Lois-of-all-trades, doing four jobs for the price of one.

She was the oldest of three sisters born to Nora and Milton Kravitz. Milton, a world famous dermatologist, taught at the university and had a lucrative practice in affluent Palo Alto. Coming from modest means, Milton, and to a lesser extent, Nora had evolved or devolved, Lois said, into pretentious snobs. "I can't believe I'm related to them."

Well after Lois and I became involved, she told me the story of her parents' initial reaction to our relationship...

"Are you sure that Arnie's the right one?" Milton asked exhibiting his characteristic bad judgment. "After all, he couldn't get into an American medical school."

Lois reddened. "How can a smart man say something so stupid?"

Nora bristled. "Don't talk to your father that way."

Lois never hesitated to speak her mind, so her outburst should not have surprised Milton, but it did. In his own defense, he replied, "I only want what's best for you, Lois. I think you can do better."

"Listen, both of you. I love Arnie. I'm going to marry him if he'll have me. Arnie is the best thing that ever happened to me. You judge without knowing a thing about the man. If you can't appreciate how fantastic he is, and how happy we'll be together, you'd best think carefully before you speak, that is if you expect to see me or your grandchildren…"

I'd looked into her tear-filled soft brown eyes. "Screw `em."

I walked two blocks in the bright sun to Brier Hospital. Automobiles filled every available curb space for blocks around, as paid parking was limited and expensive. Homeowners had parking permits attached to their cars, while interlopers, hospital workers, played hide-and-seek with parking control officers who marked their tires and ticketed those who hadn't moved in two hours. Many hospital employees had stacks of parking tickets.

I entered the hospital through an ER. They were having a bad day. gurneys lined the hallways and staff scurried from room to room with the intensity of the highly motivated, but over-stressed.

The medical staff office assigned a street level room with large, east-facing windows for our QA meeting. I served as chairman. We watched the lunchtime escapees rushing by, seeking an hour's relief from their stress.

The committee was responsible for insuring that patient care did not fall below a minimal practice standard. This approach to QA stood in sharp contrast to my experience at the university where our goals were not the minimum, but the highest level of care. In a good community hospital like Brier, there was only so much the QA process could do with private practitioners. We monitored every aspect of hospital care that affected our patients. Docs were our primary focus, but we monitored other elements like nursing and hospital systems.

Cindy Hines, an RN, worked for the department of medicine and family practice. She coordinated QA activities, performed assessment studies to see how well we were doing, and served as liaison with the hospital.

"What's on tap today?" I asked Cindy as I took my seat.

She sat at the head of a U-shaped table behind a stacked hospital chart fortress. A woman in her 40s, she looked much older due to premature graying. She'd worked the wards, intensive care, and served in nursing administration. She was the regimental Sergeant Major of nursing, a pro.

Cindy smiled. "If I said, 'the usual' would you understand?"

"You bet. Maybe we've been doing this too long."

Brier's QA committee had matured over the years. Warren Davidson, the chief of medicine, had persuaded me to chair the committee. I resisted his offer because I wasn't the traditional hard-ass usually assigned to this job. In retrospect, I think

Warren was right. Often the mixture of an open mind and a little diplomacy was more effective than a full frontal assault.

The committee members arrived and ate their lunches while reviewing the charts they'd present today. Most charts they'd reviewed in detail before hand, others they'd see today for the first time.

We ran through thirty hospital records. Several minor items of concern came up that only required a brief letter to the involved physician. Two cases were more serious and involved an intractable issue — being available to the nurses for hospitalized patients.

Sharon Brickman, the head of cardiology was a tough, take-no-prisoners reviewer. While at times she went overboard with harsh criticism and sadistic remedies, she was usually correct in her assessments.

"Physician 884994 (we used numbers to prevent bias) has been here multiple times for the same damn thing. I'm getting sick of it and more than a little annoyed that he's ignored our warnings. This time his patient in the coronary care unit went into a dangerous heart rhythm and the nurses couldn't find him for two hours. This is 2011, and with beepers and cell phones. It's inexcusable. I recommend that we restrict his privileges for any acute care unit, and require that he use an appropriate consultant."

Ernie Charles, a family practitioner in his late sixties, was a man who could find no wrong in anything a fellow physician did. I had tried, with Warren's assistance, to remove Ernie from the committee, but he had the full support of the family practitioner lobby.

Why the knee-jerk reaction to criticism of a physician? Why protect physicians under any imaginable situation, and not their patients? I didn't get it.

Ernie stared at Sharon. "You're always ready to jump the gun. You bring out the cannons when a peashooter would do the job. I know this guy, and I assure you that if Arnie or Warren speaks to him in strong terms, the problem will resolve."

Sharon tightened her jaw. "We've done that already, twice in fact, and he's still at it. You and I have been on this committee together for years, and I've yet to see you take a stand against any physician malpractice. You made excuses for that psychopath, Joe Polk, who finally killed a patient before we acted. I'm not going through that again."

"You're in the wrong profession, Sharon. You have a real flare for the dramatic."

After ten minutes, the committee voted to approve Sharon's recommendation with one vote in opposition.

I grabbed the next chart. "The second case involves the same issue, but this is a first for this doc, so if you agree, I'll send her a strongly worded letter."

Sharon shook her head then leaned over to me. "Make it a Poison Pen Letter, Arnie."

Chapter Five

Connie Rinaldi was eight when, in an instant, her life changed forever.

For their traditional Christmas Eve dinner in Grass Valley, the Rinaldi family traveled the Sierra's mountain roads onto the single lane path that led to her grandparents' secluded forest cabin.

The light snow fluttered through the trees to cover the forest floor. It started while they were eating and it looked like they'd have a white Christmas.

"We'd better get ready to leave," said Tina, Connie's mother. "We don't have chains and it's a two and a half hour trip back to Berkeley."

Connie had eaten too much and was a little sleepy, but she felt fine until she stepped from the warm house into the bitter cold. Instantly, she couldn't breathe. She grasped the rail and stared, wide-eyed, back at Joseph, her father.

"What's wrong, Connie?"

She tried to answer, but couldn't utter a sound. In full panic, she struggled and gasped for breath, but heard only short squeaks, wheezes that fought to pass through her constricted airways.

Her aunt Agnes, a registered nurse, took one look at the girl. "It's asthma, and it's bad. We've got to get her to the hospital right away."

"Call an ambulance," Connie's mother cried.

"No," said Joseph. "We can get to the hospital well before they can ever find this place."

They put Connie into her grandfather's four-wheel drive Subaru and eight minutes later helped her into the emergency room at Sierra Nevada Memorial Hospital in Grass Valley. When the triage nurse saw Connie's oxygen-starved blue lips, she rushed her into a treatment room. In seconds, Connie received an Adrenalin shot and inhaled medication to open her airways. In an instant, she could breathe. She coughed and wheezed loudly as she started to move air into and out of her lungs.

That memorable Christmas brought the first of many asthma episodes that would haunt Connie through her teenage years and into adulthood. She went to specialists. They tried the full range of medications; only cortisone insured an uneasy truce with the disease, but left her with complications: weight gain, a swollen face, and acne. Finally, after a pulmonary specialist completed his detailed evaluation, he diagnosed Connie with far-advanced lung disease carrying the label: chronic bronchitis with asthma.

Through her teenage years, Connie fought to control her weight, but circumstances made it difficult to impossible. It wasn't enough that she came from a family of chunky Mediterranean women, cortisone made the weight problem worse. Whether by vanity or self-discipline, she managed to keep her weight in the 120 to 140 range, not bad for a 5 foot 6 inch woman. Her shapely figure, dark skinned and black-haired Italian looks made her popular with the boys... "voluptuous," they said. In her junior year, she fell hard for Gino Martini, a Nicholas Cage clone.

They partied and dined with friends and Connie subscribed to *Brides Magazine*. Everything was well Connie thought until she went to Sacramento State College to study psychology while Gino remained in the bay area to work.

"I can't make it this weekend," Gino said one Thursday night.

"This is the fourth time you cancelled out, is anything wrong?"

Gino coughed. "It's a long trip up and back. I'm just beat."

Right, she thought, it's a whole sixty or seventy minutes.

His phone calls became less frequent, and the excuses less convincing, and finally, he stopped calling. Friends at home eventually told her that Gino had been seeing a vivacious blonde for the last few months.

Connie couldn't say his action surprised her, she'd wondered what this gorgeous guy saw in her, but the loss was devastating. She withdrew into food's loving embrace. Her weight ballooned to 200, and then to 220 lbs.

Connie's mother never gave up. "You're so beautiful. You'll find someone who'll appreciate you."

Right, Mamma, Connie thought. I feel the warmth of my mother's love, but I couldn't deny the bloated image in the mirror.

Chapter Six

Antonio Ruiz, Tino they called him, was Beverly Ramirez's cousin. After five troubling years, he was through with the gangs.

Tino's life had changed that day nine months ago when his sister Maria slammed open the door to their apartment screaming and sobbing. "They killed her. They killed Angela Rodriguez."

Tino stood. "Angela! What happened?"

"She was sitting on the stoop playing with her dolls and they shot her. Another senseless drive-by shooting. Three...she was only three-years-old."

As he watched his sister collapse in tears, his mind flashed, enough, I've had enough.

In reality, Tino never fit into gang life. He was too thoughtful and introspective. He took constant abuse for having his nose in books. Several gang members were illiterate, and nobody read anything but sports and pornographic magazines. They called him *el profesor*, sometimes with affection, more often with disdain.

Facing a cocaine possession sentence, Tino lucked out when the judge gave him counseling, probation, and community service. He took the opportunity to extend the forced separation from the gang into a major life change. After completing his GED, Tino started at Diablo Valley Community

College (DVC), and applied for a part-time position with Horizon Drugs.

Beverly came into my office one morning. "Can you help Tino?"

"I don't know. He's a gangbanger, Bev. The stigma of that life is tough to overcome."

"He was never really one of them. In that neighborhood, gang membership was essential if you planned to survive."

She looked at me with dark, pleading eyes, and I knew I was dead. Beverly, once an employee, was family.

"I'll call Henry Fischer. We're one of his oldest and most reliable customers. Maybe he'll help Tino with a job."

When Tino went for his interview, he'd dressed carefully in pressed chinos and a blue denim shirt buttoned to the top to hide his tattoos. He'd cut off his ponytail and had neatly parted his thick black hair.

Henry Fischer stood behind his large teak and chrome desk staring down at the younger, smaller man, an act of intimidation. "Have a seat, Mr. Ruiz."

"Thank you, sir."

"Let me be frank with you, Antonio, if it hadn't been for Dr. Roth's call, I'd have never agreed to see you. Let's say I'm doing him a big favor. You haven't made much of your life, have you?"

Tino recognized Henry's strategy for what it was. Confrontation was the currency of gang life — and Tino was an expert. "Please call me Tino, sir, and yes I agree with you. I've changed that now. I'm out of the gangs and three quarter time at DVC. I'm smart and hardworking, and if you give me a try, I won't disappoint you."

"I'm a careful man, Tino. I don't like taking risks, but I'll give you a chance. Screw up once, you're out of here."

"Thank you, sir. You won't be sorry."

They put Tino to work unpacking shipments and stocking shelves. For the first two months, they checked and rechecked each order and counted each shelf item. He'd catch them staring at him, peering around corners, and listening to his phone conversations.

Tontos...fools, he thought, smiling to himself. If I were going to steal, I'd have walked away with half your inventory already.

"Okay, Tino," said Henry, one day after work, "I think we can get more out of you if I train you as a pharmacist's assistant."

Chapter Seven

Debbie Ann Wallace lived in a shadowed past that said, "If you think you're happy, think again — it won't last."

She grew up as the youngest of three girls with a cold, rejecting mother and a brutal father.

Her rape at age twelve by her father's friend was her life's sentinel event. It permanently altered her sense of herself, of the world, and especially of men.

Trying to talk with her mother was a waste of time. "Oh, grow up, Debbie Ann. Women aren't worth a damn in this life…get used to it."

Debbie never did.

She spent years trying to trust, trying to feel safe, trying with psychiatrists and women's rape survivors' groups. Nothing changed until Matthew Wallace entered her life.

Debbie was a junior at UC Berkeley and Matt a graduate student at the School of Public Health in the dual degree program, M.S.W. and M.P.H. He supported himself as a teaching assistant, and although neither believed in love at first sight, it happened. The wonder was, that Debbie, instead of facing the urgency of a blossoming relationship, found Matt moving at a snail's pace. Neither would deny the animal attraction, but somehow Matt understood, she thought. He moved gradually with friendship and affection first, and then with infinite patience toward their union.

By the time, she graduated, and they married, Matt accepted the assistant directorship of The Contra Costa County Child Protection Services.

Debbie took a fifth grade teaching position with the Concord School district. She loved the kids and they responded in kind making her one of the school's most sought after teachers.

One evening after clearing the table and sharing the dishwashing, they moved into the den for coffee.

Both enjoyed their work, and shared their experiences. When Debbie listened to Matt's tragic cases and the heartbreak, her mouth dried and she felt flushed. Her eyes welled. "How do you deal with it every day? It makes me crazy to hear about these kids, their misery, and the brutality of their lives."

"You never get used to it." He reached into his briefcase, extracted a thin blue binder, and dropped it on the table. "On top of it all, this is my operating budget. It's a joke. What kind of world do we live in where child protective services must fight for funding, fight bureaucratic obstructions, and public apathy? My work makes a difference. That's what keeps me going. I tell myself I'm helping to save children, and despite all the frustrations, that's enough for me. At least I hope it's enough to see me through in the future."

"Don't say or even hint at that. Your optimism is the one constant in my universe."

Debbie resigned with the birth of the first of her three kids. She knew she'd return to teaching someday, but for now, her children were priority one. The family settled in Lafayette, five miles from the Caldecott Tunnel that separated the east bay from Contra Costa County.

While taking a shower, Debbie felt something in her right breast. Her breasts were lumpy for sure. Dr. Roth had told her that it was fibrocystic disease and it made examining her breasts difficult. She continued to feel her breast, hoping it would go away; it didn't.

In full panic mode, Debbie Wallace was waiting at my office the next morning. She looked at me expectantly. "It's a lump, Arnie."

Her breasts were cystic and fibrous making manual examination and mammography problematic. Her breasts felt universally lumpy to me, but once I thought about cancer, I needed to follow through. Not doing so would be like smelling smoke, and failing to check it out. Delay and it might be too late.

She returned to my office the day after the mammogram.

I smiled and held up the radiologist's report. "Good news, it was negative."

"What do you mean, negative? I feel something, how could it be negative?"

I picked up two mammograms. "Come with me, Debbie." I placed the two films side by side on my x-ray view box. "Yours is the one on the right. What do you see?"

"I see all that white streaky irregular stuff on my mammogram. What's that?"

"Mammograms show tissue density. The denser the tissue, the more the x-rays are absorbed, creating the variations in black and white that make up the image. Fat hardly absorbs the beam at all, so it shows up as black. Breast tissue, particularly the thick breast tissue of a young woman like you, shows up on an x-ray as shades of light gray or white. The white on your films reflect fibrocystic disease. Tumors being especially solid also show up as dense whiteness."

"If tumors are white, and my breasts show all this white stuff, how can you see the tumor?"

"That's exactly our problem. Small tumors can hide within the white and we wouldn't see them until they were quite large. The whiteness we see here," I pointed to her x-ray, "means that what you're feeling is likely to be fibrocystic disease and not cancer. Here's the report."

Debbie read the report carefully. When her eyes reached the bottom, she looked up at me. "What's this starred note on the bottom of the report?"

"It's a disclaimer. They're an unfortunate fact of life in modern medicine. It means that no test is 100 percent accurate. It's a way for radiologists to cover their asses to protect themselves should cancer show itself later. In the world of rampant malpractice judgments, trial lawyers make disclaimers necessary."

"Excuse me, Dr. Roth, but none of that means a damn thing to me. Just tell me I'm okay."

"I wish I could, Debbie, and the odds are overwhelmingly in your favor. If we take one hundred women with lumps in their breasts, do all our imaging techniques, mammograms, ultrasounds, and MRIs, and we get negative reports, 1 to 3 percent of these women will still have cancer."

"One to three percent sounds pretty high when you're sitting in my position."

"I agree, but we're stuck, especially in patients like you Debbie with cystic, fibrous breasts. Keep checking your breasts. Once a week is enough. We'll repeat the mammograms as often as needed. I'll order a biopsy if we see something suspicious."

"I don't like all those x-rays. Are they safe?"

"Mammograms are a special type of low dose x-ray. When combined with special high-resolution film, we get spectacular images. In experiments, it takes x-ray doses hundreds to thousands higher before we see a statistical increase in cancer."

"I'll keep checking, Doctor, but that's a hell of a way to live."

"I know, but try not to obsess about it. One warning: if you're constantly examining your breasts, you can aggravate the inflammation and a lump can persist or enlarge."

Two months later, Debbie returned. "I tried to ignore it at first thinking it was my imagination, but it's still there, I feel it. It's larger. I know it."

A quick examination told me Debbie was right.

This time, the mammogram showed a small mass, suggestive of a tumor. When I said the words she feared the most, "We need to do a biopsy," Debbie's eyes glazed over and she slumped in her chair. I managed to catch her before she hit the ground.

Matt saw Debbie's fear—abject fear. She was frantic, but frozen in place. Their lives were no longer under their control. They sought safe haven—there wasn't one.

Matt, an optimist by nature, felt helpless, as he was unable to control his own fears gathering momentum and speeding to a brick wall finish line, toward the worst possible scenario.

"We're going to make it through this, no matter what it takes," he said with the conviction he didn't feel.

Debbie reached for his face and stroked it gently with her hand. "I love you, Matt. I'll always love you." She placed her head on his shoulder and wept.

Chapter Eight

I began ICU rounds on this eighth day of Samantha Goldstein's coma by confronting Richard and Marion, her parents. Their superficial impassive greetings couldn't mask their desperation.

After so many days, I marveled how they maintained hope, although having children of my own, I understood.

I entered the isolation room, masked and tying the green hospital gown behind my back. "Good morning."

Today, like every day, we met in Samantha's room. Gowns and masks hid their body language, but their eyes shone with unrelenting hope that only parents can have for their children. It was desperation, not simply born out of desire, but built on their belief that there was no way they could lose their daughter — they couldn't — they wouldn't, outlive their little girl.

I encouraged Marion to help the nurses when they bathed Samantha and changed her bedclothes. I had misgivings because the physical act of moving Samantha's extremities told Marion that her daughter wasn't merely asleep. Arranging Samantha's lax extremities was like moving a puppet.

I watched as Marion stopped in midstream when she lifted Samantha's lifeless arm. It shocked her, I could tell. She paused a moment, stared at the arm, her daughter, and continued the bed bath.

She knows, I thought.

Samantha looked asleep, a princess with her warm blond center-parted hair neatly combed and splayed over the white pillow. The clear plastic tube that we'd passed through her nose and into the windpipe, the trachea, was connected to the ventilator that whirred and clicked rhythmically as it breathed life into her.

I raised my hand to forestall their questions until I examined Samantha, knowing in advance that change in her condition was unlikely. "Give me a moment, and then we'll talk."

I shook Samantha gently — no response. I shook her more vigorously — no response. I placed my body between Samantha and her parents so they wouldn't see that I applied my knuckles to her chest, a potent and painful stimulus to see if she'd respond — she didn't. My neurological examination showed an array of abnormal reflexes, all indicating severe brain damage.

We walked into the anteroom to talk.

I shook my head slowly, but before I uttered a word, Marion trembled and moaned her deep visceral devastation.

I sat beside her. "I'm so sorry."

Richard stood erect, his lips held tight.

"I don't know what else to say. I'm a father. I have two daughters. I see tragedy and death as part of my life, yet I still don't know how parents ever survive the loss of a child."

Richard's tears ran down his cheeks. "The thought of losing Samantha is more than I can bear." He looked at the floor. "We had plans. No matter her age or the distance between us, I'd always be there for her. I'll never walk her down the aisle or be the grandfather to her children. She has so much to give; so much to experience, so much talent. How can her life end this way?"

Marion reached out to her husband, caressed his neck, trying to ease his pain.

Richard slowly lifted his head and stared at me. "What are <u>you</u> going to do?"

I recognized this as a desperate father's question, and a challenge, too.

Each family dealt with tragedy in its own way, some withdrew in quiet desperation, while others abandoned the cultural restraints that kept their emotions in check. I remember…

My chief resident smirked. "It's your turn."

"My turn for what?"

"Their daughter just died. You need to tell them."

"Find someone else. I'm not up to it."

He stared at me. I felt nauseated. I didn't know whether this was a dump, palming off an unpleasant job on an underling, or was he offering me the opportunity to learn something. Whatever his intention, I found myself unprepared for what happened. How bad could it be, I'd thought at the time, after all, they knew their daughter was dying.

The moment I entered the waiting room, my carefully planned script crumbled as I met her parents' eyes.

Her mother stood. "What is it, Dr. Roth?"

I stared at my feet. "I'm so sorry."

"Sorry...Sorry for what?"

I grasped her hands and whispered, "She's gone. It was peaceful. She didn't suffer."

She pushed my hands away as if they carried an electric current and faced her husband, "What is he talking about?"

From the back of the room came a communal moan. "No, Dear God...Jesus...Lord." A few at first, followed by mountainous waves of grief that increased in height until they crested, and crashed into the room that exploded into the screaming, shouting, and wailing whirlpool. Whatever sense of control I had, vanished in an instant, as I stood there, a mute among the disconsolate. I knew that there had to be words to ease their pain, but each hollow platitude stuck in my throat...

That experience with patients and their loved ones taught me much about death and tragedy. Mostly, they showed me how to listen to what families said, to really listen, so I understood immediately Richard's choice of words: what are <u>you</u> going to do?

I could resent the question and the implication that the decision was mine, but I chose not to avoid the responsibility. After all, I was their physician, their advisor, and I admit it, their friend.

The question suggested no easy answer for me or for them. I couldn't think of a way to be truthful to the situation, yet withhold the words that I knew would sound cold and callous. The cruelty of this truth would overwhelm any spoonful of sugar.

"I'm going to order another EEG to measure her brain wave activity. If it's like the last one, showing no signs of higher brain function, we will face a difficult decision."

Richard tightened his lips. "You're suggesting we stop treating Samantha, and turn off her respirator."

"Yes."

The icy clouds of reality chilled the room. Silence replaced their aggressive denials. For weeks, fear sustained them while denial provided comfort. Now they understood.

Richard embraced his wife, their heads side-by-side. My eyes filled in empathy for their tragedy.

After rounds, I returned to the office. Workmen blocked my private entrance. That forced me to use the front door and walk through the packed waiting room. Dozens of eyes followed my every step.

I'd have to deal with their problems soon enough. I didn't need an appetizer.

"Hey, Doc. What's up?"

"Good morning, Dr. Roth."

"Great to see you, Doc."

I nodded, waved, and made my way back to the office as quickly as possible.

As usual, they'd over-scheduled me this morning. Most patients looked okay, while others were clearly in the right place as they coughed and hacked, sharing their bacteria and viruses with the rest of the waiting room. I often hesitated with my hand on the examining room's doorknob when I heard coughing and sneezing within. Why would anyone choose to join Typhoid Mary in her den? This was an occupational hazard. It surprised me that more doctors and nurses didn't share their patients' infectious diseases. Maybe this was my unwritten contract with the fates for doing this job. I picked up the chart from its holder on the door.

Annie Franklin was a twenty-two-year-old graduate student at UC Berkeley, and the moment I entered the room she assailed me. "Dr. Roth, you must do something."

"Good morning, Annie, it's nice to see you, too."

"I'm sorry, but this cold's making me crazy. I'm supposed to be the maid of honor tomorrow. I can't walk down the aisle sniffling and sneezing with mucous dripping from my nose. I don't think the bride will find my condition fitting for her elegant wedding."

"That's a charming visual image, Annie. Let's see what's going on."

Her throat was red and the nasal mucosa looked inflamed, but her lungs were clear. "I'd say you have an upper respiratory viral illness, Annie, better known as the common cold."

Annie smirked. "Thanks, Doc, but my $120,000 education already told me that. What can you do? I'm such a mess. I can't ruin this for my best friend. Whip out your prescription pad and write for a strong antibiotic."

"Here's the news, we can't treat the common cold, and, for sure, antibiotics won't help. I'll give you nose drops and a strong, long-lasting antihistamine. You'll still feel lousy until this thing runs its course, but hopefully your nose won't drip."

I wrote two prescriptions. "Call me if the symptoms persist or if that cough worsens, and by the way, watch your alcohol consumption. Alcohol and antihistamine can lead you to embarrass yourself in other ways."

"Thanks, Doc, but I was hoping for a cure."

"Go to medical school or become a research virologist, Annie. A Nobel Prize looms ahead for you."

By the end of the busy day, I felt unusually tired and achy. Even my three p.m. dose of energy, a large cup of cappuccino, failed to perk me up. I also had a headache and a scratchy throat—so much for my unwritten contract with the fates.

Chapter Nine

As Henry Fischer sat at his enormous desk ignoring the spectacular view of the San Francisco Bay, he thought, how could a life so full of promise turn to shit?

His business and his marriage to Ruth were in trouble. He was a man of big appetites, too accustomed to, and too expectant of, the approval and the envy of others. Their sex life diminished dramatically after the birth of their first child. Before, they'd made love three or more times a week. He'd delighted in Ruth's desire for him and her uninhibited sexuality. Now, they rarely made love and, by her seeming indifference, Ruth convinced him she did it only from a sense of duty. What a turn-off! What happened to her?

Henry had his physical and emotional needs, after all. He was an attractive, affluent man, and he'd had no difficulty finding willing and enthusiastic partners. At first, he sought the company of high-class professionals who were good at their work and allowed Henry to avoid the messy emotional attachments that could complicate his life.

His current affair with Monica Kelly, his director of sales, may have been a mistake. After nine months, their relationship had become anything but detached. They worked closely together, and over time, their casual flirtations progressed from joking references about sex to reality. Monica, thirty-two and recently divorced from a local obstetrician, had no children. Her career was her life and she, too, hadn't been looking for entanglements, especially with her boss.

Henry smiled as Monica entered his private office. "You're a sight for sore eyes...just what the old man needs."

"What old man?" she asked, pulling his face to her lips, kissing him passionately, and caressing him between his legs. "That sure doesn't feel like anything an old man would be packing."

"You're too much, Monica. With you around, I never feel old."

Her tongue slid across moistened berry-red lips. "I can't wait for this weekend. We're still on, aren't we?"

"It's becoming a strain creating plausible excuses for being away. If Ruth's suspicious, I don't see it. Maybe she doesn't give a damn. The Denver meeting of the National Community Pharmacists' Association gives us reason to be away together. I can't wait to sleep with you for four whole nights."

She smiled. "I don't know about the sleep part."

Henry returned to his chair. "Any good news from your front?"

"When don't I bring good news? I've picked up three new accounts, and have substantial orders from another six. How's that?"

"You're the best, baby, but we're getting squeezed by the hospital associations, the HMO's, and especially from Medicaid. I don't know how they think we can stay in business with their drug reimbursement formulas. Our recent expansion adding five new pharmacies, and purchasing United Drugs, have put us into a bind."

"How serious is it?"

"It's serious enough. If we can't do something to increase revenues, we'll be in big trouble. Another computer glitch from Medi-Cal, and we'll have to borrow to pay our bills."

Monica shook her head. "This is a first-rate business. If you can't make it, I don't see how any pharmacy can."

"It's not rocket science. The prices of drugs are rising, and health insurers are under tremendous pressure to cut costs. We may be the first casualty."

The clock struck eight as Henry returned home that evening. Ruth sat at the dinner table correcting class homework.

"Your dinner is in the oven. It may be a little dry by now. If you'd let me know you were going to be late, I'd have waited for you."

"Thanks, Ruth. I'm not hungry." He paused for a moment and reconsidered his answer. "Okay, I'll take a few bites."

Ruth studied him as he picked at his dry chicken and shrunken vegetables. "Is everything okay? You've been unusually quiet lately."

"I have a lot on my mind. Things aren't going well with the business, and I'm feeling the pressure."

"Maybe it's a good thing that I'm working."

He stopped eating. "That may help you, but it won't do a damn thing for me. Don't you understand? We have major financial problems with Horizon Drugs. A teacher's salary won't fix that."

Ruth looked at him with disbelief. "You know very well what I meant. Why do you try so hard to misunderstand what I'm saying? I'm your wife. I want to help."

"If you want to help, write me a check for $650,000."

"$650,000! What's going on?"

Henry rattled off a litany of problems with the recent expansion of the business and the reductions in reimbursement. He used simple language, defining each term as if he were explaining something complex to a moron. He wanted to offend her, and he did.

"Why do you talk to me in this way, Henry? I'm intelligent and over the years, when you talked with me, I developed more than a passing knowledge of the pharmacy business."

"A passing knowledge won't do me much good now."

"I can talk to Daddy. Maybe he would lend you the money until your cash flow problem straightens itself out."

Henry laughed with obvious disdain. "Bert Carlin lending me money. What a joke. That prick would love to see me crawling to him for help. It would make his day…no, it would make his decade."

"Don't trash my father. He's been nothing but kind and generous to the kids and to us. What do you have against him?"

"That's easy. Nobody was ever good enough for Bertram Carlin's daughter. I'll never give him the satisfaction of watching me fail. If I go down, his precious daughter will go down with me."

Chapter Ten

Matt Wallace took one look at Debbie as she put down the phone. She stared at him and paled. "What's wrong?"

"I've never been so frightened in my life." She grabbed Matt's hands, and told him the mammogram's results. "I need a breast biopsy" She paused. "It could be cancer," she said in a whisper, as if not saying it aloud would change the reality.

Matt's reaction to the words, the image of breast cancer was like the near miss in his car, or turning around and finding his child gone in the supermarket. The hollow feeling in his stomach was his visceral concession to terror.

Needle biopsy by the radiologist revealed cancer.

Debbie and Matt met with me the next day.

They sat before my desk waiting expectantly and I pulled my chair around to join them.

"I've had too many conversations like this one. It's never easy for me or the people I care about. Breast cancer eventually affects one in nine American women, and it arrives with twin attributes, a reality, and a mythology. The reality is the tumor, its size, its location, its pathology, its hormonal sensitivity, and of course its spread. This, more than anything, determines how we're going to treat it. Then we have what I like to call the mythology of breast cancer."

"Mythology?" Debbie asked.

"I don't like the word, but it's the best one I can find. It describes our obsession with breast cancer and it's all over TV, especially on shows like Oprah. Then we have the books and articles in women's magazines with gritty stories of struggle and survival against all odds, and the tragedy of death too soon.

"The universal fear of the disease is real and rational. Women inhale it, absorb it, and assimilate it, like the air they breathe. Overall, it's beneficial and has increased awareness of the disease, raised huge amounts of money, and reversed the image of the disease from pessimistic to hopeful.

"The one disadvantage is the overwhelming amount of information available about treatment. Much is useful, but it makes life more difficult for patients by being confusing and sometimes irresponsible."

I ran them through the alternatives and, as much as I tried, I was unable to eliminate my bias for breast conserving surgery—maybe I shouldn't try to be objective.

"I'll leave you alone for a moment. Take as much time as you need. Talk it over. If you need more time to consult with others, that's okay too."

Debbie and Matt sat side-by-side. Matt grasped her hand. "What's going to happen?"

"You heard Dr. Roth. I'm going to have a lumpectomy. It makes the most sense to me. They'll remove the tumor and its surrounding tissue. Then they'll operate on my right armpit to examine and remove any affected lymph nodes. What do you think?"

"I trust Arnie, and I trust your judgment. Who's going to do the surgery?"

"Julie Kramer. Arnie says she's the best."

She squeezed Matt's hand. "I'm trying so hard not to think the worst, but you of all people know how difficult that is for me."

"You're the best and I love you. I'll always love you. This will work out. I know it."

Debbie lay on a gurney in outpatient surgery waiting for the orderly to roll her into the operating suite. Matt stood on one side, Julie Kramer, the general surgeon, on the other.

Julie took Debbie's hand. "The surgery won't be difficult or too uncomfortable. I can't guarantee it, but I think that this is going to be Stage I or II disease, and you should be fine. We'll know more when we see what the tumor looks like under the microscope and we examine the lymph glands in your armpit. Nevertheless, you'll need radiation afterward."

Matt turned to Julie. "What about chemotherapy?"

"That will depend on what the pathologist finds."

For two days, Debbie stared at the phone each time she walked by. She'd picked it up several times to call Julie and nearly broke her neck racing into the house to answer a telemarketer. Imagining the worst, she slept four hours the first night and two the next.

Finally, Julie called. "Good news, it's Stage II. I'm not going to recommend chemotherapy."

By the fourth week of a seven-week course of radiation therapy, Debbie was sleeeping better and had caught up on her soaps.

The radiation oncology department was deep within the bowels of Brier Hospital. It loomed dark and forbidding. Patients of all ages filled the large reception area awaiting—no dreading—their turns as if they were cued up for root canals. Nobody smiled. Nobody laughed. Nobody made eye contact.

After her first treatment, Debbie met Matt in the waiting room. "The procedure didn't scare me…much. I barely felt anything. What made me feel special," she smirked, "was the staff scurrying from the room to get to the safety of the lead wall before they turn on the machine.

"The place gives me the creeps. I don't know if a good interior decorator could help, but the radiation oncology department's message is oppressively solemn, as if you're entering a church or a mausoleum. Huge whirring and buzzing machines loomed over me, aimed at me, and made me feel as if I was a bug under a dissecting microscope."

When Debbie stood before the mirror each morning, it wasn't the small lumpectomy incision that disturbed her. Instead, it was the hideous purple indelible ink markings on her skin, the target zone for those radiation beams.

I'm ground zero, she thought.

After four weeks, the side effects, though mild, were predictable. The skin over her breast and upper arm had first taken on a rosy hue, like sunburn but lately the skin had darkened. She felt mild nausea, fatigue, and a scratchy soreness in her throat.

More troubling than anything, was the realization that she was no longer in control of her life; that she was somehow less than she was before. Hugs and kisses from Matt were satisfying but an inadvertent touch anywhere near her breast made her pull away painfully. The message was clear to anyone as perceptive as Matt, and he did not approach her sexually.

"Don't think for a moment that I'm not interested. I know you're not ready, and that's okay."

"That not okay. I love you. I want to make you happy. I want to make love to you, but... this is all my fault."

"You're remarkable. Don't be so hard on yourself. Only you could find a way to blame yourself for something out of your control. I'm focused on getting beyond this and to our future together."

Debbie caressed his cheek. "Three more weeks to go...piece-of-cake."

Disease is ingenious for its creative ways of torturing humans. I'd cared for patients with every variety of illness. On top of the list were the illnesses I feared the most, the ones that made it difficult to breathe like emphysema, chronic bronchitis, asthma, and heart failure, and those neurological diseases that paralyzed or destroyed control over one's body. The worst and the most pernicious of all was cancer. In decades past, the diagnosis carried a finality; you had cancer and eventually, you died.

"Today, with progress and the promise of treatment, we talked of cure, we began to expect, to anticipate cure. Although we couched our prognostications with disclaimers, the statistics, the maybe's and the perhaps's, cancer patients rapidly embraced the idea of cure, and make it their own, setting themselves up for disappointment and chaos.

It shocked me to see the look on Deborah Wallace's face when she returned to my office eighteen months later in despair.

"It's back," she said without emotion, although her eyes were red from crying.

She was right, of course. When I examined her right breast, I found a small, hard nodule at the lateral margin of her lumpectomy incision. Biopsy confirmed the diagnosis.

To make *Wellcare* happy, I did the blood tests, the CT scans, the bone scans, and the x-rays locally, but I decided to send Debbie for a consultation at UC Medical Center in San Francisco.

"I'm sending you to UC, Debbie. Stanley Becker is a world-class breast cancer physician. He'll evaluate your case and then present it to Tumor Board where we'll benefit from the best minds available. They even have access to experimental protocols for treatment, although I know your treatment will be a standard approach. At the end, we'll get their specific recommendations for treatment. Either I'll carry them out or I'll have one of our own cancer specialists work with us."

I remembered the first time I went to Tumor Board as a medical student. My patient was a young man with pancreatic cancer. The entire situation was tragic: his age, the devastating disease, his young family, and their hopelessness. The meeting shocked me for its cold-blooded approach to cancer, the brusque recommendations presented in a casual manner when everybody knew what it meant for the patient.

I recall my chief resident's words after the meeting. "They've got to guard themselves from becoming involved in the emotionality of cancer, and to protect their objectivity…to do their job." I didn't buy it, and still don't. Maybe it takes a certain kind of person to work with cancer patients every day.

Debbie sat with her arms crossed. "When I felt it, I knew what it was immediately and I died. Matt was worse. We thought we were through with this…what a joke." She laughed bitterly.

I held Debbie's hand. "For selfish and practical reasons, I've never lied to you, and I never will. First, I'm a bad liar, and second, you'll know that what I tell you will be the absolute truth."

"You told us what we needed to know. You warned us about the first five years, and that we shouldn't do exactly what we did. We convinced ourselves it was gone. You can't tell us anything today that we don't already understand."

Oh, yes, I can, I thought. Maybe I'm overly paternal, but I'm trying to save them from the burden of knowing too much. That, too is part of my job.

Chapter Eleven

When the cruel buzzing alarm clock jolted me awake, I knew I was sick. My stuffed head, scratchy throat, and headache told me all I needed to know. Disease had no respect for physicians. It's your turn, Dr. Roth.

I pulled the covers over my head. "You go in for me this morning, sweetie."

Lois sat up in bed and rubbed her eyes. "If I could, Arnie, I would. Maybe Beverly can lighten your afternoon schedule so you can finish early?"

I pulled the blanket back exposing my face. "I hate that. Patients have waited weeks for an appointment. I don't want to disappoint them."

I lingered in the shower soaking up the intense heat. I dressed and came to the kitchen table where Lois had hot coffee ready.

She placed her lips on my forehead. "I think you have a fever. What's your schedule like today?"

"The usual, except, this morning we terminate life support for Samantha Goldstein. That's a hell of a way to start a day."

"How long has it been?"

"She's been in a coma for three weeks. Yesterday's EEG showed minimal brain wave activity. Clinically, she's brain dead. All hope is gone, and I think the family understands."

"I couldn't do it."

"That's one hell of a comment. Do you think I enjoy this?" I lowered the coffee cup too quickly and spilling some on the table.

She touched my arm. "I'm sorry, Arnie. I know how tough this is for you."

"In spite of all we know, all modern medicine has to offer, we failed Samantha and her parents."

"This isn't your fault."

"I know that, but the way they look at me every morning breaks my heart. They trusted me with their daughter's life and I failed them. I shouldn't feel guilty, but I do."

"What else could you have done?"

"Nothing."

I tried not to feel more guilt as our family started the morning with our familiar preparations for the day ahead. Ours was loving family life at its best. It was a life we took for granted. Now, as I thought about the Goldstein family, it was hard to feel secure about anything.

A gloomy sky and the thick ground fog matched my mood as I drove to work. My headache resisted the three aspirins I took at breakfast.

Samantha's relatives crowded the ICU waiting room taking turns at her bedside, each saying goodbye.

I walked to the nursing station and stared at Beth Byrnes. "Are you ready?"

Beth nodded and accompanied me into the room. She hugged Samantha's parents.

After my final perfunctory examination, I turned to Richard and Marion. "It's time."

"Please, a minute more." Marion sobbed, holding her daughter's hands and placing her head on Samantha's chest. Richard stood behind his wife and caressed her neck and shoulders.

"It would be better if you waited outside," I said, knowing that even in the severely brain damaged, the primitive part of the brain would struggle to keep her alive...not the picture I wanted for this family's final memory of their daughter.

Richard took Marion's hand. "We want to be here to say goodbye."

I placed my hand on his shoulder. "Please. Say your goodbyes now and leave the rest to us."

Marion's mouth tightened. "I don't see why we can't be here,"

I kneeled before her looking into her eyes. "I've been through this more times than I care to remember. In all ways, it's awful. Trust me; it's better to carry your memories of Samantha as you see her now, in peace, at rest."

Marion grasped the bed rail with both hands. "I'm staying."

Richard placed his arm around his wife, pulled her close, and led her from the room.

Marion turned for a final look as they passed through the doorway. Beth followed, walking them back to the waiting room.

When she returned a minute later, she nodded. "Do you want me to...?"

"No, I'll do it."

I listened to the ventilator's rhythmic clicks. Air whirred through its bellows and into Samantha's lungs. I watched her chest rise and fall with each cycle, and then, with a moment's hesitation, my hand hovering over the glowing red switch, I clicked the ventilator off, leaving the room in deathly silence.

Samantha's chest remained still, but within a long moment, her mouth opened in its final gasp. Her back arched and her neck extended as her brain fought for survival. Two minutes later, the cardiac monitor alarmed as her heartbeats flickered chaotically across the screen and finally nothing remained but death's infinite straight line.

My eyes filled and my head ached as I left Samantha, dreading the short walk to the waiting room.

Depression followed me through the day, worsened by my blossoming cold. My headache, at first a background discomfort, moved to the forefront making it difficult to concentrate. I must have missed several patients' comments as more than one asked, "Are you okay, Dr. Roth?"

At 4:30, I entered the brightly lit examining room for my third from last patient. My head was killing me. I felt slight nausea, and when the lights themselves were painful, I knew at once that I had encephalitis.

I excused myself and started to enter an empty examining room when I saw Beverly. "I'm sick, Bev. Call Lois and call Jack Byrnes. I need to get over to the hospital. I think it's encephalitis."

The nausea returned suddenly, and I rushed to the sink, retching. My head felt like it was about to explode, my neck ached, and the room spun. I reached for the instrument stand and knocked it over. It hit the floor with a loud metallic crash. Somehow, I managed to get myself to the examining table before everything went black.

Chapter Twelve

The wailing siren had Lois's heart racing. Her stomach cramped with fear as she turned the corner and pulled into the office driveway. She reached the door just as the siren blare died and the ambulance screeched to a halt at the curb.

Beverly waved at Lois. "He's in here. Jack Byrnes is waiting at Brier ER. He said that we're to get him over there STAT."

When Lois entered the examining room, Arnie lay stretched out on the table.

"Arnie, Arnie! It's Lois."

He moaned and turned, nearly falling off the narrow table.

Lois grabbed his head between her hands and yelled, "Arnie...Arnie. Wake up."

He tried to turn again, but she couldn't tell if his movements were purposeful.

The EMTs charged into the room, took Arnie's vital signs, slid him on a gurney, and rushed him out the door. In less than two minutes, they were on their way to Brier only blocks away. Lois knelt beside Arnie as the ambulance sped away, sirens blaring.

Moments later, the EMTs whisked Arnie into the ER and rolled him to Trauma I, where Jack Byrnes and the ER physician stood waiting.

They transferred Arnie to the hospital gurney then Jack examined him and the nurse again took his vital signs. Arnie responded to voice and to painful stimuli, but still not in a purposeful way.

Jack continued his examination. "What happened, Lois?"

"He thought he had a cold...a runny nose, sneezing, and headache. Moments before he went out, he told Beverly his eyes were light sensitive and that he thought he had encephalitis."

"So much for diagnosis. We'll do blood tests, a CT scan, and a spinal tap."

Lois turned to Jack. "What's going to happen?"

"I don't know, but Arnie's healthy. I can't see any reason why he won't be able to fight this off. We'll treat him with everything in our arsenal."

Lois stared at Jack. "Samantha Goldstein was young and healthy too, and look what happened to her."

"I know."

Lois collapsed into the corner chair and wept. "Jack, help me. I'm so frightened. I can't stand to see him this way."

Jack sighed. "I won't lie to you. This scares me, too."

The blood tests showed nonspecific signs of infection, the CT scan was normal, and the spinal tap revealed white blood cells of the number and type consistent with viral encephalitis. Jack treated

Arnie with antiviral agents, and cortisone to reduce brain swelling.

Lois called her sister Sally to remain with the kids. Lois stayed by Arnie's bed, gowned, gloved, and masked. She tried repeatedly to awaken her husband, but he didn't respond.

By the next morning, Arnie remained asleep, however, when Lois shook him for the fifth time, screaming his name, he sat in bed and said in a slow and matter-of-fact way, "Lois...Lois." He paused, looking around. "This is ICU, isn't it?"

"Of course it is. What do you remember?"

Arnie spoke in a monotone. "I remember the headache and the pain in my eyes with light. I was sure that I had encephalitis."

Lois ran to Beth's office to tell her that Arnie had awakened, but when they returned, he was asleep again. They tried, but could not awaken him.

This cyclical pattern continued for a week, hours sleeping followed by lucid minutes.

Jack sat with Lois. "That's why we call encephalitis, sleeping sickness."

Each time Arnie awakened, Lois felt relief, only to have it evaporate when he fell back to sleep.

Jack studied Arnie's chart. "This is more difficult than if he remained unconscious. I know it's hard, the ups and the downs, but each awakening encourages me that the virus has caused no permanent damage to his brain. I'm looking for a change that will indicate sustained improvement."

Lois winced at the icy term permanent damage. It was doc talk, Lois understood, so she said nothing. She wiped her reddened eyes. "Each time, I want to believe that it's finally over, that Arnie's finally back with us."

Lois dipped the washcloth in cool water and wiped the perspiration from Arnie's forehead. Maybe it was a reaction to her touch, but the right corner of his lip quivered. She removed her hand, and the twitching stopped. As she was about to touch him again, the spasm at the corner of his mouth returned and spread to his right cheek, and then to the entire right side of his face.

Lois gasped and reached for the nurse call button screaming, "Get the nurse in here now, he's having a seizure!"

The steel bedsprings squeaked and the frame rattled. Suddenly, the bed shook violently as Arnie's head reared backward and his trunk arched in a whole body spasm. Then, his body convulsed rhythmically. Pink, blood-tinged foamy fluid oozed from Arnie's mouth and nose as the nurse entered, grabbed a padded tongue depressor, and rammed it between Arnie's teeth.

Jack rushed to the bedside with a Valium-filled syringe in his hand. He grasped the thrashing arm, shoved the needle into the IV port, and injected. In twenty seconds, the seizure ended abruptly.

Lois looked expectantly into Jack's eyes.

"It's the encephalitis. I've controlled the seizures with Valium and will begin medications so it won't happen again."

"What does it mean, Jack?"

"Nothing good, Lois. Nothing good."

The seizures broke the pattern of sleep and awakening and Arnie slipped into a deep coma.

Friends, relatives, and patients, had managed to fill most of the available wall and counter space in Arnie's room with get-well cards, flowers, and plants. In the center, Lois placed Amy and Rebecca's Get Well Daddy drawings.

After two weeks, they moved Arnie to a private room adjacent to the ICU. Lois spent hours each day at his bedside, clutching his hands as if he'd disappear if she released them.

Arnie and Lois's lives were so intertwined, that they had found it difficult to determine where one ended and the other began. It wasn't the romantic fantasy of fulfillment by the blending of personalities or of one soul completing the other. Lois found it difficult to explain herself to others, but each time she looked at Arnie, she had to smile.

How can I go on without his love, without his touch, without his laughter, and without sharing my life with this incredible man? With so much at stake, she fought the intrusive, distressing thoughts — evolving truths rejected by her soul.

While he remained in a coma, the physical therapist splinted Arnie's hands in a normal position to prevent contractions. Twice daily, the therapist came to put Arnie's extremities through a full range of movements. They attached muscle-stimulating electrodes to force contractions and preserve muscle tone and strength. Jack placed a thin clear feeding tube through Arnie's nose and into his stomach. Thick cream-colored liquid tube feeding dripped into Arnie on a regular schedule that simulated mealtimes.

Each day was like the last. Their words read like a script. "Any change, Jack? — No, I'm sorry, Lois."

The staff of Brier Hospital, physicians, nurses, and others, Arnie's fans, continued to express concern and then disappointment. Soon, Lois noticed that life for others, in spite of their real concern and their love for Arnie, had drifted back to normal.

Having a choice, nobody could live this way. Like an unending war, you could forget about it until the evening news reported twenty of our troops killed. The people would have their transient moments of angst, and then they'd return to blissful oblivion. Lois understood but resented the loneliness and isolation of her mission. Only Jack, Beth, and Beverly remained steadfast beside her, saving her from the added pain of going it alone.

Lois sat with Beth. "I don't think I could do this without you. I can't thank you or Jack enough."

"It's what you guys would do for us. It sounds trite, but that's what friends are for."

Jack Byrnes felt the pressure. Although he was doing everything possible, Jack, an activist physician at heart, found passive waiting difficult to impossible.

I'll never get used to it, he thought.

Since most of his patients were in ICU, the sickest of the sick, death hovered nearby. It was the merciless specter, indifferent to the tragedy of their deaths. Irrational as it was, Jack's struggle against death remained personal.

One evening, Jack led Lois into the nurse's lounge. "I'm getting another EEG. Arnie's brain waves looked okay. They show only the slow waves we expect in coma. Maybe he's developed seizures that interfere with his level of consciousness. It's a long shot, but I'm playing all the odds."

"How long can he go on this way?"

"I don't know what you mean," Jack said with consternation.

"No, Jack, it's only a question. We'll go on for as long as it takes. For as long as Arnie has any chance of recovery."

Chapter Thirteen

The UC Medical Center was a crowded gray and tan high-rise complex that sat atop Parnassus Heights south of Golden Gate Park. Debbie and Matt Wallace arrived as bone-chilling fog rolled over the hills and into the city.

Once they diagnosed Debbie's breast cancer, events moved so fast that she and Matt could barely keep up with the logistical demands much less the emotional ones. Julie Kramer, Debbie's surgeon, had her scheduled for surgery the following week.

Today, they were seeing Dr. Stanley Becker, chairman of the department of oncology, and one of the nation's leading cancer specialists. They sat in his sterile waiting room and flipped through outdated *Time, Newsweek, Sunset,* and a variety of car enthusiasts' magazines.

Stacks of brochures spanning the broad breadth of cancer were scattered about the room. The bulletin board had postings on patient oriented seminars, professional meetings, newspaper clippings about the university, and a directory of cancer support groups.

What am I doing here? Debbie thought. I don't want any part of this world.

The receptionist rose from her desk. "Doctor Becker will see you now."

The large office had a sitting area with easy chairs, a couch, and a small conference table.

How many tears had been shed here? Debbie wondered.

The twelfth floor widow immediately behind Dr. Becker's desk revealed the brick wall of the adjacent nursing school.

Dr. Becker unfolded his sixty-year-old lanky body from the chair behind his desk and approached them with his hand extended. "Stan Becker."

"I'm Matt Wallace and this is my wife Deborah."

"Call me Debbie, please."

Becker smiled. "Let's move over to the conference table. We'll be more comfortable."

He's friendly, Debbie thought, but so restrained that I can't read the man. He lives in cancer's black shadow. What should I expect?

Becker wore an Armani suit; the work of an expert tailor who'd fashioned the garment to fit his long arms and legs.

"How's Arnie doing these days? He's a special guy."

"Haven't you heard?"

"Heard what?"

"Arnie has encephalitis."

"How bad?"

Debbie shook her head. "Bad."

"I hadn't heard a thing. I'll give Brier a call." Becker paused for a moment then faced Debbie. "How are you dealing with this so far?"

Debbie didn't know how to respond. She sat with her head down in thought, and then looked into his eyes. "I'm not dealing with it. I'm living through it."

"I've been at this for a while," he said smiling, a genuine smile this time. "I've seen it all. Take my word for it, as dark as it looks now, you'll get through it. Brier has wonderful support groups with women like you who will understand.

"Arnie's office sent your complete chart including the surgical report, the pathologic examination and the slides, and your complete diagnostic evaluation. I'm presenting your case to the Tumor Board today, but I've been through this so often that I'll tell you in advance, what they'll recommend.

"First, you'll have a mastectomy. Julie Kramer will discuss technical details with you regarding immediate reconstruction. She did her surgical residency here. Don't tell her this, but she's one of the best surgeons we've trained at the university. We tried to get her to stay on the teaching faculty, but she had her heart set on private practice. If technical considerations allow it, she'll reconstruct your breast at once. Second," he hesitated before delivering the grim news, "you'll need to undergo a full course of chemotherapy."

Becker stood and walked to the credenza next to his desk and grabbed a thick bound notebook. "Much of this will sound like a foreign language to you, but the information packet, more like a book, will tell you more than you ever want to know about chemotherapy. I'm going to recommend a full course of two powerful anticancer drugs, Adriamycin and Cytoxan. We call it the AC protocol. Therapy with the drug Taxol will follow."

"Chemotherapy scares the hell out of me. How bad is it really?"

"Anyone who tells you that it's a stroll in the park is lying. These are powerful drugs designed to kill cancer cells, but since these drugs affect all the cells in your body, they'll make you sick…very sick. We've gotten much better controlling side effects, but still, it will be unpleasant for a time."

Debbie looked into the doctor's eyes, her voice cracking and barely under control. "What are my…"

"What are the chances of surviving your breast cancer?" he interrupted. "Considering the type of tumor, your age, and my expectation for your response to chemotherapy, your chance of surviving five years is close to 90 percent."

"I'd prefer 100 percent, but that's not bad, is it?"

"I'm not big on pep talks, they don't endure, and so let me simply say that a life-affirming attitude is a potent force for success. Spend your time with the optimists and ignore the gloom and doomers. You'll sail in a sea of opinion, part of it will be on course, much of it can send you adrift, and, if you're not careful, you can sink in it. Hail me any time you need help in navigating these unchartered waters."

They talked for another thirty minutes then Matt stood and extended his hand to Dr. Becker. "I appreciate the time you've spent with us today. You may be sorry you made yourself so available to us."

"Never. One more thing, you won't offend me if you ask for another opinion. If you want one, let me help you. I know the best oncologists in California and around the world. I'll arrange for you to see as many as you like." He paused again. "I don't want regret over 'what ifs' to be part of your care, now or anytime in the future."

Chapter Fourteen

Little remained of the life that Lois and Arnie Roth shared. Her daily hospital trips were exercises in futility. Arnie simply looked as if he were asleep. For the first few weeks, Lois remained frantic. She knew that nobody could maintain this level of fear and anxiety indefinitely, yet any degree of relaxation, any moment of pleasure with the kids or with the hospital staff, felt like betrayal. If she only could maintain her focus, her determination, then Arnie would get better.

She watched as the physical therapist lubricated Arnie's skin and joints with peppermint oil. Afterward, he put those joints through the full range of exercise movements to prevent contractures.

When the therapist worked hard to move Arnie's joints, he remained motionless, serene. That must be painful, she thought.

Jack and Beth Byrnes shared Lois's despair, but tried not to show it. Beth was okay with long periods of handholding and silence. Jack maintained the facade that somehow, he had things in hand. He needed to be in control, and tried to remain upbeat.

"I'm not ready for any of this," Lois said. "I live each day in fear that we'll lose him, yet I dread even more that he won't be the same Arnie when he awakens. That would be…"

Jack squeezed her hand. "I can't help myself. I'm an optimist. The last thing I want is to give you false hope, but when I put it together, look at Arnie physically and especially neurologically, I think that optimism is justified." He paused. "How are the girls doing?"

"Amy is too young to understand. She just wants her Daddy. Rebecca understands all too well, and she's devastated. The pain of Arnie's illness has brought us closer."

Four weeks passed. Arnie remained unresponsive. Jack came every day and the exchanges with Lois became strained. Each sensed what the other felt: disappointment and despair. For Lois, anger came as an extra burden. While she knew nobody would blame her, she felt guilty.

At Jack's instructions, the nurses placed headphones on Arnie and they played his favorite music for hours each day. Lois read books and magazine articles aloud.

Jack placed Arnie's chart in the rack. "Lois, don't be upset, but maybe it's time to send Arnie to a coma care facility."

"Don't tell me *Wellcare's* pushing you to transfer him. He'd love that."

"They are pushing, but I don't give a shit what they say. I believe that everything we're doing at Brier can be done better in a place designed for patients like Arnie."

"Patients like Arnie," Lois exploded. "Don't think or talk about him in that way. That's Arnie Roth lying in that bed. He's your best friend. He's my life. He's my…"

Lois burst into tears, but slowly regained control. "I know, Jack, but it's like giving up…accepting that he'll remain this way. I can't stand it. I won't do it."

"I'll ask around. Remember," he said without conviction, "this type of facility may be the best thing for Arnie in his present condition. We'll discuss it again when I have more information."

One morning, a week later, Lois was sitting at Arnie's bedside, gazing through the ICU window at the east bay and the distant city.

Beth carried fresh bagels from Saul's kosher deli in downtown Berkeley. "Jack brought these in for the staff. He won't be happy until we're all in Weight Watchers. I grabbed some cream cheese, and you'll find lox and smoked whitefish in the lounge."

Lois tore an onion bagel in half, took a bite, and smiled. "Arnie loved…I mean he loves bagels and lox."

What is that aroma? Fresh bagels, like Nana made. Then later, no, it's smoke…a fire somewhere. I roll out of bed, walk to the door, and look down the shadowed hallway.

It's like a painting with symmetrically contracting walls creating the illusion of distance. Gray-yellow clouds revolve in a slow-motion cyclonic pattern obscuring the hall's end. From time to time, the clouds part long enough to reveal a large steel door.

When I enter the mist, my face feels cool and I smell peppermint. I grasp the knob and the door trembles in anticipation.

"Daddy...Daddy," comes the plaintive cry beyond.

"I'm coming girls," I reply. I again grab the knob. This time it's hot to touch, and shakes as it melds with my hand. As I turn the knob, the door rattles and suddenly bulges toward me. Some force was pushing from the other side, trying to escape. I step back reflexively with dread.

"Daddy...Daddy,"...voices behind the door. "Come get us."

My hand returns to the knob. I gradually turn it until it clicks. The door suddenly swings open with force enough to send me reeling backwards. The expelled air is warm and fetid, the smell of death.

I turn to see Lois and the girls standing before the doorway of our home. Their wide eyes and Lois's hand to her mouth tells me something's wrong.

I feel it approaching from behind, and just before I turn to see what it is, Lois screams, "Don't look back...run, and whatever you do, don't look back."

I run, but soon feel its hot breath on my neck.

"No Daddy the girls scream," as I trip and fall to the ground.

Arnie thrashed in bed screaming, "No...No!" He'd raised his arms as if he were fighting off an assailant.

Shocked, but pleased to see Arnie move and hear his voice, Lois hugged her husband. "It's okay Arnie. I'm here. You're all right. It was a dream, a bad dream."

I sat upright and looked around the room. "It was on me. It was so real. It couldn't be only a dream, could it?"

"You've been out for quite a while, sweetie. It's incredible that you're back with us."

"Out? Back? What are you talking about?"

Just then, Jack arrived. "My God, Arnie, you're back!"

I stared at Jack. "Back from where? What am I doing here?"

Lois broke into tears while Jack studied me. "What's the last thing you remember?"

"It's hazy, but I recall the office, a headache, the sensitivity to light...It was encephalitis, right?"

"No question about it. You were lucky to get through it."

"I was out for a while, I know. How long was it? A few days?"

"Arnie, you were in a coma for a little over a month."

"A month! A month. That's not possible, Jack."

"Ask Lois. She was here most of the time."

I turned to Lois and grasped her hands. "Are you okay? The kids?"

"I'm fine. We're all fine." Lois paused. "It was horrible. You were so sick…I thought I'd lost you…" Lois wept.

"Don't," I said. "The worst is over. What happened with my patients?"

"Your internist and family practitioner friends either came in to run the office or agreed to see your patients in their practices. Everybody's fine."

I slumped back on my pillow trying to digest everything. After several minutes, I sat upright. "Maybe my worst patients will decide not to come back."

"No such luck, Baby. Your loyal patients await your return, especially Missy Cabot. She's been asking for you and asking…and asking…"

Chapter Fifteen

Connie Rinaldi was in for her fall checkup in preparation for what was likely to be another challenging winter for her bronchitis. She worked as an elementary school psychologist in Berkeley. She loved the job, but in winter, sick students felt obligated to share their bugs with everyone.

Jim McDonald, her internist, entered the examining room. "How's it going, Connie?"

"I'm doing well."

"When was your last attack?"

"May, I think. Every spring, all that pollen kills me."

"It's time for your Flu shot, and this year, I'm giving you *Pneumovax*, the pneumonia vaccine."

"Forget it, Doc. The last time I took the flu vaccine, it nearly killed me. The reaction was so bad, I think I'd rather have the flu."

"That's probably what happened, Connie. You got the flu. This vaccine contains dead virus and never causes disease."

McDonald picked up Connie's office chart and flipped to her pulmonary function tests. "Look, Connie, your breathing tests show that each bronchitis and asthma attack has cost you lung function. You don't have enough reserve lung capacity if you're unlucky enough to catch the flu or develop pneumonia."

Connie half smiled. "I feel so good after talking with you, Dr. McDonald."

"Don't give me a hard time, Connie. I wouldn't suggest it to you if I didn't think it was important. The flu shot we give every year, but the pneumonia vaccination should last for at least five years."

Connie smiled. "Get me down to a lower dose of cortisone, and we have a deal."

"I'll try, but I'm not making this a quid pro quo. Roll up your sleeve."

As far as Connie could tell, the flu vaccination gave her a transient low-grade fever and a little aching. She couldn't discern any physical effect from the *Pneumovax*.

When Connie returned to school after the Christmas holidays, the kids arrived with the usual mix of infections from simple colds, influenza, and a variety of upper respiratory infections.

They should have enough common sense to cancel assembly, she thought, as she sat in the crowded auditorium listening to a chorus of coughs and sneezes.

"You look like you're coming down with something," Connie's mother Tina said one evening three weeks later, staring with concern at her daughter.

"That wouldn't surprise me, Momma. The kids breathe and cough on me every day; it's an occupational hazard."

"Maybe you should call Dr. McDonald."

"No, Mamma, not yet. The doctor gave me a whole bunch of medications that I need to use first. I've been through this a thousand times; I know what to do."

"Your Daddy and I, we worry too much. We can't help it."

"I had the flu shot and the pneumonia vaccine in the fall. That should protect me."

When Connie's cough became productive, she was concerned. She kept a clear plastic cup next to her bed to see the phlegm's color. If it turned green or yellow, she could be in trouble. For three days, she coughed and wheezed more than usual, but this morning, when she awakened, she knew at once that whatever she had, it had taken a turn for the worse. She wheezed heavily and failed to respond to her inhalers and aerosol machine. The cup showed thick green phlegm with specks of blood.

I'd better get on antibiotics, she thought.

By the next morning, she wasn't any better, so she called Jim McDonald.

"I'm having another attack," she said filling him in on the details.

"How bad is it?"

"I have it under control."

"Are you sure? I'd prefer to err on the side of caution."

"No, I'm fine."

"Connie?"

"No, Doc. I'll call you…I promise, if this thing gets any worse."

"Look, Connie, I trust you. You're smart and you've been through this many times before, but don't forget that it can get out of control quickly and you'll wind up in the hospital."

"I don't want any part of that, Doc."

"Call me every day until it clears. I'm in my office reading my mail every morning at 8:30. I'll tell the service to put you through immediately."

"You're worse than my mother, Doc. Thanks for caring so much."

"Just call."

Connie called the next morning. "It's about the same, Doc. I'll talk with you tomorrow."

Jim McDonald forgot the expected call from Connie until his nurse stuck her head into his office. "We're ready for your first patient, Doctor." It was 9:15 in the morning.

"Give me a minute," he said as he picked up the phone and dialed Connie's number. The answering machine picked up after the sixth ring with her cheery message. He dialed her at school. "This is Dr. McDonald. I'd like to speak with Connie Rinaldi."

"I'm sorry, Doctor," the school secretary said, "but Connie didn't come in this morning."

"Did she call in sick?"

"No, and that's unusual. She calls if she's going to be late or if she's too sick to work. We're a little concerned. "

Me too, he thought as he dialed Tina, her mother.

"It's Dr. McDonald, Tina…"

"What's wrong?" she shouted.

"Have you heard from Connie?"

"No, tell me what's happening, Doctor."

"She didn't call me this morning as she promised, and she didn't go to work or call in."

"Dear God…" she cried. "We'll go right over."

"Call me immediately when you get there."

Twenty minutes later, while Jim McDonald was examining his first patient, his nurse banged on the door. "It's the phone, Doctor, an emergency!"

Jim put the phone to his ear and heard the crying screams of Mrs. Rinaldi. "She's all blue. She won't wake up. What should we do?"

My God, he thought, she's dead! "Is she breathing?"

"I think so, but it's high pitched wheezes. Do something, Doc."

"I'm sending an ambulance. Stay with her and let them in when they come. They'll take her to Brier Emergency."

Eight minutes later, the EMTs burst into Connie's bedroom, took one look at her, and placed her into the ambulance. They raced with sirens blaring toward Brier.

An EMT was on the radio, shouting, "We're four minutes out. This is a bad one. Asthma, I think.

She's cyanotic with blue lips and hands. She's barely moving any air. Get ready."

Jim McDonald worked through his morning awaiting the emergency room's report. When he tried to reach the ER physician, the nurse said he'd call the moment he was free.

At 11:30, Herb Fine, the ER physician, called. "We've loaded her up with cortisone and bronchodilators and she's breathing better. The x-rays of her chest show bilateral pneumonia and the examination of her phlegm suggests that she has pneumococcal infection. I've started antibiotics."

"Does she need to be in the ICU or the respiratory care unit?"

"Maybe not the ICU, and the RCU would be my first choice except they're full with influenza and pneumonia cases. They've been so for a week."

"Okay, put her on the medical ward. I'll see her in about a half hour. Thanks for the help, Herb."

When Jim arrived at noon, he went immediately to the fifth floor medical unit to admit Connie. Joseph and Tina Rinaldi sat at her bedside. Tina was holding her daughter's hand and crying.

Connie looked up as Jim approached the bed. Thank God she's awake, he thought.

She pulled the clear plastic oxygen mask away from her face and with a wheezy whisper said, "I was fine when I went to bed, Doc. I'm so sorry," she sobbed.

Jim placed the mask back on her face and smiled. "Don't blame yourself. I should have forced the issue a lot earlier. Maybe we could have prevented this."

"No," she said in muffled tones, "I should have listened. I never learn."

"What's wrong, Doctor?" asked Tina.

Jim signaled her parents to walk with him into the hallway. "It's pneumonia, and it's bad."

"Bad. What does that mean?" said Joseph.

"Well, this kind of pneumonia wouldn't be a problem for anyone with normal lungs, but as you know, Connie's lungs are far from normal. I think we got it early enough for her to respond to antibiotics, but it going to be iffy for a while."

"Why pneumonia?" Tina asked. "I thought you vaccinated her against pneumonia."

"I did, but maybe it's a strain that the vaccine did not cover. I'm not sure."

Jim wrote Connie's admission orders. She'd receive potent intravenous antibiotics, large doses of cortisone-like medications, and vigorous inhalation treatments. He asked Alan Morris, a pulmonary physician, to consult to see if he had any other suggestions, he didn't. This time, they knew that Connie was skydiving without a reserve parachute.

Chapter Sixteen

Brian Shands ran the original Horizon Pharmacy. Henry Fischer met regularly with him.

Brian was the product of suburbia and Myra and Bruce, his 60s challenged parents. Since he was old enough to walk, Brian's mother and father were determined not to repeat the overindulgences of their own parents. Brian and his younger sister Karen spent hours in the minivan or the big SUV shuffling from lesson to lesson and game-to-game.

When Brian looked back at his formative years, he couldn't remember any significant amount of free time, time to play, time to do nothing, or time to stare at the wall or out the window. In fact, the few moments of solitude he recalled left him ill at ease. Why didn't he have something to do? He filled those moments with fantasy games and comic books.

As much as he tried, Brian couldn't remember failing at anything. Nobody won or lost at baseball or soccer. His parents managed to find a way to approve and reward every accomplishment, however minor.

School bored Brian. He read by the age of three and soon found an interest in American historical figures, especially the presidents. At his parent's prompting, Brian would challenge adults with an encyclopedic knowledge of arcane presidential trivia. Brian obsessed over his history books, but failed to recognize, as did his parents, that his behavior by the age of seven had changed from cute to boring or worse. His demands for attention became rude and inconsiderate. He was overtly disrespectful to his parents, who joked at this behavior, thinking that Brian's precociousness justified his disgusting and insulting comments.

When Brian reached age nine, even his parents couldn't ignore the problem.

One evening, while his parents entertained three other couples, Brian took front stage and challenged all with his trivia. Eyes rolled upward and scowls appeared — not again, they thought. Finally, Myra said, "That's enough, Brian. Why don't you go to your room?"

Brian looked at his mother with disbelief. "Why don't you shut up?"

Myra recoiled and her eyes widened with shock. After an embarrassed tittering laugh, she said, "That's not funny, Brian. I don't want to hear that language in this house."

Brian sneered. "Get a life, you bitch," then stormed from the room.

He'll grow out of it, she thought, and over time, his behavior seemed to moderate.

In high school, he achieved straight A's. He assumed the persona of Michael J. Fox on Family Ties. He participated in the debate club and became its president. In addition, he joined the John Birch

Society, the U.S. Junior Chamber of Commerce, and the National Rifle Association.

Brian hated the school jocks, their arrogance, and especially their popularity with girls.

Willie Howard, the star linebacker, was in constant academic difficulty. One day, after overhearing Willie fret at the next table over upcoming examinations, Brian said, in a voice too loud, pointing with his head toward Willie. "Too much inbreeding in that family's gene pool."

The laugh at Brian's table was short-lived as the room suddenly became silent. Willie rose and strode slowly toward Brian.

Willie loomed over a stunned Brian. "What did you say, you son-of-a-bitch?"

Brian froze. His hands shook and he paled. He couldn't think up a glib comment or utter a word.

Willie grabbed Brian by his shirtfront, and pulled the smaller boy up, until Willie stared down, their faces separated by inches.

Suddenly, the football coach and a male teacher grabbed both boys from behind.

The coach held Willie firmly, and whispered into his ear, "Don't do it, Willie. He's not worth it."

"Look," said a football player, pointing to a puddle on the floor by Brian, "he peed in his pants."

They all pointed and laughed.

Brian reddened as they pulled Willie away, straightened his shirt, and left the room without a word. He wouldn't forget this day and his humiliation. He'd avoid Willie in the future, but vowed revenge at the first opportunity.

Three months later, when an anonymous tip led school officials to Willie's locker, they found Dianabol, a performance-enhancing steroid. After weeks of scandal, news headlines, investigations including blood tests, that showed no drugs in Willie's system, the authorities concluded that someone had planted the drugs in the locker.

Brian watched in amusement.

Brian obtained a modest academic scholarship to the University of Utah, but at the end of his second year, his father's business failures robbed Brian of the financial resources needed to continue in the business administration program. To continue in school, he transferred to the school of pharmacy. This department offered partial financial support, but he needed to work and take on additional educational loans.

Brian met Lilly Bender, a cashier at Bernard's Pharmacy in Salt Lake City, where he moonlighted. When he first came to work, Lilly lit up in an immediate attraction to Brian, his dark hair, eyes, and his seriousness that contrasted with her usual dates. He was lean and dominated over her five feet, two inches.

"You're too serious, Brian. Don't you have any fun?"

He blushed. "Don't have time for fun, Lilly."

She looked up at him with doe-brown eyes. "There's more to life than school, you know. I can add a bit of excitement, honey," she crooned, "try me."

Brian still considered himself a virgin since he'd ejaculated on the teenage hooker before penetration, a humiliating memory that still haunted him.

Lilly, a thin, pale, but attractive college dropout was completely comfortable in her sexuality and took pleasure in Brian's education. She taught him virtually everything he knew about sex, and how to please a woman in bed.

On impulse, he married Lilly after graduation and accepted a position in the East Bay of San Francisco at Horizon Pharmacy. To his embarrassment, Lilly worked in Wal-Mart as a cashier until she had their first child, Melodie. They remained heavily in debt, and although Brian had a stable position, it was worlds away from his fantasies of material success. Over time, he became convinced that his marriage was a mistake. He felt trapped by circumstances out of his control. His goals now appeared out of reach.

Brian's title as chief financial officer far exceeded his actual responsibilities. His education and interest in business administration made him a wizard with the books, and he knew how to evaluate the many business profit and loss sheets that came the way of Horizon in its expansion.

"We're getting killed, Henry," came Brian's opening salvo.

"You're not telling me something that I don't know. We're making greater than 16 percent margin, pretty damn good for the industry, but it's not enough."

"You can read the P&L statements as well as anyone. Our capital expenditures, the delay in opening new pharmacies, and the rising prices of drugs are making this a tougher business every day. Walgreen, Rite-Aid, CVS, and that tiny competitor, Wal-Mart, are mounting aggressive marketing initiatives. They're killing off five percent of local pharmacies every year."

"We've done well over the last few years with our agreements to supply Brier Hospital, local clinics, and physicians' offices with drugs and medical supplies. We made a fortune with our contracts for chemotherapy medications, EPO for dialysis, cancer, and AIDS patients, and a whole range of hospital supplies, but now…"

Brian's deal with Henry was to share the profits from Horizon Pharmacy over a certain dollar amount per month. In the last three months, they'd exceeded that target once and only by a hair. Brian, extravagant by nature, aspired to a fat income and he was having difficulty in meeting his own strongly held professional targets, and his family's material needs.

Brian placed the P and L sheets on Henry's desk. "How badly do you want to turn this around, Henry?"

"What kind of question is that?"

"It's a simple question when you face losing everything you've worked years to create."

"I wouldn't murder anyone, if that's what you mean."

"Nobody's talking about murder, but many drugs are far too potent...I'll show you the published studies. We could dilute them while maintaining their effectiveness, and by the way, greatly increase our margins."

"Maintain their effectiveness?"

"The drugs I'm talking about don't have absolute doses," Brian said with a thin smile. "We titrate them, that is physicians adjust their doses to obtain a specific effect. The only thing that the users could notice is that they are using more medication to obtain an effect."

"I don't know if we can get away with that. They'd catch on eventually."

"Not if we're smart, and by smart, I mean not too greedy."

"We could go to jail!"

"Choose your poison, Henry." He paused for a thoughtful moment. "You wouldn't need to know."

"I'll think about it. Outline the details for me to review, and then we'll talk again."

Henry decided to go along with Brian's suggestion before he left—after all, what choice did he have? Everyone makes compromises, he thought. I'm no different. Even Teddy had to deal with the devil in Germany, at least until he could get his family out.

Bankruptcy loomed over the horizon. Teddy's business, bankrupt?

Henry needed to rationalize his decision. His investors, people who held him in high regard, people who trusted him would lose everything. More than one hundred employees, many who have been with Horizon for over twenty years, would lose their jobs. He couldn't imagine the humiliation. Worse of all, he would hear from Bert Carlin, Ruth's father.

He would love this—rubbing my nose in it.

Pharmacists substitute cheaper drugs or supplies to increase their profit margins, and nobody gets hurt. This is no different.

The next morning, Brian and Henry sat over coffee. "I'm turning day-to-day operational control to you, Brian. I expect that you'll do your best to boost our margins in a totally ethical way. That's the tradition of Horizon Drugs."

"Of course," said Brian. "I'd never do anything to compromise our sterling reputation."

"I'm going to make this work," said Julie Kramer as Debbie Wallace returned to the office for her third visit. "That should do it," she said as she injected more saline to expand the small bag in Debbie's breast. "The scaring from your radiation made immediate reconstruction difficult, but I think we have enough space now."

"I'm so nervous Julie," said Debbie, "what will it look like?"

"I'm not going to tell you that it will look exactly like your normal breast. It won't. At first, it will look a little unnatural, but as it heals, as gravity exerts its effects, and your new breast fills into your bra, it will look nearly normal. We might need to do a little nip here or a tuck there, but you'll look fine."

The surgery went well, but Debbie's postoperative pain was severe especially when she moved her arm. After six days in the hospital, she returned home to begin chemotherapy. She stood naked before her mirror and grimaced at the oddness of her chest. Her new right breast, black and blue from the surgery, sat an inch higher than her left, and compared with the smooth graceful curve of the left breast, the right was lumpy and irregular. The puffy pinkish healing fresh incisions looked uneven. Julie promised this would recede over time.

Each time Matt tried to look at her breast, Debbie turned away.

"I love you," he said. "Don't shut me out."

"I love you too, but I'm not ready."

It surprised Debbie how quickly she recovered from the surgery. She needed to adjust to Arnie's absence.

Jordan Goodman, Brier's busiest cancer specialist, agreed to administer her chemotherapy as outlined by UC's Stanley Becker. The Brier oncology-hematology program used a converted supermarket, a large outpatient facility, three blocks from the hospital.

The huge parking lot was half-full when Matt drove Debbie in for her first chemotherapy treatment. As they walked toward the East Bay Comprehensive Cancer Center, the traffic on nearby highway twenty-four rumbled in the background. They grasped each other's hand, turning Debbie's fingers white with the pressure. The chemotherapy, like her mastectomy, was life affirming and while it came with an array of emotions, one stood out— fear.

"I'm frightened," she said.

"Me too, Baby."

"I can't stand the dread, the hopelessness, and the loss of control over our lives...it's unbearable."

"I have the irresistible urge to get back in the car, pack our bags, and get the hell out of town," said Matt, "but hope's distant voice of keeps me going."

"Everything that's happened in our lives changes us, the good and the bad," said Debbie. "I recognize for the first time, something that only the neurotic obsesses about when they focus on all those who take our lives in their hands every day. You know them, the airline pilot, the taxi driver, the operator of the thrill ride, and those who control what we eat, drink and breathe."

"And our physicians," said Matt, opening the door to the clinic.

"I trust them, just as I trust you, baby, it's as simple as that. They want me to get better. That's enough."

They approached the receptionist, identified themselves, and gave her their insurance information. Katy Howard, a nurse in her late twenties, introduced herself, brought them into a small examining room. Katy took Debbie's vital signs, and had her sign a six-page Authorization to Perform Chemotherapy form. Most of the document contained a long list of possible side effects ranging from trivial to, as the clinic's attorneys insisted, death. She wasn't sure if they fostered informed consent to help her or protect the clinic...well, yes she was sure.

Debbie could see that Katy was a caring nurse, so she downplayed her reaction to the clinic's questions. As if she were giving a Miranda warning, Katy read from the card. "Are you sure you understand the risks of this treatment, the side effects, and that you have a right to another opinion or a more detailed explanation of these medications...if so, please check this box, and sign here," she said pointing to the form.

"You're kidding, of course," said Debbie, with a broad smile as she held up the document.

"I'm sorry, Mrs. Wallace. They make us do this, or we can't give you the treatment."

"I know," she paused, "and please call me Debbie. I'm sure you understand I'm not all that glad to be here, and this scares the hell out of me."

Katy took Debbie's hand, nodded. "Come with me."

They walked together into a room the size of a small theater at a multiplex cinema. A circular nursing station stood in the center of the room while at its periphery, against the walls, were leather recliners fully occupied but for one. Fluids in glass bottles or in plastic bags ran through clear plastic tubes and into veins.

Katy tied a print blue floral patient gown around Debbie's neck. "This is to protect your pretty clothes, I love that dress, it's so cute, and it goes with your blue eyes."

Debbie looked around the pale yellow room. They'd decorated the walls with photo reproductions of Ansel Adams and Edward Weston. Most patients slept, maybe that was the best way to deal with chemotherapy.

As she sat with her right arm extended, Katy cleaned it with disinfectant and inserted a small plastic catheter into a vein. She hung a bag of salt solution and ran a small amount in to assure the correct placement of the catheter.

"We've got to make sure that the catheter is securely inside the vein because if chemotherapy drugs escape, they can be extremely damaging to the tissues."

"Damaging to the tissues," she said, "and you're pumping it into me. That's encouraging."

"I understand how you feel, but we're after cancer cells."

Katy injected two medications into Debbie's IV. "The doctors have designed these to prevent side effects." Next, she hung a glass IV bottle with a hazy fluid. "We'll run this in over three hours and then you're out of here."

"How will I feel?"

"Most of the time, patients feel well, but if you feel sick, push the call button and I'll give you something. Try to relax if you can. Sleep, read, watch TV or listen to music."

Debbie somehow managed to fall asleep during the third hour of treatment, waking only when Katy removed her IV. "We'll see you in three weeks."

Katy gave Debbie three vials of medication to counteract the predictable side effects of the chemo and a five-page list of complications and treatment advice. "It's going to get rough, but I know you can handle it."

Chapter Seventeen

"Arnie, take it easy," Lois said.

After three days assuring Jack that I was stable, he had moved me into the skilled nursing facility for aggressive rehabilitation.

I had no idea how difficult it would be. I could barely sit upright, and when I did, dizziness and weakness overwhelmed me. At first, I blamed this on the effects of prolonged bed rest, even as they'd used electrical simulators to maintain my muscle tone.

It's a joke to think that technology can mimic the effects of gravity by stimulating a few muscle bundles.

I noticed that weakness wasn't my only problem. I had difficulty coordinating my muscles, an aftereffect of encephalitis. I wouldn't be returning to work for a while.

To prove my mind was intact, I worked the *San Francisco Chronicle's* daily crossword puzzle, which I completed easily. I tackled the *New York Time's* puzzle, which left me in my usual state of frustration. Lois and I spent time reminiscing about our past. My memory, it seems, was better than hers was, or less selective. Women remembered a few things better than men did, especially any insult, perceived or real, even if it happened eons before.

I wanted to go home, but my limited mobility and the physical therapy I needed made it necessary for me to stay in rehabilitation. Although Lois and the kids came every day, it wasn't home.

Sandy Katz, my physical therapist, came from the Marquis De Sade school of Rehabilitation. This was odd since when we first met, she looked like a shy high school student with auburn hair in pigtails. Her awe at caring for a respected physician lasted thirty seconds.

At our first session, she shook her head in disappointment. "Don't be such a pussy, Arnie. Let me see you sweat."

I sweated and wobbled between the parallel bars, unable to support my weight for more than twenty seconds. In retrospect, Sandy Katz was just what I needed. I'd been an athlete with natural gifts, so I never worked as hard as others did. In my weakened condition, PT with Sandy was more difficult physically and more challenging emotionally than anything I'd done before. Over time, I got rid of the wobble, and my rubber legs were replaced by saplings, and finally by tree limbs. Among my life's accomplishments, walking again, unassisted, was my proudest achievement.

On the day of discharge, Lois and the kids came to drive me home. Sandy marched into my room pushing a wheelchair. "Have a seat, Doc. It's time to make room for someone who needs our help."

I hugged Sandy goodbye. "I can never thank you enough, but if you think you're going to get me in that chair again, you'd better get someone a little bigger to do it."

"Don't be a pain in the ass, Doc, you know it's hospital regulation."

I kissed her on her rosy cheek, turned, and walked out. "Tell them to sue me."

As I walked into the bright sunshine, all my senses were fine-tuned. The air was rich with Jasmine and roses, more distinct than I'd ever noticed before. Maybe this was another benefit of my newfound freedom.

"Let me drive," I said as we approached our Toyota Sienna minivan.

Lois slid quickly into the driver's seat. "I don't think I'm ready for that."

I sensed a musky aroma. "What's that smell in here?"

"That's 'new car smell'. Becky chose it when we went to the car wash to get the van ready for the big day."

Becky pouted. "Don't you like it, Daddy? I picked it out myself."

"I love it, sweetie. Daddy's nose must be really sensitive today."

Lois turned and gave me one of her looks.

The powerful tang made me uncomfortable. "That's pretty potent, Lois."

"I think they make that stuff up in a New Jersey lab along with thousands of scents and flavors in our soaps, perfumes, toiletries, beverages, and food."

I enjoyed the ride home and felt my eyes fill as we pulled up to our tri-level redwood house and parked in the garage. When I walked through the kitchen, I breathed in a strong pine scent. My mind flashed to my childhood home, and my mother scrubbing with Pine Sol, her favorite. "You cleaned the house for my homecoming."

"You're surprised. Let me introduce myself, Lois Roth, your wife."

"I guess that shouldn't surprise me. You're the one who straightens up for the cleaning lady."

Amy grabbed my hand and dragged me down the hall. "Come Daddy, I even cleaned my room for you."

When we entered her room, it looked uncharacteristically neat. She made the bed herself I saw by the uneven cover and the sheet dangling from one side.

"Whose room is this?"

"Oh, Daddy."

I picked up the scent of Windex. "You cleaned the windows, too, I see."

"How could you tell?"

"I haven't seen those windows so clean since you were six."

"Oh Daddy, you know I'm only five," she laughed still holding my hand and now hugging my thigh.

When we returned to the kitchen, our eight-year-old, Becky, stood quietly studying her feet.

"Can I see your room too, Becky?"

"Sure Daddy."

I followed her to a similarly neat room. I detected the smell of fresh paint. Somebody had hung two pictures on her wall; one was a pencil still life of our back yard with the flowers and trees beautifully rendered while the second was a watercolor of a little girl standing alone in a field of grain, dark clouds overhead. Becky's message was clear, fear and loneliness. I forgot how talented she was and vowed to sign her up for more art classes.

I scanned the room. "You did a terrific job."

"Daddy," she hesitated, and then began to cry. "I was so afraid..." she rushed into my arms.

"It's okay, Becky. I'm fine. Please don't worry. I'll never leave my little girl."

When I returned to the kitchen, I grasped Lois's hand. "Do you want me to see your room, too?"

Lois grinned. "Oh, don't worry, you'll be seeing a good bit of that room. We've got a lot of catching up to do."

"I may not be the man you're used to right now, Baby. Give the old man some slack."

"Don't worry," she smiled sensually. "I'll do all the work. You relax and enjoy."

I went into the great room and collapsed into my recliner, savoring the strong leather aroma as the seat cushion whooshed under my weight.

I turned and adjusted my pillow, struggling for sleep. The flashing 12:00 on the alarm clock said we'd been through a power outage. I flipped on the nightstand light, examined my wristwatch, and reset the clock to 2:15 a.m. Lois's snore was soft and regular — white noise. I was almost asleep when the first scent molecule reached my consciousness — the acrid odor of fire. For ten seconds my mind ignored the message, and then I sat up, alarmed. I shook Lois, "Wake up — wake up!"

She groaned. "What is it, sweetie?"

"Can't you smell it?"

"Smell what?"

I stood, glanced around the room. "Something's burning."

"I didn't smell a thing — go back to sleep."

I returned to bed fully awake now, sampling the air...the faintest trace of smoke then moments later, the undeniable fumes of fire. I turned on the bedside lamp again and when I gazed at the closed door to our room, traces of smoke seeped in from beyond. Now sirens sounded in the distance as I touched the door handle and retracted my hand immediately from the searing hot knob. "Daddy...Daddy...," came the plaintive distant wail. "Lois...Lois..." I screamed. "Get up!"

I grabbed the shirt atop my dresser, wrapped my hand to protect it from the heat, and reached for the doorknob.

"Don't," Lois shouted as she grasped my shoulders pulling me backward as the door swung inward *engulfing me in smoke and flames. I began coughing and choking then...*

"Arnie...Arnie...wake up...wake up."

"What happened?" I said fighting for full consciousness. "Lois...it was horrible...so horrible. The smell...the fire...the kids!"

"It was a dream, sweetie. Everything's fine except for the potatoes au gratin. They ran onto the oven burner, stinking up the house."

A dream, I thought...that was one hell of a dream.

Chapter Eighteen

For Debbie Wallace, Katy Howard's warning, 'it's going to get rough', ranked as the understatement of all time.

Predictably, after each chemotherapy infusion with Adriamycin and Cytoxan, she became deathly ill with nausea and vomiting, often lasting for up to six hours.

Debbie pulled her head from the sink and wiped the stringy mucous from her mouth. "That was the eighth time in the last thirty minutes. I can't take much more."

Matt ran the washcloth under the cold water and wiped her face.

Debbie grasped his hand. "Oh God, that feels good."

She recalled Matt's comment about seasickness, when you had it, you were afraid you weren't going to die. Three days ago, she laughed at the joke. Nothing seemed funny anymore.

"If the nausea wasn't bad enough," she said, "I feel so weak afterward. That scares me more. I feel helpless. All I can do is stay in bed."

This was the specter of cancer she feared the most.

Debbie thanked God that Matt and her closest friends didn't attempt to cheer her up — she'd have killed the first one who tried. Instead, they let her take the lead, provided sympathetic ears, sat by her while she cried, and shared the everyday events of their lives.

I'd give anything to be able to focus on trivialities, she thought.

Two weeks after each treatment, she felt better, and by the third week, nearly human. Unfortunately, that only made her dread the next round of chemotherapy.

Her beautiful chestnut hair fell out in clumps each time she brushed it, and soon she accepted the inevitability that getting rid of it all would be best.

"Are you sure you want me to do this?" Matt asked as she sat at the kitchen table with a towel over her shoulders.

"I'm sure."

She closed her eyes as the electric clippers vibrated over her scalp. Tears streamed over her cheeks. Debbie remembered her reactions to seeing the bald women of chemotherapy. While she'd been saddened and frightened by the sight, she was a caring woman and had empathy for them. As she thought back, she hated to admit it now, but she'd felt an element of revulsion, too. Maybe it's in my genetic code — to react that way — like any human faced with the specter of disease and death.

She had endured the best medicine had to offer, but chemotherapy acted as if its intention wasn't salvation but destruction.

The term 'side-effect' was like calling a tsunami, a ripple on the ocean's surface.

Chemotherapy became the disease itself relentlessly affecting all of her body—collateral damage, to borrow from the war metaphor.

I might survive cancer, she thought, but not the treatment.

The faces of Debbie's children hid nothing of their despair…cancer was their nightmare, too. Her eight-year-old didn't fully understand what was happening to her mother, but all understood the dramatic change in Mommy's energy level, her prostration following each chemotherapy treatment, and the striking changes in her appearance.

Kelly, her five-year-old, stared at Debbie this morning as she posed before her mirror trying on several wigs. "What happened to your pretty hair, Mommy?"

"It's the medicine, but don't worry, it will all grow back. Meanwhile, I need your opinion." She posed for her daughters with several wigs. "Which one do you like the most?"

"The blonde one," said Heather. "It makes you look like Beyoncé."

She kept explanations to the girls casual. They couldn't fully understand, so she used their questions and their behavior to monitor their emotional reactions and as a guide to what they needed to know. The younger child knew that Mommy was sick. She missed the many activities they shared, but she knew nothing about the effects of the disease. Even Heather, who knew a little about breast cancer, and what death meant, could not relate these things to her mother. She had become more attentive to Debbie, more helpful, and showed anxiety only when her mother was her sickest after chemotherapy.

"The kids have been amazing, Matt," she said one night as they prepared for bed.

"It's a tribute to you, Deb. You've kept it together. You gave them the luxury of security."

"It's so hard," Debbie said, crying and seeking the safety of his arms.

Matt resisted the impulse to say something; to reassure, to remind her of what the docs had said, and to tell her that everything would be okay. Instead, he kissed her. "I love you. I'll always love you."

Debbie completed the cycles of Adriamycin and Cytoxan, and met with Dr. Jordan Goodman for the next phase, the home stretch.

Jordan sat at his desk with her chart. He smiled. "I know it wasn't easy, but we're exactly where we should be in your treatment. We're ready to start the second, and I hope, the final phase in treatment, Taxol. This is a compound extracted from the bark of the Pacific yew tree. It's a potent anticancer drug that received FDA approval in 1994 for individuals with your tumor."

"Please don't tell me that the side effects are as bad as the first combination of medications."

"It's hard to predict how anyone will respond to a specific drug, but in general, Taxol may be easier on you than the others. Keep in mind, however, that with this final step we've increased your chances of beating this thing to more than 80 percent after five years."

Debbie tried to smile. "You say 80 percent survival, I think 20 percent recurrence and…"

"By type of tumor, your response to the first course of treatment, and my experience, I think it's much higher. People are too used to the 80 percent chance of rain from the weatherman. If our reliability was like theirs, I'd worry too. It's not. We do much better."

At first, the Taxol infusions produced similar ghastly side effects, and one she hadn't had before, mouth sores. They were painful and produced large amounts of mucous, frequently choking her. She found it necessary to carry a washcloth or tissues at all times.

How can Matt watch this? It's disgusting…I'm disgusting, she thought as she wiped the stringy mucous from her mouth.

When Matt rubbed her shoulders, she wept.

She lifted her head from the sink after vomiting for the third time in fifteen minutes. "I'm sorry. You shouldn't have to deal with this."

Matt hugged his wife. "And if I were sick, you'd be out playing tennis, right?"

I'm so lucky, she thought, to have Matt. I must find a way to make him know it, but she knew he already did.

"Hang in there, Baby. We're nearly through this nightmare."

After the second cycle, the side effects had diminished. I'm practically there, she thought.

Chapter Nineteen

Jim McDonald made rounds on Connie Rinaldi and received frequent detailed phone reports from the nurses during the day. For the next three days, she teetered at the abyss then stabilized. Jim felt better until the repeat chest x-ray showed persistent infection in both lungs.

She should have responded, he thought. What's wrong?

On morning rounds, day four, Connie looked terrible. She'd again become less responsive, the oxygen saturation in her blood had declined, and she struggled more than ever to breathe. She needed to be in ICU, but the unit was packed. He'd have to call Jack Byrnes, the ICU director for a bed.

The severe influenza epidemic had Jack Byrnes's ICU in full triage mode, too few beds for too many sick patients. Setting priorities, deciding which patients needed the ICU the most, put Jack on a collision course with Brier Hospital physicians.

"Jack," pleaded Jim McDonald, "you have to find an ICU bed for my patient, Connie Rinaldi. She's too sick for the medical floor."

"Look, Jim, I don't like this any more than you do. I'll see Ms. Rinaldi and make an assessment. If she's sicker than anyone in ICU now, I'll transfer someone out and make room for her; otherwise, you'll have to make do. We simply don't have enough acute care beds."

"If they were sicker than Connie, they'd be dead. She almost coded this morning. If she dies because we treated her on the ward rather than ICU as I recommend, all of us will be liable for her death."

"Don't give me that crap, Jim. I know what's at stake, and I know that triage is not only necessary, it's essential when we have limited ICU beds. I'll look at her right now. You'll have my answer in thirty minutes."

"I'll wait in the doctor's lounge."

Jack went to the fifth floor medical ward to see Connie Rinaldi.

"You look beat, Jack," the charge nurse said.

"I am. I may be the next victim of this epidemic. Can you get me Ms. Rinaldi's chart."

She returned with the chart and a cup of coffee. "She's too sick for us, Jack."

"So I hear."

Jack reviewed her chart, and examined her briefly. "My name is Dr. Byrnes. We may need to move you up to the intensive care unit."

Connie looked up through watery frightened eyes, but didn't respond. As she struggled with each breath, Jack noted her ashen color, blue lips and impaired mental status. Jim was right. He'd have to push someone out of the unit and suffer the ire of that patient's physician. He'd try persuasion first, but he knew that all the patients in the unit were very sick, and that no physician would willingly relinquish the security of an ICU bed.

During Jack's review of Ms. Rinaldi's chart, he saw that her sputum and blood cultures teemed with pneumococcus, the infecting organism. Pneumococcus was the most common severe bacterial infection causing pneumonia and physicians, especially old-timers, called the infection, 'the old man's friend' because in the past, it brought death to the elderly and debilitated. Hospitals were seeing less of this organism and this type of pneumonia due to the administration of *Pneumovax*, a highly effective vaccine against pneumococcus. Connie Rinaldi, like several of his sickest patients in the ICU, had received the vaccination, yet developed the infection. That was odd.

Jack rang the doctor's lounge. When Jim answered, he said, "That's one sick lady you have there, Jim. Give me a little time to find a bed and we'll transfer her."

"Thanks Jack and I appreciate your help."

"By-the-way, Jim, don't you think it's a little strange that she has pneumococcal infection when she's been vaccinated?"

"It should be unusual," said Jim, "but this is the third patient I've seen recently who developed this infection after receiving *Pneumovax*. Maybe we have a bad batch out there?"

Maybe, thought Jack.

The signs of change were subtle at first, but when Henry drove up in a new Lexus SC 430, Ruth Fischer knew that something was different. Her questions over the last few months about Henry's business problems evoked only glib responses.

"I'm entitled to know what's happening, Henry. It's my ass on the line, too."

"You worry too much, Ruth. I told you that I'd take care of it. Thank God that Medi-Cal claims came through with those delayed payments and that the new Regency Drug store opened with a bang."

"What about the $650,000 that you needed?"

"It's no longer a problem."

"Where did you get that much money?"

"I didn't get that... ," Henry stopped, a scowl on his face. "Don't give me the third degree, Ruth. I don't like it. I told you I dealt with this."

"Now you really have me worrying. What are you hiding?"

"I'm not hiding anything. I'm trying to run our business the best way I can, and excuse me, but I don't like being second guessed by a rank amateur."

"Why are you being so deliberately offensive, Henry? What are you hiding? I have legal rights here. I'd prefer to keep this discussion between us and avoid attorneys, but if you force me..."

Henry stood. His face was red with rage. "Don't mess with me Ruth. You have no idea what you're doing or what damage you can cause."

I've never seen him so angry, so out of control, Ruth thought. What's going on?

As Ruth rose to leave the room, she turned to face him. "This is far from over, Henry. Count on it."

Chapter Twenty

Maybe it was the near death experience, but after two weeks at home, life never felt so joyous or as rich as it did now. My heightened senses were confronting the world anew. Food never tasted so good, Lois' skin never felt so soft, my children never smelled so sweet, and music, its beauty, touched my soul as never before.

I was sitting on Jack Byrnes's examining table when he walked in. "How's it going Arnie?"

"It's crazy, but I can't recall ever feeling better in my life."

Jack wasn't a primary care physician, but because he was smart and compassionate, he'd become a doctor's doctor and cared for Brier physicians and nurses.

After he listened to my heart and lungs, and felt my abdomen, he did a neurological examination testing muscle strength, reflexes, and sensory perception. When finished, he smiled. "Can't find anything wrong with you, Arnie. You're life of leisure is over. You can get back to work like the rest of us."

"Encephalitis was one hell of a trip. It scared us all, especially the kids. The experience gave me new insight into what it's like to be that sick. That's called learning the hard way."

Jack slapped me on the back. "Anyway, get back to your office and let me see you again in three months."

"Thanks for everything, especially for how you and Beth helped Lois. We can never thank you enough."

"Buy us dinner sometime, and let me pick the place. Maybe you'll treat us to Chez Panisse?"

I hugged Jack. "You're on."

I'd surprised him, I thought, as he initially stiffened, paused, and finally hugged me in return.

Monday morning and my staff had strung a banner across the entrance. "Welcome Back Arnie!" They applauded as I walked in.

I felt my face turn red. "Thanks guys. You don't know how good it feels to be back."

After a few hugs and handshakes, I knocked on the wall to get everyone's attention. "I'd like to thank you all for your help in carrying on while I was away. You did a terrific job. We're a team, and I know that for me this is more than a place to work. In spite of all our problems, I look forward to coming here each day, and you're the reason why."

I paused for a moment, grabbed a stack of envelopes from my briefcase, and handed them out. "You'll find a small token of my appreciation here."

Beverly Ramirez stood. "Wonderful having you back, Arnie, we missed you. You won't mind if we run out and cash those checks before we start today?"

I stared at Beverly and smiled. "Don't tell me…Missy Cabot's in the waiting room."

The staff erupted in laughter.

My return to work was seamless. It was satisfying to do once again all those things I took for granted. My enthusiasm was boundless and my mood, ebullient. What had irked me in the past, I ignored. I even enjoyed the moments of silence while stuck in bay area traffic — that, more than anything else, said that nearly dying had changed me.

At Debbie Wallace's request, I agreed to resume her chemotherapy.

Debbie stood outside the examining room. "I'm so happy to have you back, Arnie. Thank Dr. Goodman for me , but his chemotherapy clinic's depressing."

"It's good to be back."

When I entered the examining room, I sensed body powder's strong aroma, a common occurrence as many women showered and powdered themselves before coming to the office. I wished more patients paid attention to their hygiene. In addition, I sensed something else, a more subtle tangy scent like that of tonic water — quinine?

After examining Debbie, she sat before my desk while I finished reviewing her course under the chemotherapy protocol, and her recent laboratory results.

"I'm pleased with your progress. I know you may not feel terrific, but chemo is tough. You know that better than anyone. Side effects following the more recent treatments have been easier, is that right?"

"The last two infusions of Taxol weren't bad at all. I must be getting used to that miserable medication. How many more, Arnie?"

"Two more should do it. Then you can get back to a normal, happy life."

"Excuse me, Arnie, but with breast cancer, a normal life, if I live so long, will be decades ahead."

"I'm as close to breast cancer as I can be without having it myself, and I can tell you that I like your odds for a long life. The happiness part is up to you and Matt. Let me see you again in a month."

Debbie gave me a hug. "Thanks, Arnie. I'm so happy to have you back."

Chapter Twenty-One

People complain about routine. Even those living 'exciting' lives like doctors, lawyers, rock stars, and racecar drivers, find tedium in their day-to-day activities. That wasn't true for me, at least not for this moment as I released the pause button on my life, and pressed play.

After my third month back at work, the encephalitis faded into memory. I felt relaxed and more satisfied with my life than ever before.

My office was as busy and frustrating as usual. I still fought with the HMOs, and I resumed the QA Committee's chair.

In the past, when the sun bathed me in a light of pure joy, I dreaded the dark storm clouds I knew lurked just over the horizon. Now, I savored each sunny day, heedless of the worries that troubled me in the past. With the blackjack dealer showing a ten, I'd hit sixteen knowing I'd bust. Now, I knew that the next card would be a five or less.

When I returned home after a particularly busy afternoon in the office, Lois greeted me with a hug. "How was your day?"

"I think I saw more patients today than ever before, but it was okay." I moved my head in a lateral arc, sniffing the air. "Leg of Lamb, honey, with Worcestershire sauce, and rosemary, right?"

Lois stared at me. "That's amazing. All I can smell is the lamb itself."

"It smells awesome. I can't wait."

"We've got another thirty minutes before it's done. I'll get you a glass of wine, brie, and crackers."

When Lois opened the refrigerator door, a rancid stench hit me. "Something's rotten in there, Lois."

"I don't smell anything."

"You're save leftovers in plastic bags, and then forget them. Throw them out or let's do a search and destroy mission from time to time. Who knows, maybe we'll find a cure for cancer."

Lois gave me a smirk and walked away. "Go with God, my son. Enjoy your reconnaissance."

I rummaged through the refrigerator. After removing the known and recognizable, all that remained were a half dozen Tupperware containers and one plastic-wrapped furry-white alien substance that exuded a ghastly essence. I turned my nose away, held the thing between my index finger and thumb in my outstretched arm, and extended it toward Lois.

"Eureka!"

Lois turned from reading *Prevention* magazine. "Very good Arnie. Feel free to do this any time."

"Do you have any idea...?"

"None," she interrupted.

"What about these Tupperware containers?"

"Go to it with that talented nose or toss it all."

Afterward, I sat at the kitchen table reading the mail and sipping the icy wine. It was a Double Oak Chardonnay from our wine club. I savored the dominant buttery flavor with a hint of oak and pear. We had a glass of wine most nights. Lois purchased wine by price. Somehow, she managed to find a decent yet inexpensive wine. The only expensive wines we drank were gifts, though on occasion we'd splurge on a good bottle of Champagne.

Lois reached over to the mail. "Two of your favorite catalogues came today."

I thumbed through the Sharper Image catalog, before scanning the Victoria's Secret, which came six times a week. "I enjoy the artistry of their professional photography."

"Right."

I went to the refrigerator, filled my glass with ice water, and returned to the table. I took one sip and grimaced. "Something's wrong with the water. It tastes terrible."

Lois came over and took a sip. "It tastes fine to me, Arnie."

"Something's wrong. You'd better call the water treatment people out to check the system. It tastes like iodine, chlorine and something foul."

"I'll call them in the morning."

Dinner was delicious.

"You really did it this time, Lois."

"What do you mean, by 'this time'?"

"No. I think it's both of us. The lamb was succulent with a pungently sweet tang. It tasted better than it smelled."

"You're getting into this taste thing, Arnie."

"Taste is complex and starts with our tongue taste buds for salty, sweet, bitter, and sour, and the new one, umami."

"How can we have a new taste bud?"

"We don't. The Japanese first described it a hundred years ago as the receptor for MSG in Asian food. When you combine taste bud sensation with smell, the result is what we commonly call taste. Then, when you add the satisfaction of chewing and the relief of hunger, the result is a splendid sensory symphony."

As usual, I ate too much and nodded off in front of the television.

I felt a tug on my arm. "Play Chutes and Ladders with me, Daddy."

I nodded and joined Amy on the floor for the next thirty minutes. She smiled then giggled in triumph over her dad.

"Can you help me with my homework?" Rebecca asked.

"Sure, sweetie, as long as it's not math."

"Oh Daddy, you know it's math...I hate math."

"Well, I wasn't too crazy about math myself. If I could learn it, you can, too."

Her math book couldn't be more than a few years old. It had a faded cover, many torn pages, and a distinct musty aroma as if it had been sitting in a damp place for decades. The first time I helped Becky with her math, it was immediately obvious that while numbers never change, math teaching did. Before I could help her, I first had to understand how they did it today.

After an awkward start, we completed her assignment.

I remained before the TV, not really watching. I gave the girls their final goodnight kisses before Lois put them to bed.

Lois collapsed at my side onto the soft couch. "I'm glad that's over. Give me a moment to restore my energies."

I stared at the TV, and then pushed the remote's off button preferring silence and the moment's intimacy.

Lois stirred then lowered her head into my lap, closed her eyes and slept. Suddenly, I felt a familiar stirring in my groin. I felt relieved that this part of my anatomy had come through encephalitis unscathed.

Twenty minutes later, I was still erect.

Lois stirred, and then did her best Mae West impersonation. "Is that a gun in your pocket, or are you just happy to see me?"

She raised her head and moved to sit astride me. "How about a lap dance, big boy?"

I lifted her into my arms and carried her to the bedroom. "Why go for fantasy, when you can have the real thing."

Chapter Twenty-Two

Two nurses and an orderly wheeled Connie Rinaldi into the ICU and transferred her to bed five. One look at the purple-blue and unresponsive woman had the staff in crash mode. When they stuck the electrodes to her chest, the cardiac monitor showed a rapid and irregular heart rhythm.

Beth Byrnes turned to the ward clerk. "Get Jack on the phone, stat."

The ward clerk pointed to the phone.

Beth pushed the blinking line. "Connie Rinaldi just got here and she's ready to code."

"Get a stat electrolyte panel and blood gases. I'm on my way."

Jack called Jim McDonald who'd returned to his office. "If we don't do something, she's going to code."

"I'm stuck in the office, Jack. Can you take over? Get Alan Morris, the pulmonary doc to see her again."

"Okay, Jim, but when you come back this afternoon, don't be surprised to see her intubated and on a ventilator."

Jim hesitated. "I understand. Can you ask her nurse to get the Rinaldis' phone number? I'll try to explain what we're up against and what we're going to do."

Jack Byrnes had the operating room on the line. "Get me an anesthesiologist right now. We need to intubate one of our patients before she codes."

"They're all in surgery," said the operating room director. "I can get you somebody in about thirty minutes. Will that be okay?"

"That may be too late," Jack said prophetically, as the ICU code blue alarm sounded.

Jack rushed to Connie's bedside. The nurses had removed her pillows, lifted her torso, and placed a resuscitation board behind her back.

Beth lifted her stethoscope from Connie's chest. "Her heart rate spiked to over 200 and her pressure's down to 60 systolic. She's not moving any air. We had no choice, but to push the button."

The nurses were trying to breathe for Connie with an Ambu bag, but her lungs were so stiff and the airways so filled with mucous that they were having little success.

Jack removed his lab coat and shifted position to the head of the bed. He removed the headboard. "Get me the intubation tray."

Beth opened the tray while Jack donned green gloves.

"Extend her neck," Jack shouted as he grabbed for the stainless steel curved laryngoscope blade and placed it atop the battery pack. As he started to insert the blade into Connie's mouth, he shouted, "She has an upper dental plate. Get the Goddamn thing out now!"

Beth reached into Connie's mouth and removed the denture.

Jack guided the blade back over the tongue and then, lifting the soft palate, tried to visualize her vocal cords. The laryngeal area overflowed with frothy blood and mucous.

Jack's heart raced. His mouth was dry and he felt the first cramps of fear in his abdomen. "I can't see a damn thing. I need suction."

Beth handed him the vacuum wall suction catheter and he swept it rapidly through Connie's mouth and throat.

"Take it easy, Jack," whispered Beth. "You'll get it."

He reinserted the blade trying to find her vocal cords, but all he could see was the fleshy soft palate. "Somebody push down on her larynx, I can't see shit."

Beth placed one finger on each side of the thyroid cartilage, the part of the neck laymen call the Adam's apple, and pushed it down toward the back of Connie's neck.

Immediately, the two white vocal cords appeared in Jack's view and he pushed the endotracheal tube through. "Got it! Someone inflate the cuff before we lose it."

Jack breathed easier as the respiratory therapist attached the ET tube to the ventilator and turned it on. He smiled as the machine provided Connie's first good breath and her chest rose in reaction.

Jack listened to Connie's lungs. "Suction her out then let's begin bronchodilators. Get a stat portable film to check the tube's position and draw a set of blood gases."

Three hours later, Jack stood with Jim McDonald and Alan Morris. "The tube's in the right place and her blood gasses, although poor by anyone's standards are a hell of a lot better than they were before."

Jim looked at Alan. "What do you think?"

"She's safe for the moment. I don't know how she'll respond to more vigorous treatment, but I'll make one prediction; it's going to be difficult to impossible get her off the ventilator." He hesitated a moment. "I know things happened precipitously, but in a woman with advanced lung disease, maybe we've done her a disservice by putting that tube in, especially if we can't get it out."

When Jim entered the ICU waiting room, the Rinaldis rose together, looked at him expectantly.

In muted tones, Tina asked, "How's my baby doing?"

"She's out of danger for the moment, but we had to insert a tube into her throat so she could breathe. This will give us and her a chance to bring this infection under control."

Joseph, Connie's father, pumped Jim's hand. "Thank God, Doctor."

Please sit for a moment. "I don't like to bring this up, but with Connie so sick, we need to understand what she'd want if things don't go well."

Tina turned to Joe. "What is he talking about?"

"I'm not sure," he responded. "I'm sorry, Doctor, but you're not suggesting that we stop treating our daughter?"

"Absolutely not," Jim said, and then he girded himself for what was to come. "We'll do everything possible, but we'll need your help. You know Connie best. You know what she'd want if she gets worse."

"We're still not following you, Dr. McDonald. We've known you for a long time and we trust you, so just say it."

"Let me give the worst case to make the point. This is only an example. It's not about Connie. If something were to happen to a loved one and they had extensive brain damage to the extent that they had no chance of meaningful survival, would you wish to continue treatment. Would you keep a person like that going by keeping them on a ventilator, providing them with nutrition and other treatment to keep them alive at all costs?"

"Like that young woman in Florida?" Joe asked.

Jim nodded.

"I'm Connie's father and I love her more than life, but if we were sure that her mind was gone, that everything that made Connie, Connie, we wouldn't try to keep just her body alive. We're religious people, but doing that would be a disgrace to the memory of our daughter. If she dies," he hesitated wiping a tear away, "it should be with dignity and peace."

That's a relief, thought Jim, but it barely touches on the complexity of keeping someone alive on a ventilator where her mind's intact. God help us if we have to deal with that one.

Jim moved his gaze between the Rinaldis, fixing each for a moment. "Connie knew that she has a severe form of lung disease, and that she might require a ventilator. Did she ever discuss this with you?"

"No," said Tina, "but I know my daughter. She's a fighter. I do know one thing for sure; Connie wants to live."

Chapter Twenty-Three

For the first time in his life, Tino Ruiz had things going his way. He'd arranged his schedule to accommodate his classes, and although the work left little free time, he'd never been happier. His fear about handling the college curriculum faded. He discovered that the classes interested him and he aced the examinations.

Tino's training as a pharmacist's assistant was going well. His bright mind captured the complexity of the dosing system as he read extensively about the more common prescriptions he filled. More significantly, he felt that Henry Fischer and Brian Shands no longer looked at him as if he were about to steal the silverware or rape their daughters.

"Why don't you fill these," said Brian one afternoon. He handed Tino a stack of prescription forms. "I'll deal with the refills." The pharmacy was bustling with prescriptions, their normal heavy load, plus those written because of the influenza epidemic.

Tino worked closely with Brian and had learned much, but something about the man made him uneasy. In his gang days, Tino learned to respect first impressions about people. It saved his ass several times. Brian was secretive about his activities and spent hours alone in the air-controlled clean room. Since airborne particles can carry bacteria and viruses, the clean room eliminated them, a critical step in making up IV fluids, and other injectables. Once, when Tino tried to enter to get medication, he found the door locked. Suddenly, Brian opened the door and shouted, "When the door's closed, it means don't disturb me, comprende amigo?"

"Of course. I needed to get sterile water from storage."

In addition, Tino noted that Brian lied. A few were the-check's-in-the-mail lies, small deceits to explain their failure to supply medications or fill prescriptions when promised. Others were senseless lies over trivialities, and several were major-league, like failing to log in supplies received, and falsifying records subject to examination by the state's division of pharmacy inspectors.

Was this business as usual, Tino wondered, or was something else going on?

I looked at the wall clock that showed we had ten minutes left for the QA meeting. Anything else, Cindy?"

"Yes, Arnie. We have mostly minor stuff to deal with, but we can deal with it after the meeting. We do have another request, an unusual one. The pharmacy committee is on a rampage to reduce cost. In their review, they noticed an unusual drug usage pattern, a costly one."

"What is it, and what do they want us to do?"

"One of the most expensive items in our formulary is EPO, a powerful stimulator of blood production. In the past, we used it primarily to treat anemia in patients with kidney diseases, but now they're dispensing it for AIDS, a variety of cancers, and to boost a patient's blood count before surgery to avoid transfusion and its risks."

"It's a revolutionary drug," I said, "and a real advance in treating a difficult problem."

Cindy passed out a spreadsheet. "Take a look. The pharmacy's budget for EPO has gone up nearly 100 percent. They want us to find out why."

I scanned the data. "The hospital lives and dies by Medicare, Medicaid, and private insurers' reimbursement formulas for this drug. The current usage pattern makes the economics of this drug a break-even or a losing proposition. Simply, they're asking us to look into the reasons behind this increased usage."

"Since we use the drug is more widely now, are they sure they have a problem, Arnie?" asked Jim McDonald.

Cindy Hines shook her head. "They've looked at its use in all these groups and it's an overall increase in per patient usage and not an increase in a particular new patient group. They can't figure it out."

"Cindy and I will meet with specialists who prescribe EPO the most and look at its usage in a systematic manner. I'll bring the evaluation criteria back to you next meeting for discussion before we begin the study."

When Cindy first received the request about EPO usage, it drew her attention at once…

Cindy divided her life between job and work with the Special Olympics. She'd been engaged to Mike Kelly, a husky, athletic Berkeley cop who'd been shot in the abdomen during a drug raid seven months earlier. She'd been through the wringer with Mike during the horrendous first stages of his injuries. He'd undergone multiple surgeries and was near death several times until his condition finally stabilized. She loved Mike, and continued at his side into rehabilitation.

Cindy had been Mike's guardian and protector throughout. Experience told her that even in a good hospital like Brier, mistakes were inevitable. She'd questioned everything, berated physicians, nurses, technicians, and virtually anyone interacting with Mike. Incredibly, she performed her watchdog function with grace, good humor, and kept on good terms with everyone.

After five weeks in rehabilitation, Mike became depressed and withdrawn.

"It'll pass," Cindy told him. "Be easy on yourself. Look at what you've been through."

"Look at me," he replied as he gazed down over his flat abdomen, disfigured with multiple healing scars and two foul smelling yellow rubber drains. "I weigh 120 pounds. Half of what I was before being shot. These infections will never heal."

Cindy held his hand. "Part of your problem, Mike, is that your blood count is too low. Maybe that's why you're healing so slowly."

"Why can't they do something about it?"

"Let me talk with your doc. I think you should be on EPO, a genetically engineered medication that builds red blood cells."

"It'll take more than medication to pull me out of this, but I'll do anything if it'll help."

They began Mike on EPO, but his blood count increased only a little. "We'll step up the dose," said his physician.

Why isn't it working, thought Cindy? Mike can't buy a break.

After two more weeks, Mike said, "EPO's one hell of a wonder drug. It hasn't done a damn thing for my blood." He hesitated a moment, and then turned away. "It's no use, Cindy. Nothing works. This whole thing is a fucking waste of time."

She grasped his hands. "God, Mike, you've come too far to give up now."

He pushed her away, grabbed the rubber drains, pulling them upward. "Look at me, Goddamn it Cindy, look at me. I'll never be the same. I'll never be me again."

She sought psychiatric assistance and soon they were giving Mike Zoloft, a powerful antidepressant.

Mike smirked as he swallowed his first dose. "You're kidding."

"It's going to take a few weeks, but the Zoloft will help."

"Will it allow me to play basketball, go fishing, or camping, or go back to work?"

While Mike slept, Cindy visited with others in rehab, making friends with many patients, especially the children. Rehab introduced Cindy to Special Olympics.

Into the second month, Mike slept fifteen hours a day, and awakened sullen and angry. In spite of increasing doses of EPO, his blood count remained low. His doctor increased the dose further.

Early in his illness, Mike had regular visits from Berkeley cops, but in rehab, the number of visitors had dwindled to his partner and a few close friends. Visiting with Mike was never easy. Nobody knew what to say or how to deal with his anger.

"They're my friends. You should see the way they look at me. Their eyes...they can't stand to be with me, to smell me, or to have me remind them that, but for the grace of God, any one of them could be lying in my place."

When Cindy pulled into the rehabilitation facility on a Sunday morning, flashing police lights and fire department vehicles filled the parking lot.

What's wrong? she thought rushing to Mike's ward.

As Cindy approached the nurse's station, the head nurse, Betty Atkins approached stone-faced.

Cindy felt sick. "What's wrong?"

"I'm so sorry."

Cindy tried to rush past Betty, who held her in place.

"It's too late, Cindy. Mike's gone."

Cindy felt faint. She grasped the sofa's arm and sagged into its soft cushions.

"What happened?" Cindy whispered, tears flowing from her eyes.

"I don't know how or where he got the gun, but Mike shot himself."

The police interviewed Cindy, and Internal Investigations questioned the cops who'd visited with Mike, but without success. The gun had its serial numbers removed, but the FBI lab was finally able to identify the pistol as a weapon confiscated ten years earlier by the Berkeley P.D. during an arrest. They had sent it to the property room from which it disappeared.

Mike's suicide devastated Cindy. She survived through hard work and dedication to a life helping others…

The pharmacy committee's request to study, EPO, sent Cindy's mind back to Mike and the drug's failure. Something was wrong.

At our next monthly QA meeting, Cindy Hines took the pharmacy records on EPO usage and brought the associated medical records for me to review. I'd met with the kidney and cancer specialists, the largest users of EPO.

I began by pointing at Cindy's cart stacked high with charts. "Cindy will pass these out. Look them over to see if you can find any explanation for the excessive use of EPO. I went over them quickly and to my eye, their use was appropriate. We don't understand why these patients require so high a dose to achieve the desired effect."

One by one, the reviewers reported that they could find nothing in these records to explain this phenomenon.

Jack Byrnes picked up Cindy's data sheet. "Maybe the drug company has changed its manufacturing method or there's something wrong with the product. I suggest we obtain the EPO from our usual sources and return them to the manufacturer so they can assay them for potency."

"That may take a while," I said, "but I can't think of any other course of action."

After the meeting, Cindy stared at the stack of charts. Mike hadn't responded well to EPO either, she thought. Could this be why?

The Infectious Disease (ID) committee met the next day at noon, in the same room. Edith Keller, an ID specialist, chaired. Cindy Hines supported this committee as well.

Edith held up the data folder. "We've recently had our tenth case of pneumococcal pneumonia in previously vaccinated patients. That's distinctly unusual, as vaccination is highly effective in preventing the infection. We pulled the records on all patients receiving the vaccination in the last five years. When you look at this group, it's immediately obvious that it's those vaccinated in the last two years who are getting the infection. We took the analysis further and compared their risk factors, their ages, and all other parameters. The groups are virtually the same except for when they received the *Pneumovax*."

"What about UC or Sanford," asked Jim McDonald, "are they seeing this problem?"

Edith shook her head. "No, but two other east bay hospitals have had a few cases."

"This is serious," Jim said. "We give *Pneumovax* to our high risk patients since they handle this infection poorly. While it's not as bad as it was in the past, people still die from this type of pneumonia. *Pneumovax* saves lives or at least it should."

"Either something's different among these groups and we're not seeing it," said Edith, "or something's wrong with the vaccine."

"Can we measure antibodies to pneumococcus in these groups?" asked Karen Small, a family practitioner.

"We can get the *Pneumovax* manufacturer to do this or we can find a reference lab," said Edith. "That may not help us, since low antibodies won't tell us if it's the vaccine's fault or it's the patient's fault. We need to know why this is happening before someone else dies."

Chapter Twenty-Four

She feels pretty, I thought, as I watched Debbie Wallace entering my office a month later. She wore a floral sundress and her chestnut hair with small butterfly barrettes had reached the pixie-cut length. She'd taken care with her makeup and her red toenails shone in her dressy strap sandals.

"You look terrific, Debbie. It's wonderful to see you this way."

"I feel good, too." She pulled up on a lock of her hair, "and it's coming back."

"How are things at home?"

"We're back to normal, or what we call normal for our family." Debbie paused for a moment then stared into my eyes. "I focused too much on being cured and when the cancer came back, it was more than I could bear. Now, I don't think about it."

"That's normal, but what you mean is that you don't obsess about it."

"No, Arnie. Once I got through the last treatment cycle, it just isn't part of my consciousness. Intellectually, I understand that this is the ostrich approach to illness, but I feel so good that for better or worse, I've taken the plunge. I chose not to post a five-year calendar and mark off each day until I'm sure the disease is behind me."

"Okay, I'll worry about it."

Debbie smiled. "Good. What's next?"

"I'll see you for routine examinations quarterly, then once a year we'll do blood tests and x-rays." I stared at her for a moment and locked her eyes. "You'll call me right away, if anything develops."

Debbie smiled again. "You worry too much, Arnie. I'll be fine."

After I finished my office hours, I walked to ICU. Jack Byrnes sat at the nurse's station reviewing a thick medical chart.

"I think you're glued to that chair, Jack. Every time I come in here, you're in the same spot."

"Sometimes I get that same impression that my life's at Brier. The rest is a side show."

I pulled Sarah Jackson's chart from the rack and sat beside Jack. I'd admitted her yesterday with a urinary tract infection that spread into her bloodstream, making her blood pressure unstable. Changing her antibiotics had done the trick. As I glanced across the room, a strong familiar aroma caught my attention and instantly my mind flashed to my tour as a medical officer in Desert Storm...

They brought the Iraqi prisoner to our medical clearing company for treatment. The black-bearded teenager was dirty and wasted. It looked as if he'd been ill for weeks. His right leg was heavily bandaged with a filthy encrusted gauze dressing that reeked. He'd suffered burns over 20 percent of his body, but most of those wounds had healed.

I stood by the gurney. "Charlie, cut that dressing off, and prepare yourself."

Charlie Hicks was a veteran medic with years of experience. He was my right-hand man. He struggled with a bandage scissors to slice through the thick dressing. The last cut released the dressing and the room filled with a fruity, grape-like aroma that I recognized as the product of the bacterium called pseudomonas. We covered our noses and turned away.

The egg-shaped leg wound measured five by three inches. I directed the high intensity light directly onto the large skin ulcer for more detail. A white sheen covered the wound. After staring at it for ten seconds, I thought I saw fine flutter on its surface. I stared again and the wound undulated with a wavy, rippling movement. I folded a piece of sterile gauze into a surgical clamp, drew it across the wound, and gasped. As I pulled the white membrane away, the wound was alive with shiny, crawling maggots that had eaten the damaged, infected tissue, leaving a bright pink healing surface called granulation tissue.

Charlie turned, grabbed a stainless steel basin, and vomited...

"What's the matter, Arnie? You look green."

I shook my head, clearing it of that vivid memory — no, it was more than a memory. I had relived the experience. My hands trembled. I stood. "Come with me Jack."

Jack looked puzzled, but rose and followed me to the first ICU bed on the left.

"Stay with me a second, Jack. I know that pseudomonas is in the unit somewhere. I'll never forget that disgusting sweet stench."

"I don't smell a thing, Arnie."

We walked past the first four beds. Each time I stopped, swung my head in an arc, and inhaled — nothing.

Then we came to bed five, Connie Rinaldi on a ventilator.

Jack turned toward me. "She's having an exacerbation of severe chronic bronchitis."

I stopped and stared. "It's here. It's pseudomonas and it's coming from her lungs."

Jack leaned over Connie and sniffed. "I know that odor, but I can't detect it here."

"Take a sample of the fluid from the breathing tube. You'll find it. I'm sure."

His "Okay, Arnie," carried disbelief as he broke the connection between the breathing tube and the ventilator to get a sample.

"I'll send it to the lab. They'll place it on a microscope slide and stain it with dye. Then we'll have an idea what it is before the cultures come back in a day or two."

Fifteen minutes later, the bacteriology lab called back. "It's a gram negative bacillus Dr. Byrnes. It looks like pseudomonas to us."

Jack stared at me. "I don't know what's going on here, Arnie, but you may have saved Connie Rinaldi's life."

Chapter Twenty-Five

Henry Fischer rolled off Monica Kelly flushed with satisfaction. He lay next to her in the warm afterglow of their lovemaking.

Ain't life grand, Henry thought.

Monica smiled. "You're spoiling me."

"I'm the one getting spoiled." He paused for a moment. "I know we agreed that this was only for fun, no strings attached, but I'm enjoying this too much to keep our relationship recreational."

She caressed his cheek, and smiled. "I made a promise not to get involved, but I guess I was kidding myself...I am involved. Maybe it's because you have so little left of your marriage that I imagined what might be ahead for us."

"Dealing with Ruth won't be easy. She's smart and can be vindictive. I can only assume that she has her suspicions about me, and I know she has questions about Horizon Drugs. She can screw things up for us if we're not careful."

"Then let's be careful."

Horizon Drugs was back in stride. They'd weathered the squall and clear sailing lay ahead. Their cash-flow problems were behind them, and their profitability soared 50 percent. His meetings with Brian Shands, once unendurably depressing, had become a joy as the black ink overflowed the pages of their accounting book.

Henry lifted the glass of Champagne he'd iced for the occasion. "You're a genius, Brian. At this rate, we're going to retire our entire debt in six months."

Henry's agreement with Brian was making his young partner a rich man, but Brian wanted more.

Be smart, Brian thought. Don't screw this up.

"I couldn't be more pleased, Henry. Everything's going better than we thought." Brian paused, and then continued, "I don't want to cause problems, Henry, but when I first joined you, my deal came with the implied promise that one day I'd share in Horizon Drug, that is, have an equity position."

"I think you've earned a position in the company, Brian, but I'll need to deal with the timing and work out the agreement with our shareholders. You know I can't act on my own. I have responsibilities to the partnership."

Brian recognized bullshit when he heard it, but he knew that it was a mistake to push Henry too hard, too fast. "Henry, you're too smart to let this get between us since you already agreed that I've earned a share of the action. I know you'll find a way to make this happen."

Henry worked through the permutations of keeping Brian happy. It would be simple and clean if Brian didn't get greedy. In addition, Henry recognized that forces beyond their control bound him and Brian together.

Tino Ruiz was on the schedule to work late.

Brian slipped on his sports jacket. "Can you close, Tino? I've got a date, and I'm late."

"No problem. I'll see you tomorrow afternoon."

A date? Tino thought. Brian has many dates for a married man.

Soon after Brian left, the private line rang. "Hi, Tino. It's Lilly. Is Brian there?"

Shit, Tino thought. I can't hurt her. "He just left. I think he has a meeting."

"If he comes back or phones in, please have him call me."

"Sure Lilly."

After a moment's hesitation, Lilly said, "How are you doing, Tino? How's school?"

"Straight A's, Mrs....I mean Lilly. Thanks for asking."

What a sweet woman, Tino thought. That fucking Brian Shands.

Tino placed the large medication jars back on the shelf, refilling those whose levels were low. He checked the vials, labels, instruction sheets, and phone-in prescription pads, and restocked those that were low. When he looked for more prescription labels, he could find none. He checked the storeroom for the packages with the name, Colfax Printers, the company that did all their printing, but found none. As a last shot, he looked toward the clean room, but hesitated remembering Brian's admonitions. Finally, he entered, checked the shelves, and then saw a box turned at an angle showing the word, 'Printers'.

There they are, he thought.

When Tino brought the box down, he saw the full name, Colonial Printers, with a return address of Guadalajara, Mexico. He lifted the lid and examined the contents. Inside, he recognized the printed labels for three drugs, EPO, Taxol, and *Pneumovax*. These weren't the common usage labels affixed to prescriptions, but exact replicas of the proprietary brand labels. Perhaps Brian used them to replace labels damaged in shipping or in preparation, or is it possible they were for something else?

He replaced the lid and returned the box to its exact position on the shelf. He'd ask Brian for more labels tomorrow, but would say nothing about his discovery.

I never thought it would come to this, thought Ruth Fischer as she stood before the smoked glass door that read, Sam Spade Detectives, Reggie Brand, Owner: Confidential Investigations, Surveillance, Criminal and Civil, Cheating Spouses.

All she knew of private investigators came from movies and television, so it surprised her to see a thin, balding man in his late forties sitting behind a large oak desk. He looked like a bookkeeper.

He stood and extended his hand. "Reggie Brand,"

"Ruth Fischer," she said staring at the man.

"I know," Reggie laughed. "I'm not anyone's image of the hard-nosed private eye. That's what makes me effective. I look ordinary. What can I do for you?"

"This is embarrassing. I've never done anything like this before."

"Few women have. Tell me what you need."

"This isn't a matter of finding out my husband's been cheating. I assume that as a fact. What I want to know is how long and with whom. In addition, I share considerable material assets with Henry Fischer, much more than the usual community property. I have a significant position in my husband's business, Horizon Drugs, and I want to protect those interests. He's hiding things from me. I need to know what and why."

Reggie smiled. "The first part will be simple, that's my bread and butter. The second part is problematic."

"Problematic?"

"You may be in a better position than I to look into his business affairs. I'm afraid that combing through public records trying to get inside information may not get you what you need."

"I want this done without his knowledge. Is that possible?"

"Anything's possible with enough time, enough cash, and a degree of ethical insensitivity."

"I don't care how you do it. Get me the information," she said, extracting her checkbook.

Lilly Shands had spent hours cooking Brian's favorite dish, roast duck. She set the dining room table for two with her best silverware and crystal. The candles, lit two hours ago in expectation of his arrival, had melted as had her joyous anticipation for the evening.

She had her head down on the table when Brian entered and threw his coat and briefcase on a chair. She wore the white with roses sundress that he loved. The first time she'd worn that dress, he had the full skirt up and her panties off in moments.

Lilly looked up as he entered the room.

"God damn it, I forgot," he said, shaking his head.

"I told you this was an important night. It's our anniversary and I wanted it to be special."

"It's no big deal, Lilly. Can we eat now?"

"It's too late," she cried. "It's all dried and ruined."

Brian frowned and pointed to the gift-wrapped package next to his place setting. "What's that?"

Lilly stared at him. "It's no good Brian. I can't go on this way. You're never home, and when you are, you act like a stranger."

"I've been busy with work, Lilly. I work hard for all of us. Don't be so spoiled."

"Spoiled. I do everything for you. I live for you and the baby. What more do you want from me?"

"I'm sorry, Lilly. You know me. When I'm into something, I let it take over my life. I'll do better, trust me."

Lilly raised her head focusing her eyes on Brian. "You haven't touched me in three months, Brian. Three months! At one time, you couldn't keep your hands off me."

"Don't be such a pain-in-the...I don't have the energy to deal with this crap..." he paused. " I'm sorry, I'm just tired."

"Let me get you something," she said as she walked into the kitchen.

Brian shook his head in disgust, although he had to admit that with her narrow waist and full hips, she sure looked good in that dress.

Chapter Twenty-Six

Since discharge seven weeks ago, my life gradually fell back into a routine. I finished morning office hours early and drove home to join Lois for lunch. When I arrived, a service van with a large blue water drop on its side, the logo for Crystal Pure Water, sat at the curb.

Finally, I thought. We'll get to the bottom of our water problem.

"Lois, I'm home."

She came out from the kitchen, gave me a kiss and a hug. "The water man is almost through, and then we'll have lunch."

"Caesar salad with grilled chicken, cloves and mustard...no, make that Dijon mustard. And, if I'm not mistaken, key lime pie for dessert."

"Arnie, you're freaking me out with that nose of yours."

"Me too, babe. I don't know what it is, but my nose is working overtime."

I heard a knock on the door from the garage and when I opened it, the Crystal Pure man, Greg Waterford, entered. "Hey Doc. It's good to see you back in action."

"What did you find, Greg?"

"I've been over the equipment, top to bottom, and I can't find a damn thing. Maybe something got past the system, but it's okay now. I took the extra step of back-flushing the deionizer and the charcoal."

He opened the kitchen tap, let the water run for three minutes. "Give it a taste, Doc."

Even before I took a sip, the water emitted the aroma of decaying organic material. The sip was worse. I grimaced as I flashed back to Iraq where my canteen's disgusting water sat in desert sun for several days. "This is bad, Greg, maybe worse than before, it's putrid."

"Putrid," said Lois, taking a sip, "it tastes fine to me."

Greg took a sip. "I can't taste anything wrong with this water, Doc."

I felt my face redden. "It's either my imagination or I'm going out of my mind, but that water tastes like shit to me."

Lois looked at me strangely. "Arnie, calm down. Nobody thinks you're crazy. There must be a simple explanation."

Shaken, Greg handed me his clipboard with his water test readings. "The total dissolved solutes was fifty, virtually distilled water, and the rest of the tests, pH, nitrates, etc., are normal."

I grabbed a bottle of purified water that I kept in the refrigerator. I took a sip. "This tastes fine to me. It's the water here…don't you understand?"

Greg looked at Lois and shook his head. "I'm sorry, Doc. I'll have my boss out tomorrow morning. He's been in the business for twenty years; maybe he can figure this out."

After Greg left, Lois sat next to me. "This isn't like you, Arnie. We have a problem, but one way or another we'll figure it out. You must have read about or come up against patients with conditions that effect taste."

"I'm sorry, Lo. It's as if somebody demanded that you ignore the evidence of your eyes. Maybe it's more than my nose that's sensitive these days."

Lois walked to my side and caressed my neck. "Normally it takes a lot to make you this angry, Arnie. What's up?"

"Don't know. I'm constantly on edge." I hesitated a second then continued, "When I rotated through the Ear, Nose, and Throat service as a medical student, we learned of a condition called dysgeusia, a distorted sense of taste. I'll look it up, but as I recall it includes things like dental, ENT, or gastrointestinal problems, certain vitamin deficiencies, and the effects of medications. Maybe Jack will have an idea, but Lois, in my heart, I think my nose is heading for bloodhound or beyond."

When I returned to my office after lunch, I concluded that this heightened sensitivity had changed my relationship with those chemicals in my environment scientists call odorants. Unless you were on a sensory mission, sniffing for a gas leak or smelling your child's diaper, our olfactory discoveries were passive, sensing random odors, the fragrant, and the disgusting.

Suddenly, these encounters were becoming active, and instead of awaiting the collision of drifting molecules with my olfactory epithelium, the smell sensors, in my nose, I found myself going out on the battlefield to greet them. It was crazy by any definition. I found myself sampling everything like a kid with his first microscope.

I entered each room breathing in, sampling its molecules. I surreptitiously examined each patient's emitted ambiance (I didn't think that sniffing at my patients like a bloodhound would go over too well). I approached each olfactory challenge with (pardon the expression) a scent of adventure and discovery.

An afternoon of this insanity drew me to conclude that while my sense of smell soared, anyone who spent time obsessing about an activity like smelling everything in the environment may not be in the best position to judge the breadth of that curious newfound skill.

I made one additional observation; I'd begun to smell things foreign to me. Whatever had happened to me, I now carried a diplomatic passport, one with special privileges into an unseen world.

My next patient was Phyllis Carter who'd been with me from the beginning. She was in her mid fifties, thin, pale, and chronically depressed. Today, she came for a routine checkup. When I first met her eight years ago, she'd been from shrink to shrink for diagnoses ranging from bipolar disorder, to personality disorder, to unipolar depressive illness. She'd been on multiple medications, all of which produced intolerable side effects, forcing her physicians to abandon them well before she completed a reasonable therapeutic trial.

"This is what I have in mind, Phyllis," I said into our third recent meeting. "I can send you to another psychiatrist or, if you're willing to work with me, we can try Prozac again."

"Prozac didn't do a damn thing for me, Doc, except make me feel like shit."

"All the antidepressants require an initiation period before you feel their antidepressant effects. I don't think you took any of these long enough or at sufficient dosages to say they didn't work."

After she agreed to try Prozac again, I spent a good part of the next month holding her hand, encouraging and cajoling her to continue.

As we approached the end of the fourth week, she returned to the office, and whirled into the consultation room in her new outfit. "It's a miracle, Arnie. Over the last two days, it's as if someone lifted a heavy weight from my shoulders. I can't remember when I felt so good."

The effect lasted several years, and then gradually her depression returned. I tried several other antidepressants, with some effect, but none as good as her initial response to Prozac. Finally, I sent her to see Ross Cohen, an experienced psychiatrist, with the thought that she might need another category of drugs called monoamine oxidase inhibitors (MAO), problematic drugs, best prescribed by someone with more experience than I had.

She had an excellent response to the MAO called Nardil, and continued under Ross's care.

When I entered the examining room, Phyllis sat on the table in a gown. I immediately smelled Shalimar perfume, body powder, and hairspray. When I examined her throat, I caught a whiff of a musty-metallic and acrid aroma. I checked her teeth and gums for any sign of decay or inflammation, but everything looked normal. I questioned her about food, vitamins, herbal supplements, etc., but Nardil was her only medication. I'd have to research the association between this aroma and Nardil.

Afterward, we met in my office. "I'm setting you up for routine blood tests, a urinalysis, and a chest film. Make sure you keep up with your gynecologist for Pap smears and mammograms. I'll see you again in six months or sooner if you need me."

My last patient of the day was Janine Joseph, new to the practice.

"Arnie, you're going to love, Janine," said Beverly Ramirez, my office nurse. "She's so sweet and charming."

"Why is she here?"

"She recently moved to Berkeley with her two little girls and got your name through friends. She's asking to join our practice."

When she entered my consultation room, her charisma stunned me. Besides being physically attractive in her floral pink flowered sundress, her smile, and attentive wide blue eyes said, that for this moment, I was the most important person in her life. Who could resist the seduction?

"Thank you for agreeing to see me, Dr. Roth. I've heard wonderful things about you."

She wore an appealing floral perfume that I didn't recognize. "What's that fragrance you're wearing, Ms. Joseph?"

She smiled seductively as she stared into my eyes. "Please call me, Janine. Givenchy calls it *Very Irresistible*. Do you like it?"

"It's lovely," I said. "I think I'll get some for my wife."

"She'll love it."

Beneath the obvious floral bouquet was something else, a delicate, but acrid ammonia-like aroma, that I couldn't identify. Something about it made me uneasy.

I took a complete history, unrevealing except for many years of migraine headaches.

"What have you tried for your migraines?"

"I've tried everything. Nothing worked."

"What do you do for your attacks?"

"The doctors gave me Vicodin. That's the only thing that helps me."

The ammonia-like aroma recurred and my mind grappled with a particularly apt cliché: this doesn't smell right to me.

"What about the ergot drugs?"

"They make my fingers go into spasm."

"What about preventive measures, like beta blockers?"

"They make me depressed."

"What about Imitrex?"

"It doesn't work and it makes me nauseous."

The ammonia-like smell of her fabrications increased ever further. "If you'll excuse me for a moment, I must check on a patient in the hospital. It'll be only a moment."

I walked to the front desk. "Where's Janine's information sheet, Beverly?"

"Here it is, Arnie. What's wrong?"

"Did she bring any old records?"

"No."

"I'll be in my office calling her last physician."

"Dr. Ostrow's office, can I help you?"

"This is Dr. Roth calling from Berkeley. Is Dr. Ostrow in?"

"Why yes, doctor. Can I pull a chart for him?"

"Yes," I said. "I'd like to talk with him about Janine Joseph."

"My, my," she said with a chuckle. "Doctor will be right with you."

A moment later, the phone clicked and I heard, "Ben Ostrow here, can I help you?"

"I'm calling about Janine Joseph."

"That didn't take long, did it?"

"You know Janine?"

"Do I know her? She a piece of work. She's the best con artist I've ever seen. How much Vicodin have you given her?"

"None. I only met her today."

"You're a smarter man than I. It took me nine months to catch on. Dozens of doctors have come before us and many more will follow."

When I hung up the phone, Beverly said, "Well?"

"She's an addict, Beverly."

"My God," said Beverly, "what a waste. How did you know?"

"I just knew."

"Are you a mind reader?"

"If I were, I'd never admit it."

When I returned to the consultation room, Janine smiled brightly. "Is everything okay, doctor?"

"I just talked with Ben Ostrow."

Janine's smile disappeared. "What did he say?" she said with coolness.

"Exactly what you knew he'd say."

She rose and began walking for the door. "Well, thank you for your time, Dr. Roth. You seem like a nice man."

"Thank you, Janine. Why don't you let me help you?"

She smiled the smile that would send any man's heart a flutter. "You're sweet, but I've been through it a hundred times; inpatient, outpatient;

voluntary and court-ordered; as well as every form of standard and alternative treatments. I'm an addict. I'll always be an addict."

"I'm not going to try and convince you otherwise, but you need to store one fact somewhere in your memory. People who persist in their struggle to overcome an addiction, will, in spite of failing repeatedly, eventually succeed. That time may come for you, and if you are so inspired, you know where to reach me. Good luck."

Chapter Twenty-Seven

Saturday morning. I slept soundly and for the moment, all was well with the world. I left Lois in bed and moved to the lounge chair near the open window. The morning sun shone through the blinds and the air carried an aroma of freshly cut grass. I inhaled deeply, raised my legs, and looked around at what Lois and I had accomplished, our lives, and our kids. I flushed with satisfaction. The lyric, you don't know what you have until you lose it, was too near reality and as close as I ever wanted to get.

Amy folded herself into her favorite beanbag chair listening to the music box we gave her for her birthday. It played a charming version of Disney's "It's a small world," but after the umpteenth play, its charm grated on my nerves. I had the irresistible urge to take a sledgehammer and silence the damn thing.

When Lois entered the room, I gestured discretely, a pantomime of pointing to my ears in pain and closing the music box.

"Why don't you go to your room for a while, sweetheart. Maybe I can get Daddy to take us out for lunch."

After Amy left, I said, "If I hear that song one more time, I'm going to check my blood sugar and put myself on insulin."

"What about lunch?"

"We'll see."

"You promised to take us," Becky whined as the clock approached noon.

Lois looked at the girls then at me. "Daddy's not in the mood for fast food, sweetie."

"But you promised," Becky cried, soon joined by Amy's tearful, "You promised, Daddy."

Lois rubbed my back. "Come on, Arnie. You like Burger World."

"Tolerate is a better word."

We loaded the kids and the dog into Lois's minivan and drove downtown. It was a bright, but hazy day and, judging from the traffic, everyone had the same idea.

I pulled into the drive-through line about twelve cars deep, listening to the family's meal preferences.

Becky leaned over my seat back. "Don't forget to get a burger for Archie."

Archie, our Golden Retriever, had his nose fused to the vent. His tail wagged in anticipation.

Suddenly, a foul, pungently sweet stench hit me. My mind flashed back to Fort Carson, Colorado, where I served as a battalion surgeon...

Two soldiers carried a PFC into the dispensary. The young soldier writhed in pain. Beaded sweat soaked his OD shirt and covered his face. When I approached the examining table, he pointed. "It's on my butt, Doc. It's killing me."

When he turned face down, I saw a large shiny abscess, a red three-inch circular swelling with white-gray spot in the middle. The abscess was bulging and getting ready to rupture. When I touched it, he screamed in agony.

"I'll fix this in a minute," I said as I froze the surface of the boil with ethylene chloride spray, then lanced it with a scalpel and watched as the infected material erupted from the wound with the foul stench of infection. I gagged.

He screamed. "It's gone Doc...it's gone...thank God, it's a miracle."...

I jerked the wheel to the right breaking away from the drive-through line and left the parking lot.

"What are you doing, Daddy?" Becky shouted, suddenly shocked.

Lois looked at me strangely. "Arnie, what's wrong?"

"We can't eat here today, Lo...trust me. Let's go to McDonald's."

Like the long pause before Claude Raines said, "Round up the usual suspects," I awaited a reaction.

"McDonald's...yeah...yeah," Becky shouted.

"Happy Meal...Happy Meal," Amy peeped.

Lois looked my way, smiled, and then shook her head.

When I opened the next morning's paper, the headline shouted: Seven people hospitalized with food poisoning after eating at Burger World. State health inspectors promise a complete investigation.

This new reality, this sensitivity distracted and confused me. If I had the time to isolate myself from normal life, there's a chance I could make sense of the chemicals assaulting me every day. It was all new. Familiar aromas had subtleties, flavors, and hues that gave me a new appreciation for their essences. The aliens who crossed the frontier of my consciousness came, it seems, in infinite varieties; aromas from the sublime to the repulsive, and every shade between.

Now, when I took Archie for his evening walk, I had insight into his world. His twitching black nose sensed from afar the places he'd visited before. He learned the history of each geographic spot by placing that nose to the ground, and he freaked out from time to time at an unseen terror.

I was a gourmet trapped in the world's best restaurant, and at the same time a worker confined to a meat rendering plant. I became an overindulgent olfactory overachiever. As much as I tried to dampen it, the sensory overload was taking its toll.

Chewing gum, strong breath mints, and dousing myself with Old Spice aftershave lotion brought respite by overwhelming my senses and erecting a short-lived sensory barricade. Scientists of smell called that desensitization or sensory exhaustion. This phenomenon explained why factory employees working in foul-smelling environments, eventually lost their ability to sense the chemicals that surrounded them.

Monday, after I saw the last patient, Beverly Ramirez stuck her head into my office and sat next to my desk. "What's wrong, Arnie? You don't appear to be all here."

"What does that mean?"

"I know you. You focus on our patients, but lately I'm hearing that you're inattentive, and that you're not listening. Is everything okay?"

"Everything's fine. Maybe I'm not ready yet for full-time practice."

Greg's boss, and the owner of Crystal Pure Water, returned the next day. "I'm sorry, Doc, I can't find anything wrong with the water."

"I'm sorry too. It must be me."

When Lois found me handling and smelling things around the house, I had no choice but to confess. "Something's happening to me, Lo. It started after I recovered from the encephalitis, and it's getting worse."

"What is it, baby?"

"I could try to explain it in scientific terms, but to state it simply, my nose is running amok."

She smiled. "That's an interesting image."

"No, I'm serious. We laughed with my perceptions about your cooking, and then we went through the water fiasco. I'm sure the water contains something that only I can detect."

"Arnie?" she replied quietly.

"No, I'm not crazy…except for my nose, that is."

"Are you sure that's all that's going on?" she paused. "A talented nose is a gift. You should be happy."

"Parts of it <u>are</u> wonderful, for instance, last night when I came home, I knew you were horny. I sensed it."

Lois blushed. "How did you know?"

"I'd like to say I smelled it, though that's not what you want to say to any woman. It really wasn't smell, but I sensed it, felt it, and it gave me an erection. Didn't it surprise you when I came into the bedroom ready for love?"

"That's never surprised me. I adore spontaneous lovemaking. It's been a part of our lives. You have a talent for guess right about my moods."

"I love it, too, but I don't have to guess anymore, Lo. I know."

Chapter Twenty-Eight

Ruth Fischer had guarded the fantasy for as long as possible. This was Henry's mid-life crisis, they'd weather it together and go on, but soon she accepted the undeniable reality, her marriage was over. Her emotions ranged from anguish to depression to anger. She hadn't heard from Reggie Brand, but she remembered his comment when she last called.

"The investigation is going well. I'll have something for you soon."

Ruth lay in bed reading *O Magazine*, the popular guide for the woes of the modern woman, when Henry came home late again. He no longer bothered with excuses for his late nights, his unexplained weekend absences, and unusual business trips.

"We have to talk, Henry," she said as he undressed and threw his clothes over the corner armchair.

"I'm too tired, Ruth. Can't it wait?"

As he slipped into the bed, she caught the faint, but distinct scent of the perfume, Poison, not hers. They'd shared this bed for twenty years, and now she suddenly realized for the first time that Henry's nearness violated her personal zone. She'd marveled at the comfort with which loved ones shared the unity of space. She remembered a college professor, Carlos Rios, a Spaniard, and how she found herself continually retreating as he violated the gap between them, intruding on her space. Although she finally understood his behavior as cultural, and not boorish, she couldn't avoid her aversion and the desire to escape.

It's exactly how I feel now, she thought, but Henry's not innocent. Ruth threw the covers back and stood. "I won't play this game any longer Henry. I'm no fool."

"God, Ruth, not again. I'm beat. Can't this wait?"

"If you think I'm blind or stupid, you're out of your mind."

"I don't know what in hell you're talking about," he said staring at her across their bed and running his fingers over his thinning hair.

"You think I don't know what's going on with the late hours, the trips, the business meetings. Don't insult me."

"Don't do this, Ruth. This is all in your head. Don't make a mistake you'll live to regret."

She sat on the side of their bed, lowered her head into her lap, and wept.

He rounded the bed, sat beside her. "It's okay Ruth. Everything will be fine. We'll work this out."

When he tried to rub her shoulders, Ruth reacted violently as if his touch carried an electric current. She stood, grabbed a tissue, blew her nose, and wiped her tears. Ruth faced Henry and with a calm, determined voice said, "Get out."

"What?" he replied with disbelief.

"Get out," she shouted and then continued, "and I mean right now. I won't have you in this house."

"You don't know what you're doing."

"I know exactly what I'm doing."

"You're hysterical. You're not making sense. You're my wife. This is my home. You can't do this to me."

He moved toward her. She grabbed the fireplace poker and held it between them. "Get out now or I'm calling the police." She paused for a moment then added, "And the press too. I'd love to see you on the front page being escorted away in cuffs."

"You're out of your fucking mind. If you think I'm going to let you get away with this shit, you're dumber than I thought."

"Get out," she screamed reaching for the phone and beginning to dial.

He grabbed his clothes from the armchair and shouted, "Have it your way you bitch. You'll pay for this. I'm not through with you."

He left slamming the door behind.

Ruth heard Henry dress, the front door slam, and his new Lexus start and drive away. The house was suddenly silent and although Ruth still trembled from emotion, she felt relief.

Henry checked into the Holiday Inn, but slept little. He dialed home, but when Ruth heard his voice, she hung up.

Henry's mind was still reeling the previous night's events. He knew their marriage was over, but over on whose terms. Ruth's initiative to take the first step embittered him. His mind chilled with fear as he considered the consequences of a messy divorce on his business, financial, and personal life.

"You look like hell," said Brian Shands at their regular morning meeting. "Burning the candle at both ends again, Henry?"

"Fuck off, Brian. Ruth threw me out last night."

Brian laughed, shook his head, and sneered. "Well, Henry, what did you expect? Ruth's no dummy."

"Look, Brian, my life is about to get complicated. This divorce could be messy, and I think we've done well enough to resume our normal practices. Horizon's back on its feet, and our debt is nearly gone. I see no reason to take chances."

"Take chances? I don't know what you're talking about."

"You know exactly what I'm saying."

"Because you've fucked up your life, Henry, don't go screwing with mine. We're highly profitable, and I want to keep it that way."

Who the hell does he think he is? Henry thought. "This is my business, Brian, and I call the shots."

"If you think your life is complicated now, then try to mess with me, Henry. After all, this was your idea. You threatened me, my job, you coerced me, and you profited the most from our activities. That's how it will play it, and that's what will land you in jail."

My idea? Henry thought. I've created a monster.

Chapter Twenty-Nine

Irving Hodges smiled through a sunburst of wrinkles and brown age spots as Beatrice, his bride of fifty years, extended her arms in an invitation to their golden anniversary dance. Irv wore the charcoal-gray suit that he last wore for their daughter Sarah's wedding twenty years before. It smelled of mothballs.

He was barely able to button the coat and after trying several times to tie his shoes, each time gasping for breath, Beatrice said, "Put your feet up here, old man."

She wore a soft, muted floral dress extending to mid-calf and matching pumps. A heart-shaped locket on a delicate gold anchor chain adorned her neck. It held their wedding day pictures. When she opened it part way, the images in the photos beamed at each other like today, only fifty years ago. Bea never went anywhere without her locket.

Irv grumbled, "You know I can't dance a damn," as he moved onto the dance floor to the families' applause.

"You were a spectacular dancer, Irv. Remember those tea dances at the Fairmont in San Francisco?"

"You must have me confused with someone else, darlin'. I always had three left feet."

"Right," she smiled. "Now you have three left feet and two artificial hips," she hesitated. "Maybe I'm confused about a lot of other things too…could it be the Alzheimer's?"

He frowned. "Don't joke about that."

As they danced awkwardly to *The Anniversary Waltz's* three quarter beat, he looked into her dark brown eyes. "You've never looked prettier than you do tonight."

"Maybe it's time for new glasses."

"You can't take a compliment, darlin'…never could."

She looked into his gray eyes, smiled, caressed his cheek, and pulled him close for a kiss as the audience applauded.

Their three daughters arranged and paid for a two-week Royal Caribbean cruise to Mexico with stops in Cabo San Lucas, Puerto Vallarte, Mazatlan, and Acapulco.

They slept late, ate too much, walked the promenade, and dozed on deck chairs in the salty air with the books they were reading open on their chests.

"When we get home, we're going on a diet," Beatrice said patting her expanding waistline.

"As long as you don't wind up looking like those skinny, no-bottom, models."

"No chance of that. My big hips ain't never going away."

When they returned home, her abdomen was more swollen. The scale showed a gain of twelve pounds.

Twelve pounds, how is that possible, she thought.

"Who's next?" I asked.

"Beatrice Hodges, Arnie," Beverly said. "She and Irving are in room three. They're the cutest couple. They recently came back from celebrating with a fiftieth anniversary cruise."

I knew them both from my early days in the East Bay when they ran Hodges Hardware in Berkeley. They were among the earliest people to join my practice and I delighted each time they came in to see me. Fortunately, their problems were routine.

Irv had only three real interests, Beatrice, work, and target shooting.

"Why don't you come up to Chabot firing range with me, Doc? I've got a collection of handguns for target shooting."

"I'm not much into guns, Irv."

"Try it sometime, Doc. It's a challenging sport taking patience and real skill."

"I'll think about it," I'd said, knowing that this would never be for me.

Irving and Beatrice nearly went out of business when Home Depots and Wal-Marts came to town, but once they associated with Ace Hardware, their prices again became competitive and they survived. In addition, they had a solid advantage, Irv Hodges. Irv had been a carpenter and an electrician. When he 'retired' to open their own hardware store, Irv brought with him a vast fountain on knowledge that he shared with his customers, making shopping at Hodges Hardware a delight.

"What can I do for you, Doc?" he'd said that day ten years ago when we first met.

I showed him the Molley Bolts. "I need hollow wall anchors."

"What do you need them for?"

"I promised Lois that I'd hang pictures today. I'd better come through."

He pointed me toward the rack at the end of aisle one. "Use these Hellman screw anchors. They're easy and they come in several sizes depending on the picture's weight."

Like the help he gave to thousands of others, I could count on Irving Hodges to put me on the right track. His tiny store usually had what I needed no matter how arcane.

The few times I went into Home Depot, it took me three times as long to find what I wanted and their advice was either absent or wrong.

I went to Hodge's Hardware after Irv and Bea retired, but it was different now.

When I entered the examining room, I shook Irv's hand and kissed Bea on the cheek. "A belated fiftieth anniversary congratulations to you both. How are you doing?"

"That's why we're here, Doc," Irv said. "Bea's stomach has gotten big and her weight's up. I'm sure it can't be from eating too much. I ate more than she did on the cruise, and my weight hasn't changed at all."

The moment I entered a room I performed a sensory survey (it had become an unconscious act by now) and detected mostly the routine scents; soaps, deodorants, lotions, foods, and fabric softeners. Among the medley of familiar aromas were several distinct and unknown ones.

After examining Bea's heart and lungs, I came next to her distended abdomen. When I placed my hand on her belly, I knew it was full of fluid. I couldn't feel an enlarged liver or any other organ or a mass. When I placed my stethoscope on her abdomen, she jumped and grimaced. "That's ice cold."

I smiled. "It's not easy to keep it that way, Bea."

The amount of abdominal fluid alarmed me. Her health history and her examination failed to show heart, liver, or kidney disease, the common explanations for the fluid. Beyond that triad, was an array of serious and frequently fatal illnesses.

"Have a seat outside, Arthur. I need to do a vaginal examination."

Irv frowned. "Are you sure that's necessary?"

Beatrice smiled. "It's nothing, sweetie...had one or two before."

I returned to the examining room after Beverly draped Beatrice and put her up in the cold stainless steel stirrups. She'd spread her legs wide in preparation for the examination. While a vaginal examination meant many things to women, to most it was uncomfortable and embarrassing.

I donned my gloves and approached the table. "This won't take but a few minutes."

Beatrice spread her legs farther apart. "No problem, Doc. Get to it."

"If I hurt you, you'll let me know. Pain's not necessary."

Her vaginal examination was normal. I took several Pap samples and then went on to the bimanual examination where I felt for the contents of the pelvis through the vagina and the abdominal wall. The large amount of fluid in her abdomen made the examination difficult and Beatrice grunted several times as I struggled to examine her.

"I'm sorry. Hold on for a few minutes more."

Beatrice smiled. "It's okay, Doc. Do what you need to do. Just don't get lost in there."

I couldn't feel her uterus, not surprising at her age, but I felt fullness in the right side of her pelvis. My pulse raced. Maybe it was only an ovarian cyst, I thought in denial.

"I feel something on the right side, Beatrice, but with so much fluid, I'm not sure. I'm ordering a pelvic ultrasound examination and I need to remove a small amount of fluid from your abdomen for analysis."

Two days later, I stared at the reports. The ultrasound revealed a mass on Beatrice's right ovary, and the fluid analysis showed cancer cells. Beatrice had ovarian cancer.

Chapter Thirty

Soon, I began to indulge my newly expanding olfactory skill by seeking out those places offering the greatest sensory satisfaction.

I was on my way home from making rounds Sunday morning when I suddenly found myself at the bakery, drawn there by its pungently sweet aromas emanating from fresh baked breads, cakes, and cookies. I couldn't recall driving there.

I soaked up the aromas, in a trance-like state, until Herbie, the baker, interrupted. "What can I get for you, Dr. Roth?"

How could I choose from this world of infinite delights?

I waved my arm in an arc. "Pack it all up for me, Herbie. I'm taking it home."

Or I was at the Deli, Italian or kosher, the hedonistic havens erupting with streams of scent, and sensory satisfaction appropriate to my status as a sensual savant of smell.

Corned beef, pastrami, honeyed hams, marinades of infinite variety, stuffed peppers, chopped liver, and pickled herring brought images of lunch with Louis Roth, my grandfather. "I love it here, grandpa. It smells so good."

"Kosher deli's the best, Arnold. Trust me, if you like it, you don't want to wind up in Corpus Christi."

Lunch with Nick Martin, my best friend, in his father's deli, brought the redolences and the images of antipasto, Genoa salami, Provolone and Mozzarella cheese, and of course gnocchi.

I was the mad maven, the cognoscenti of these glorious emissions. Only one thing could surpass this experience, the marriage of these delights with my taste buds. Olfaction was a charming long distance romance, but I was eager for the honeymoon.

You'll excuse the especially apt sensory cliché that this wasn't all roses, as every delight had its offensive mother-in-law. They found me with equal regularity. I'll not offend you with the specifics, but the world's full of disagreeable aromas. Often and without forewarning, the odor transported me to the rendering plant or the sewage processing facility whose putrid stenches made my urge to escape irresistible.

One evening, I sat before my computer searching the Internet for information about the olfactory system. "The only thing I learned about smell in medical was the basics. Maybe it's because our culture says that there's something vulgar about odors."

Lois smiled. "It's a scentsitive subject, if you can ignore the pun. Look at women's magazines. It's one thing to deride the offensive body odor of someone with poor personal hygiene, it's another to disparage all natural human aromas. The manufacturers designed the manipulative

195

marketing schemes to convince women (and men too) that they'd never catch a guy/girl or make a friend, or get the job unless they cloaked themselves with their artificially created fragrances. It ignores the fact that I love the way you smell, Arnie, and I love the unique aroma of each of our girls. I'm only guessing, but I have reason to believe you don't find my taste and smell to be unpleasant."

"That's a scentsational image, babe."

Lois groaned.

"Smell's role in disease is leading to a better understanding of the process. A variety of illnesses are associated with unique odors, and the loss of the ability to smell is linked with certain psychiatric illnesses and with Alzheimer's in particular."

"Dad lost his sense of smell early in the course of Alzheimer's."

I studied the computer screen. "Here's a study of changes in penile or vaginal blood flow when researchers exposed subjects to different aromas. How come we didn't get to participate in these studies when we were in college?"

Lois laughed. "Bad timing. It's good to see how we're expanding the use of our tax dollars."

"Guess what aromas produce the greatest increase in penile blood flow in men?"

"Perfume?"

"Partly right. Lavender is on the list, but also on top are pumpkin pie and cinnamon buns."

"I guess I know what to cook when I'm feeling horny."

"What about women?"

"I haven't got the foggiest."

"Good and Plenty, you remember, the licorice candy."

Lois laughs. "So that's why Bobby Howard insisted on buying them for me at the movies."

"I think the surveys and their conclusions in *Cosmo*, *Elle*, and *O Magazine* sets the stage or the bedroom for disappointment. I'm guessing that you and I are more active sexually than most, but who really knows. What I learned about sex as a kid was worthless. What I learned in medical school was better, but if you want to know what's happening in the average bedroom, I see only two approaches; become a professional who deals with sexual problems or a woman in an intimate group of female friends like the ladies in *Sex and the City*."

Lois and I never talked much about sex. It wasn't as if we avoided the subject, it just wasn't necessary. We made love frequently, but not on a schedule. With all the complexities of work, children, and modern living, sexually, we remained in sync. She always responded to my needs with joyous acceptance. Any hint of interest on her part brought me to full arousal in seconds.

"I don't know if it's cause and effect," Lois said, "but your libido and your sense of smell are on the same accelerated trajectory."

"You're complaining?"

"Never. In fact, it's, as the kids say, awesome."

"The medical literature describes a relationship between smell and sex. People with anosmia, the loss of the ability to smell, have diminished sex drives, while surveys correlate sexuality with our sensitivity to smell."

"I love your smell. Sometimes when you're not here, I grab your sweatshirt to get that unique Arnie aroma."

"I found an interesting study in the British Medical Journal suggesting that smell and sex are complementary. After sex, the body produces increased amounts of the hormone prolactin. That in turn stimulates stem cells in the brain to form more olfactory lobe nerve cells."

"With your nose, Arnie, you ought to have a hell of an olfactory lobe by now. Let's get a CT or an MRI so we can hang it over the mantelpiece or post it on You Tube."

"Maybe there's a picture of another part of my anatomy we'd want up on the wall, babe."

"You mean your nose?"

"Of course, what else?"

Each trip to the supermarket was a sensory safari. The produce and bakery sections were delightful with their individual aromas, splendid bouquets, and the amalgamation of scents. Many aromas had an affinity for each other, often producing a unique symphony of fragrances, while for others, their fusion brought the disharmony of a Chinese opera.

When we went to the food market, Lois's shopping strategy for choosing fruits and vegetables amazed me. Shopping has been her responsibility, not because this was 'woman's work', but simply because she savored the task, especially when she could do it at her leisure. She enjoyed inspecting labels, checking calories, fat, and carbohydrate content with each selection.

After several minutes observing this painfully slow process, I usually complained, "If you don't need me, I'll be out in the car reading."

Lois especially enjoyed selecting fruits and vegetables. After visual surveillance, she grasped each item, gave it a gentle squeeze, and then brought it to her nose for final approval. I'm not sure why, but after a few constructive comments about her selections, Lois reassigned me to the produce section.

I've made sure to keep cilantro at arms length, never fully understanding how anyone could eat the vile aromatic herb. Even before I developed this new sensitivity, I could smell it immediately during transit through the produce section, and was happy to get away from it as quickly as possible. Now, as I looked at the vegetables, five aisles away, the strong, ammonia-like, urinous soapy cilantro smell made me feel like vomiting. I had to send Lois back for the veggies.

As I rounded the corner and turned into the next aisle, a young woman was pushing a cart with a boy who looked about three years old. He sat in the child seat squirming and dangling his legs with delight. One whiff was all it took, and thoughtlessly I said, "You'll find a present for you in that diaper," and started away.

"Excuse me!" she shouted.

I blushed. "I'm sorry, but that's pretty potent stuff your son has in there."

"Why of all the nerve. Mind your own damn business."

I should have let it go at that, but instead, a demon possessed me. "It is my business when you let your child stink up this store. You may find the aroma appealing, but I can assure you that others do not."

She turned equally red, thrust her middle finger into my face, and then wheeled her cart away. This new sensory skill was turning out to be of doubtful advantage, a costly ride into uncharted territory.

The next morning during rounds on the fifth floor medical unit, I visited Sarah Jackson. I'd transferred her from ICU last night.

"Hey, Dr. Roth, how are you doing this morning?"

"Doing well, but more to the point, how's my favorite patient?"

"Aren't you too much," she smiled? "I'm sure glad to get out of that noisy ICU and back to civilization. When can I go home?"

Before I can answer, Ritchie Brown, Sarah's nurse entered the room. "Hey, Doc, how's our girl doing?"

As he leaned over to check Sarah's IV, the strong, unique scent of marijuana hit my nose.

He looked fine, I thought, but if he's loaded...

"I'll have Ritchie remove the IV and your bladder catheter, Sarah. If your temp stays down through the next twenty-four hours, I'll discharge you in the morning."

I looked at Ritchie, and then moved my eyes away as he caught me staring. "Can I have a word with you, Mr. Brown?"

"Mr. Brown?" he said, looking puzzled.

I walked into the small dictation room. Ritchie followed.

"I don't care what you do on your own time, Ritchie, but if you're coming to work stoned, you're in for big problems."

He avoided my eyes. "I don't know what you're talking about, Arnie."

"That's strike one, Ritchie. Don't lie to me. I can smell it. Keep this up and you're out the door."

My mind froze for a second. When I said I smell it, I meant the marijuana, but suddenly my nose detected something else. Smelling a lie was no longer a metaphor for me. Ritchie's body was emitting something distinct — the acrid ammonia-like stench of his lie.

Ritchie blanched, and then reddened. In a voice barely audible he said, "Okay, I smoked a joint last night, but Arnie," he took a deep breath, "I'd never come to work stoned. You know me better than that."

"I thought I did. Think of the hospital's liability if something happened to one of your patients and they discover that you used pot. It wouldn't matter that you did nothing wrong. Legally, you'd be dead. Your career would be over. You don't want any part of that."

"Arnie, it was one joint, and one joint only. If I was stinking drunk last night nobody would give a damn."

"I understand the hypocrisy, but I didn't make the rules, and I don't want to see you hurt, Ritchie. This is between you and me. I believe you, but for God sake, don't let anybody suspect that you're using that stuff anywhere near your job. That's suicide. If you're going to smoke, do it so that nobody can raise the question about its effect on you, change your clothes or whatever to hide the aroma."

"Thanks, Arnie. I won't disappoint you."

"You're a talented nurse, Ritchie. Be smart."

My new life was more interesting for sure, but also more complicated. Each day brought new sensory information. For a compulsive personality, it came with a burden of responsibility. The sense of smell was our first defense organ. It allowed our evolutionary single cell progenitors to avoid exposure to harmful chemicals and to move toward nutrient rich areas. Evolutionary theorists credit human brain development to this first environmental reaction that led to the development of specialized detector cells. Over millions of years, these cells became internalized with nerve cells to form the primitive animal's olfactory system.

As I entered my office this morning, a couple in their mid twenties, with a small thin girl, stood at Sarah Ettinger's door. Sarah was a child psychiatrist, my tenant, and a good friend.

I approached the couple. "Is Dr. Ettinger expecting you?"

"Excuse me," said the man, "but who are you, and how is this any of your business?"

Before I had a chance to respond, the maple syrup aroma hit me and my mind wandered back to my childhood home and a tall stack of pancakes and the Aunt Jemima-shaped bottle.

"I'm so sorry. I'm Dr. Roth, and this is my building. I was going to say, that if she's expecting you, I'd open the door and let you into her waiting room."

"I'm so sorry," Penny said. "Roger gets a little surly when we drag him to our family counseling sessions."

"I apologize," Roger said, "and yes, we'll take you up on your kind offer."

The intensity of the maple syrup aroma increased when the girl, Kirsten, past immediately before me as she moved into the waiting room.

"This may sound a little strange to you," I began, "but did any of you have maple syrup or a maple syrup product today?"

"No," said Penny, looking at me oddly.

Before I could say another word, the front door opened. It was Sarah Ettinger.

"Thanks for letting them in, Arnie. Traffic's a bear this morning."

She inserted the key into her office door and turned to the Brewers. "I'll be with you in a moment."

"Do you have a second, Sarah?" I said.

She stared at me with interest. "Come into my office. You're not going to raise my rent, are you?"

"This will sound like a weird request, Sarah, but if you bear with me, I'll explain."

She removed her jacket, hung it on a coat tree, and then plunked herself into her soft desk chair. "Shoot."

"I don't want any confidential information, but can you tell me a little about that girl."

"Why on earth do you want to know, Arnie?"

"Please, Sarah. Just a whiff of information is all I need then I'll tell you why I ask."

"Kirsten's growth and development had been normal, although in the lower percentiles. About six months ago, she started having behavior problems at school; acting out against other children and her teachers, decline in her school performance, and the resumption of bedwetting. Something's eating at this child. I've been seeing her for four months and I still can't tell if it's the chicken or the egg; have her emotional problems compromised her performance or has poor performance left her anxious and unable to concentrate?"

"What I'm about to tell you will sound odd, Sarah, but I only tell you this so you won't recommend that I need the couch."

"I don't use a couch, Arnie."

"I know. After I recovered from the encephalitis, my sense of smell has improved dramatically. As you might expect, this poses opportunities and difficulties. When I met Kirsten this morning, she strongly smelled of maple syrup."

"Maple syrup?"

"Yes, and nobody in the family had used it, spilled it, etc. I remember from a lecture that scientists have described a rare genetic metabolic disorder called Maple Syrup Urine Disease, where due to a defective enzyme, certain amino acids are improperly broken down and appear in the urine with the distinct aroma of maple syrup."

"My mind's racing back to school," Sarah said. "This is a disease like PKU, phenylketonuria, which causes mental retardation. We can control it by diet."

"Exactly. That girl needs a workup ASAP. If she has that diagnosis, we could save her and her family a lifetime of grief."

Three weeks later as I was finishing my paperwork for the day, Beverly knocked on my door. "I have someone here to see you."

I stood behind my desk.

Roger and Penny Brewer entered with Kirsten who wore a big smile, a white flowered sundress, and pink Mary Janes. She carried a small, gift-wrapped package, and with a little encouragement, brought it over to me.

"Why thank you. You look so pretty. Is that a new dress?"

She smiled, and then looked down, saying softly, "My shoes are new too."

I looked up at the Brewers. "This wasn't necessary." In an instant, I could see their disappointment, so I added immediately, "But I sure do appreciate it."

"Open it," Roger said.

I unwrapped the box labeled, Ipod touch. This was an amazing gift. One that I wanted, but felt too guilty to buy for myself. "This is too much...I mean it's wonderful...I mean I love it, but it's too much."

"This is nothing," Peggy said, "compared to giving us our daughter's life. We can never repay you for what you did, Dr. Roth." She walked to me and gave me a hug and a kiss on the cheek. Roger approached and grasped my hand as his eyes filled with tears.

My own eyes filled. I wanted to say more, much more, but words were inadequate and could only diminish this joyous moment for all of us.

Chapter Thirty-One

Into the fifth week of hospitalization, Connie Rinaldi relied entirely on the ventilator to breathe. The week before, Connie's parents agreed to replace the ET tube with a surgical procedure called a tracheotomy. During this surgery, they made an opening in her windpipe to make breathing easier. An added benefit was the possibility that Connie's might talk. That had not yet proven possible. The infection had finally cleared, but each time they tried to get her off the ventilator, weaning they called it, she became desperate — unable to breathe on her own.

The Rinaldis tried to talk with their daughter by asking her to block the trachea, but after a few seconds, Connie panicked from the stress of trying to breathe on her own. The nurses gave Connie a clipboard with a pencil attached so that she could write. It was awkward, but effective.

Connie wrote in hesitant and irregular block letters. "What's going to happen to me?"

Tina caressed Connie's hair. "The doctors say you're doing well. The infection's better and so is your breathing."

Why is the tube's still in me?

"You need it to breathe. They tried to have you breathe on your own, but I guess that your lungs aren't ready yet."

When will they be ready?

Joseph looked at his daughter, raised his shoulders, and turned up his palms in the universal gesture of the unknown.

Tears streamed from Connie's eyes. They ran onto the clipboard staining the notepaper as she wrote, I don't want to go on this way, Daddy. I can't live like this. Don't make me do this!

Joe bent over his daughter and cried.

Brier's social service department was pushing Jim McDonald on Connie's case. The hospital had collected all it could from her insurance and they were looking for a way out. Additionally, the Rinaldis were begging for answers.

For Jim, the logic was simple: Do something to improve her lung function so she no longer required the ventilator; move Connie to a long-term respiratory support unit or to home with the appropriate equipment and training, or finally, get her a heart-lung transplant.

The RCU staff met repeatedly about Connie and had recently introduced a new structured multidisciplinary program to try to get her off the ventilator. The players in the new program reacted with enthusiasm to the studies on this new approach that showed a 50 percent success rate.

Connie did not share their enthusiasm. She submitted to part of their efforts and actively blocked others.

"She's depressed," said Alan Morris, the pulmonary consultant.

Jim McDonald put down Connie's chart. "Maybe she's just taking control of what little she has left to decide for herself."

When they pushed Connie's support by adding tube feedings to the intravenous nutritional solutions, she gained weight. The staff carefully adjusted the ventilator to allow Connie's own muscles to help her breathe. In spite of her objections, they kept Connie out of bed for extended periods. On paper, she looked better, emotionally, she was worse.

Take me off this fucking machine, she wrote with a shaking hand. I want to die. It's my right to die. Tears streamed down her face.

Connie rejected everyone's attempt to reason with her. Passive, at first, she now attacked nurses, technicians, and even her physicians. She tried several times to free her arms so she could pull out the breathing tube. She fought the physical restraints to exhaustion. Psychiatric evaluation was useless and any attempt to deal with her psychopathology, whatever it was, by drugs, they rejected for fear they would further compromise her breathing. Finally, she fell into a catatonic state and refused to respond to any question or follow orders.

"We're plain out of tricks," Jim said to the Rinaldis. "It makes me sick to see that we've come so far to only to fail because we can't deal with Connie's depression. We can try antidepressants, but that will take weeks and there's no certainty that they'll work under these circumstances."

"You must try something," Joseph said.

Jim sat with Connie's parents. "Connie's situation bothers me. She's entitled to her emotions and she may or may not be rational in her decision to stop treatment. I'm not sure what I'd do if I were in her situation." He hesitated a moment, and then continued, "Let me talk with the psychiatrists again. Maybe we can come up with something."

The RCU was quiet but for five ventilators whirring and clicking. Rarely synchronous, the sounds sometimes fell into a pattern until one or another patient sighed or stirred, upsetting the rhythm.

Patricia Coleman, an experienced RCU nurse, had three patients tonight. Two were early in their clinical courses and required lots of attention. The third was Connie, who remained awake, with eyes open, but still refused to or couldn't react.

Patricia had become so involved with the two sicker patients that she had to remind herself several times to record Connie's vital signs. At four a.m., she broke away and approached Connie's bed. Something was wrong. She couldn't hear the distinct sounds of Connie's ventilator. When she pulled the curtains around the bed, she was shocked. Connie's hands were free and she was grasping the tracheal tube in her fist. The ventilator sat in silence.

"My God," she screamed, then pushed the Code Blue button, and then flipped on the bright overhead lights. In seconds, two other RCU nurses joined her and moments later, the respiratory therapy tech and the ER physician appeared.

"What happened?" the ER doc cried.

"I don't know. She must have freed herself somehow, removed the tracheal tube, and switched off the ventilator." Patricia fumbled with the plastic packaging for a new tracheal tube, but before she could insert it, the ER physician held her back.

"Wait a minute. She's breathing on her own. Let's get her on oxygen and get a set of blood gases."

When Patricia tried to insert a suction catheter into the tracheotomy to insure it was clear of mucous, Connie sat upright, pushed the nurse back, raised her right hand like a crossing guard, and mouthed the word, STOP!

Later, with Tina, Joe, and Connie crying at the bedside, Jim McDonald watched in awe as Connie activated the speaking valve on her tracheotomy. She pulled Jim McDonald close and said in a voice somewhere between a whisper and a croak, "Don't know if I should kiss you or kill you."

Jim turned to Jack Byrnes. "The more I practice medicine, the less I know."

Jack smiled. "We have to deal with surprising success and fortuitous failure, except we're unaccustomed to the successes, and find them more shocking. Success challenges the most dearly held conceit…our certainty."

Chapter Thirty-Two

Lois and I enjoyed San Francisco's gourmet restaurants. Although we earned more than a decent living, something about paying two hundred dollars or more for a dinner and wine felt obscene and left us guilt-ridden. In recent years, when we went to the city for dinner, we opted instead for ethnic dining, Chinese, Italian, Mexican, etc.

To keep in touch with the trendy foods and wines, we had FallFest, held each September in San Francisco.

"My nose is crying out to me, sweetie," I said, as I put down the 'What's Going On' section of the *San Francisco Chronicle*. "It's FallFest time, and it's saying, take me to the Embarcadero Center this weekend."

"You're on," Lois said, patting her flat belly. "I'm not eating after Thursday."

The Embarcadero Center with its five office towers, restaurants, upscale shopping plazas, and theaters, sprawled over five blocks of San Francisco's prime commercial district and hosted FallFest.

As we drove over the San Francisco-Oakland Bay Bridge toward the city, the morning fog evaporated into the light of the midday sun. My nose savored the bay's briny aromas. When we reached the midpoint at Yerba Buena Island, my nose registered the pungent aroma of roasting beans at the Hills Brother's coffee plant under the San Francisco anchorage. Traffic intensified as we approached the Embarcadero Center.

Lois studied the traffic. "I hope they're not all going to FallFest."

"I don't think so. Although weekend traffic in the Bay Area is ne'er impossible, nothing is going to keep us away from all that gourmet food and wine."

We worked our way through the Embarcadero Center canyons in the shadows of high-rise office buildings looming overhead. Soon, we found signs for FallFest parking that pointed us into an underground garage.

Brightly decorated signage directed us up into Justin Herman Plaza. As we ascended, I sampled much of the fare trapped in the elevator's air. My mouth watered and my stomach cramped with hunger. When the elevator doors parted, the refined aromas of San Francisco's creative culinary chefs — of genius — inundated me.

Hungry gourmands snacked through the open space. Green linen-covered tables for tasters had colorful protective umbrellas. Sampling altars stood at the plaza's periphery. The cream of the city's gourmet restaurants, specialty food preparers, wineries, and chocolatiers displayed their tasty treats. Chefs stood tall behind their restaurant displays wearing executive chef coats embroidered with their names and a variety of headgear, including the traditional white chef hat, the chef's toque, and a few malcontents were wearing chefs' colored baseball caps.

We ate through the selected appetizers, sampling wines and a few microbrewery local beers. These were the best the city had to offer. Their aromas were incredible — their tastes even better.

We stopped next at Ritchie's, and upscale continental restaurant. Ritchie himself was having a fine time with the tasters who were enjoying the chef as much as the food. Ritchie wore a chef's white baseball cap with three Habanero peppers embroidered on the bill, green, orange, and red. Tasters sampled small pieces of grilled lamb chops with Jalapeno pepper jelly.

"Give it a try," Richie said as we approached his table.

"It's not too hot, is it?" Lois asked.

"No, you'll love it."

Tentatively, Lois took a bite, and smiled.

I stuck the toothpick into the meat, lifted it to my mouth, enjoying the flavor before it hit my tongue.

The taste exploded in my mouth. "Ritchie, this is special. Serrano peppers, right?"

Ritchie looked at me strangely. "Right. You must have a world-class sense of taste to make that distinction."

"We love Serranos, but can't find them in the Bay Area. Where do you get them?"

"I have friends in San Carlos, Mexico. They come up with them or arrange for someone to bring them out. They're worth the effort, aren't they?"

"You should bottle this jelly, Richie. We'd buy it for sure." I licked my fingers. "I love the apricot and the pear you added. It really adds pungency to the jelly."

"That's amazing," he said. "I'd better be careful what I serve around you."

Our conversation drew onlookers. "If everything you serve is as good as that dish, we're customers for life."

"Stop showing off," Lois whispered.

We made several other stops, relishing the tastes and adding several restaurants to our 'must go' list. A small group of tasters, intrigued by my talent, followed. I was into it—putting on a show.

The cioppino scent brought us to Biago's Trattoria table where the man himself stood erect, smiling smugly as tasters oohed and aahed as the small cups of cioppino passed through the crowd. I loved cioppino and believed that its quality portends the repertoire of a gourmet Italian chef. When we finally reached the table, Chef Biago ladled the iridescent red mixture into our cups. While I passed my nose over the cioppino, Lois said, "This is good, Arnie. Isn't it?"

When I filled the tiny cup with cioppino and brought it to my lips, Chef Biago watched me, stroking his thin black mustache with curiosity.

Instantly, I had the full recipe in my mind and said, "Not bad."

Biago reddened. "What did you say?"

I looked back at Biago, and repeated my comment. "Not bad. In fact, it's pretty good."

"Pretty good?" came with increased volume and attracted the attention of nearby tasters.

This is ridiculous, I thought. Who the hell is this guy?

I decided to keep my mouth shut, and started to turn away, when Biago grabbed my arm. "I asked you a question. At least give me the courtesy of a response."

I looked back at the red-faced chef, still seeing the humor in this odd situation. "You want to fight with me about my taste in cioppino?"

Biago released my arm, but his anger persisted. "I am a chef...a gourmet chef, with years of experience, and pride in my creations. If you've discovered something wrong with my cioppino, I want to know about it."

Lois grabbed my arm and started to pull me away. "Don't Arnie. It won't do any good."

I gently shook Lois's hand away, turned back to Biago. The crowd around us was solid with interest. "I'm not crazy about your ingredients."

Biago smirked and shook his head. "What do you do, Mr...."

"It's Dr. Arnold Roth. I'm a family practitioner, and if it's okay with you, I know what I like and what I don't like."

"Tell the arrogant prick, Doc," came a man's voice from the crowd.

I signaled with my index finger for Biago to come close. "Next time, use only fresh tomatoes, use less fennel, and for God's sake, for cioppino, use Greek oregano."

"I only use the best ingredients," shouted Biago. "Stick to your own business, Doctor," spitting out the last word as a profanity.

As I leaned toward Biago, I said in a voice loud enough that people could hear, "Your creation is a little better than the cioppino you can find in jars at Nob Hill Foods, but not nearly as good as Chef Bruno Vitale's cioppino. That's where you stole...I mean borrowed the recipe, isn't it?"

"You son-of-a-bitch," Biago shouted as he lunged for me. His staff restrained him as he flailed and sputtered.

I was six inches taller and eighty pounds heavier, so I grabbed him by the smock, lifted him off the ground. "Thank your friends, Biago. You may think you're having a bad day, but I assure you it was about to get a lot worse."

Chapter Thirty-Three

Like most normal people, I hadn't paid much attention to the sensory aspects of entering a room. With my probing proboscis, the simple sniff became olfactory Russian roulette. Now, each time I entered, I hesitated for several seconds, my nose poised for the cylinder's spin and the hammer's click. For me, ordinary smells had become sensory suicide or sensory salvation.

When I placed my bet by opening the ICU door this morning, a familiar cocktail of blood, alcohol, antibiotics and antiseptics, bath powder, and tincture of benzoin greeted me. Many people don't recognize the name, tincture of benzoin, but most of my generation recognized it immediately from childhood as that acrid substance their mothers placed in the bedside steam vaporizer for colds or respiratory infections. Benzoin is a tree gum resin from the Far East that's been in use for a thousand years as incense. Now, its sticky properties made it useful in securing bandages to patients.

I was in the unit to see Vee Dent, a forty-year-old patient of Bert Kaplan, a family practitioner. I covered for him while he went on vacation. Bert had admitted Vee three days ago with acute gallbladder inflammation. She had a history of depression and alcoholism and several episodes of inflammation of her pancreas, pancreatitis, a serious and painful disorder. Jack Byrnes consulted on her case when her kidney function declined. That had improved with IV replacement fluids.

Jack sat in his usual place by the nursing station.

"How's Vee Dent doing this morning?"

"Either she has an incredibly low pain threshold or the pancreatitis is rearing its ugly head again."

As I examined her, I picked up a familiar aroma, musty and acrid, but I couldn't quite place it. She was alert and oriented to time, place, and person, and her vital signs were stable.

"This pain's killing me, Doc," she said squeezing my arm. "It's in my back now, like a knife. I can't stand it. You've got to do something." She grasped her abdomen with both hands. She'd had an epidural anesthetic, a type of spinal used primarily in obstetrics. They'd used it immediately post op for pain control and removed it last night in anticipation of smooth sailing ahead.

When I joined Jack, I said, "It's probably pancreatitis again. Any labs back this morning?"

He held up the computer printout of today's lab. "I agree with you, Arnie, and so does the lab. Her tests for pancreatitis are sky high. I'm going to give her Demerol to control the discomfort. She's going to need potent narcotics for several days to a week."

Suddenly, something upset me. I felt anxious, but didn't know why. I tried to focus my attention by writing my daily chart note as the nurse, Carla Watts, approached Vee with a Demerol-filled syringe. In an instant, it struck me. I shouted, "No! Stop!" I raced to the bedside just as Carla was about to inject Demerol. I grabbed it from her hand and extracted it from the IV line.

Carla stared at me. "What are you doing? Are you insane?"

Jack approached. "What's happening here, Carla...Arnie?"

"He pulled the syringe right out of my hand, Jack. I was about to inject the Demerol as you prescribed."

Jack turned to me, his face full of questions. "Arnie, what's up?"

"I think she's on Nardil, Jack. You can't give her Demerol."

"Nothing on her chart suggests that she's taking an antidepressant, Arnie." He turned to the nurse. "Carla, get me the medication history sheet ASAP."

Jack stared at me. "What makes you so sure she's on Nardil?"

"I just know it," I said, in a near whisper, avoiding Jack's eyes.

Carla studied the chart. "Nothing on the nurses notes, the admission form, or anywhere regarding Nardil."

"Jack, you know what can happen if you give her Demerol and she's been on Nardil...severe hypertension, seizures, high fevers...it could kill her."

Jack gave me a smirk. "Arnie, I'm an intensive care specialist. I know more about the interaction between Demerol and Nardil that you'll ever know, and I've seen its effects up close. I'd never give them together."

"You were about to, Jack. Trust me."

"Trust you? I need a reason, Arnie. You're a friend and a good doc, but damn it, I need more."

"Let's talk with Vee."

We approached Vee's bed. She looked up. "You've got to help me with this pain. It's killing me. I can't stand it!"

I held Vee's hand. "We need to ask you a few questions, and then we'll decide how to deal with your pain."

She shook her head in disbelief. "I don't have time for this shit." She paused as if taken aback by her own words and then said, "Go ahead, Doc, but make it quick."

"When the admitting nurses asked you about your medication, you said nothing about Nardil, is that right."

"Yes."

"You aren't taking Nardil?" Jack asked.

"No, no Nardil."

Jack turned to me. "Arnie?"

"You know the drug Nardil, don't you?" I asked Amy.

"Of course, it's an antidepressant."

"Have you ever taken Nardil?" I asked.

"Of course, but I stopped it three days before coming to the hospital. I was too sick to take it."

"But you didn't say anything about Nardil when you were admitted," said an anxious Carla Watts.

"They asked me what I was taking and I told them. Nobody asked me what I'd taken before or when I stopped it."

Jack turned red, and then returned to the nursing station. He sat with his head down, and then looked up at me. "I don't know how you knew, but you probably saved Vee's life and all our asses. We must stop Nardil two weeks before we can use Demerol safely. We could have killed her!"

Mixed emotions best described what I felt at that moment. Relief that we'd prevented a catastrophe, blessed that I had the skill to detect the problem, and a strange feeling of isolation from my world. This gift, and it was indeed a gift, had changed the forthright way I related to the people I cared about. I was adrift and alone in my unique universe.

Jack was completing his own note in Vee's chart when he gazed up at me. The question was all over his face. "Arnie, what's going on?"

I shrugged my shoulders and left the ICU.

Chapter Thirty-Four

Ruth Fischer was twenty minutes late for her meeting with Reggie Brand. He'd called this morning saying that he had interesting information for her.

"What kind of interesting information?" Ruth asked.

"I'll see you later."

Once Henry left her house, Ruth felt relieved, although knowing him, she expected that this respite might be short lived.

The day after Ruth threw Henry out, she had lunch with her closest friend Rachael Sims. "You've got to see an attorney right away before Henry has a chance to screw you over."

"I don't think he'll do that, Rachael, and anyway I put in a call to Bob Hughes, he can handle the divorce."

"Another lamb to the slaughter," Rachael laughed and then smirked. "Bob Hughes is a good guy, and a good attorney, but trust me, you need a Pit Bull to deal with Henry." She opened her address book, found a number. "Call Belinda Savage, she'll know how to deal with Henry and whatever shark he brings on board to bite you in the ass. Belinda's last name is particularly apt. She doesn't take shit from anyone."

"Using an aggressive attorney sets the tone for the divorce. I'd hoped for an amiable separation."

"My God, Ruth, where have you been for the last twenty years? Given the chance, Henry will screw you over royally, and he won't understand why you don't like it."

The next day, Ruth met with Belinda for a preliminary consultation. The attorney's first step was to freeze their accounts, including those for Horizon Drugs. Her prescience was remarkable as Ruth's bank called the next day. They'd received authorization to close their joint accounts and transfer the funds to Henry's newly established ones.

"You greedy bitch!" Henry shouted through the phone. "How could you do this to me? Don't all our years together mean anything to you?"

"Sure, Henry, and your attempt to close our accounts and leave me with nothing was an act of goodwill."

"Listen, Ruth," he said pleading. "I've got a business to run and ongoing personal expenses since you kicked me out. Can't we reach an agreement?"

"Of course, Henry dear. Call Belinda Savage, you'll find her very accommodating," she said smiling, and gently replacing the receiver into its holder.

That afternoon, Reggie Brand rose from his desk to greet Ruth. "How's it going with Mr. Fischer out of the house?"

"It's going quite well, I think. I'm doing much better than I thought possible. I've hired Belinda Savage, do you know her?"

"Do I know her? I thank God she's on our side, the woman is, pardon the expression, a ball buster. I'll bet she had your finances frozen, right?"

"Just in time. Henry was about to take it all."

"Well, I've worked with Belinda before. She's going to be real interested in what I've discovered."

"What is it?"

"Do you want the abbreviated version or do you want the details?"

Ruth looked at the small, mild-mannered man, but didn't know how to respond.

"By details, Mrs. Fischer, I mean photos and videotape. I don't know where you are emotionally, but viewing this material could be difficult."

"It couldn't be worse than living with the man. Go on."

Reggie opened a manila folder with a stack of high-resolution digital photographs. He slid them across his desk toward Ruth.

Slowly Ruth thumbed through Reggie's pictures snapped through office or motel windows, several through the backseat window of a Lexus and one on the beach somewhere that was reminiscent of the beach scene in the movie *From Here to Eternity*.

Reggie then turned his laptop computer's screen to face Ruth, and then played the video. The pictures were crystal clear, sharply focused, and graphic in detail. Ruth watched, captivated by the scenes before her eyes.

After ten minutes, she suddenly burst out laughing. "I didn't know the old bastard had it in him. I didn't know he could move his limbs that way. He's going to love these...maybe have copies made or post them online."

Reggie looked relieved. He had his box of tissues and the smelling salts ready, but Ruth had made the emotional transition and was ready to deal with whatever would come.

"I've spent many hours trying to get into Horizon Drugs' finances. I had a friend of mine, a forensic accountant who consults for the DA, look into Henry's business affairs. Although we can't access much of the important financials, he thinks that there's funny business going on. By what he discovered, he cannot see how Horizon Drugs has so markedly improved their financial position in such a short time. They were heavily in debt and had made overtures to lenders indicating major cash flow problems, then suddenly, profits are up and the debt's mostly gone. Ordinarily, he would suspect mob connections, but he can't find any."

"Mob connections? I doubt Henry has the stomach for that. He said they'd made up for the cash flow problems when Medi-Cal came through with delayed payments and the new stores came on line."

"We don't think so, Mrs. Fischer. My accountant says, that it doesn't add up. Something else is going on."

"What do we do now?" asked Ruth.

"Let me talk with Belinda. Since you're a principal in Horizon Drugs, and both you and Mr. Fischer will have to come to a financial settlement, we should have access to the information we need very soon."

"Thanks, Reggie, let me know what's happening."

"Ruth," asked Reggie, "what do you want me to do with the pictures and the videos?"

"Put them in a safe place, Reggie."

Chapter Thirty-Five

The troublesome events surrounding Vee Dent and Arnie's reaction, continued to bother Jack Byrnes. When he reached home that night, he collapsed on the soft sofa. Beth soon joined him carrying two glasses of wine. As they sipped the icy Chardonnay, he said, "Did you hear what happened today?"

"What do you think? Carla Watts called ten minutes after that bizarre event with Arnie. What's up with him?"

"Whatever's up with Arnie, he probably saved Vee's life and our careers. The combination of Nardil and Demerol is lethal. The mistake may be understandable in that Vee withheld vital information, but before a jury, if she died, we wouldn't have a chance."

"How did he know?"

"I don't know, and he's not saying. That by itself is distinctly unusual. More than most docs we know, Arnie is up front and honest about everything. Then we had the episode in ICU where he was certain that we had pseudomonas in the unit when everyone else was oblivious to it. He smelled it, he said. We're all familiar with the aroma of that bug, but nobody else detected it."

"Maybe he just has a world class nose. Some people are like that."

"Perhaps, but there's more; he's been erratic, distant, and inattentive, as if he's preoccupied with something. It's a stark change from the Arnie we know. Docs, a few nurses, and several patients have commented on the change. Maybe it's the residue of the encephalitis, but I've examined him several times, and I didn't note any changes. Have you talked with Lois?"

"No, but I will."

"I'm going to ask Arnie to come in for a checkup. I'm concerned. Maybe he needs a neuro-psychiatric evaluation."

It wasn't a surprise to Lois when Beth called and asked her to lunch. They'd meet at noon once or twice a month, usually alone, but at times with other close friends. They relished these conversations for their easy informality on both the mundane and the more serious problems they often shared.

"Jack's concerned about Arnie. What's happening?"

"Concerned? Why?"

"I know you too well, Lo. Don't tell me you're not worried."

What can I say? Lois thought. How do I draw the line between the privacy and my concern for Arnie's welfare?

Beth met Lois's gaze. "Arnie's more than merely a patient to us, and you're more than a close friend. We love you both. We'd do anything to help you, but you must let us in."

Tears streamed down her cheeks. "We thought it was over when Arnie recovered. We thought he was fine, but he's not."

"Tell me."

"It's difficult to describe. He's the same loving and caring Arnie, but at times, he's preoccupied. Sometimes, I can't understand his behavior."

"I hate this, but is it possible that Arnie's seeing someone?"

Lois stopped crying. She smiled then laughed. "Not a chance. I'm not one of those last-one-to-know wives, but Arnie's crazy about the kids and me. If anything, he's been more amorous than ever. It's not easy to maintain an active sex life with a full-time medical practice and a houseful of kids, yet Arnie's sexual interest is in overdrive. He's discovered a new outlet for his creative talents; sex," she blushed, and then whispered, "and it's been amazing!"

"People at the hospital have mentioned that Arnie's different somehow," said Beth. "His mind is often elsewhere, and his behavior's unusual, yet Jack says that his skills as a physician are at an all time high. He's helped Jack several times and recently he saved a patient from a catastrophic drug interaction. Whatever happened to Arnie has been a mixed blessing."

"I don't know what to do," Lois said.

"Jack's going to ask Arnie to come to the office for a checkup. Maybe we'll get answers."

Beatrice Hodges only made things worse for me when, with a typical act of kindness and love, she arrived several days after the ultrasound carrying a freshly baked vanilla sponge cake. I loved these tokens of affection from patients, but I was about to reward her kindness by destroying their lives.

I hadn't yet discovered a kind way to deliver bad news, but as usual, I tried.

Patients are often wary of test results. That made delivering them a little easier. I'd be suspicious at once if my physician called me back after I'd been through testing, but Irving and Beatrice showed not the slightest sign of concern.

Beatrice held up her creation. "I know you love my sponge cake, Dr. Roth. Here it is, fresh out of the oven."

"Thanks, but let me put it aside for a minute. I have the results of your tests." I hesitated, and looked into their eyes. "We have a problem, Beatrice. A big problem."

Irving slid to the edge of his chair, swallowed hard, and stared at me. "What kind of problem are you talking about?"

How could I tell them?

"The ultrasound test showed a mass on your right ovary, Beatrice."

"What kind of mass?" Beatrice asked.

"It's a tumor…"

Irv sat upright. "What kind of tumor? You don't mean cancer, do you?"

"I'm afraid it is. That's the reason you have so much fluid in your abdomen, Beatrice. We found cancer cells in the fluid."

Beatrice clutched Irv's hand. "Can we get rid of it, cut it out?"

"We may have to remove it, but that would be only to help with other parts of your cancer treatment. The fact that it's already in the abdominal fluid, means that cancer cells have spread beyond the ovary. Beatrice, you're going to need chemotherapy with strong anticancer medications if you are going to have a chance."

"Have a chance?" Irv shouted, the true import of what I said finally getting through to him. "What are you talking about? Have a chance?"

Beatrice squeezed Arthur's hand. "It's okay, Irv. I'm going to be fine, right Dr. Roth?"

"I can't lie to you. This is serious business. You have cancer of the ovary, Bea, and it's spread. I'm going to discuss your case with the cancer specialists, but I have several other patients with this disease, so I already know how we'll treat it. None of it will be easy, but with surgery and chemotherapy, your chances of getting through it are pretty good."

"Pretty good?" Irving asked.

"Statistics don't mean much in an individual case."

"Tell us anyway," an irritated Irv demanded.

"I can't because we don't understand the nature of the cancer cells in the abdominal fluid. We don't know if they represent the cancer's distant spread. We'll know more after surgery."

I referred Beatrice to Harvey Russo, an experienced gynecological surgeon who scheduled her at once for an abdominal and pelvic exploration.

Irving Hodges had never felt this frightened before. The years carried its fair share of illnesses and surgeries for the family, but this was something entirely different, he could lose her. He couldn't conceive of a life without Bea.

"It's almost like we're one person," he said on the night before surgery. "I can't go on without you, sweetheart."

"Don't be ridiculous, Irv, I'll be fine." She paused. "I'm not worried about the surgery. I'm worried about how fast I can get back to you."

Harvey Russo grasped the scalpel then made a four-inch midline incision in Beatrice's abdomen. He controlled the bleeding with the electrocautery and dissected down until he reached the abdominal cavity that welled up with fluid when he entered.

He inserted shiny metal retractors into the incision, and placed his assistants' hands on them. "Pull hard. I need to see what we have here."

They pulled and the wound widened revealing the small intestine and an overlying layer of fatty tissue. Harvey gradually pushed things aside and worked his way down to the pelvic area where he immediately felt, then exposed the large cancerous tumor involving Bea's right ovary.

He dissected around the uterus and both ovaries so he could remove them. "I don't see any evidence of local spread."

Afterward, as Bea's pelvic organs sat in a stainless steel basin, Harvey turned to his assistant. "Let's take a good look around."

The fact that Beatrice never had abdominal surgery before made exploration easy. "Let's take a look at the liver and the lining of the abdominal cavity to see if we can find evidence of spread."

After thirty minutes searching and feeling, and finding nothing, Harvey smiled. "She's clean. Let's close her up."

When the young scrub nurse entered the waiting room, she said, "Dr. Russo said everything went well. Mrs. Hodges is in the recovery room. Doctor will be out in about ten minutes to go over the details."

The Hodges family sat anxiously in the surgical waiting room awaiting Harvey Russo's arrival. When he strode through the door, still in a sweat-stained scrub suit, they rose as one.

Harvey looked at Irving and his daughters. "Should we talk here, or should we go somewhere for more privacy?"

Irv's stomach knotted and he felt weak. He drifted to his right as if he were about to faint.

Kathy, their eldest daughter caught him. "Dad, are you okay?"

Irv pulled himself up to look at Harvey. "Go ahead, Doctor, tell us."

"I'm so sorry," Harvey said, "I didn't mean to suggest by my question that I had bad news. In fact the results are as good as they can get considering the circumstances."

"Go ahead, Doctor," Kathy said.

"First, I removed her uterus and both ovaries. The right ovary had a large tumor attached, but I could find no signs of local spread. The abdominal cavity was full of fluid, but again we couldn't find tumor anywhere. More important, we cannot find any signs of tumor spread to other organs, especially the liver."

"You mean she's cured," Irv shouted.

Harvey approached Irv and sat by his side. "We can't use the word cure for a while, Irv. We have to assume that cells from the cancer remain and that if not treated, they will continue to grow and threaten Beatrice's life. We can control all that, if we're lucky, by chemotherapy."

"Beatrice and I have been lucky all our lives. I know we'll be lucky now."

"She'll be with us for four or five days then she can go home. Dr. Roth is arranging for chemotherapy to begin as soon as possible."

Irving's large hands grasped Harvey's hand and arm. "I can't thank you enough, Dr. Russo. You don't know what this means to all of us."

Chapter Thirty-Six

After months of hell, Debbie Wallace finally awakened intact from the breast cancer nightmare. While she labored to keep it out of her conscious mind, on occasion, a comment, an article in the newspaper, or a moment of vulnerability would breach her complacency.

When Debbie checked her naked body from all angles while standing before her full-length bedroom mirror, she saw that Julie Kramer was right about the reconstruction. She lifted both arms upward, then grasped each breast and turned, examining them in detail. Time had transformed her breast from unshapely and lumpy to the normal breast's smooth-curves. If she looked closely, she could see subtle differences. For months, she'd kept them in hiding, but now she concluded that, girls, you're ready for prime time and returned to low-cut tops she loved and to the joys of cleavage.

Matt's whistle from the doorway caught her by surprise, but she recovered immediately then slowly turned to face her husband.

"They look…I mean," he stumbled over his words, "you look fantastic."

Debbie opened her arms, an invitation he readily accepted.

She smiled. "We have about an hour before the kids get back, that is if you're interested."

"Thanks for the vote of confidence, sweetie, but I don't need an hour."

He locked the door out of habit, and then dropped his clothes in a heap on the carpet. As he approached his wife, she spread her arms and they embraced. For the first time in months, Matt felt the invisible barrier separating them disappear. He never doubted his love for this woman, but time and events had taken their toll on the best part of their marriage, its intimacy. He missed it, missed her, missed the security and comfort of sharing his life with this incredible woman, but thank God, here it was again. While they made love, and amid the passion, Matt's mind luxuriated in the stillness of that moment, the moment when he finally accepted that all was well with the world.

Tino Ruiz worked late again. He'd closed the doors of Horizon Drugs and was cleaning up and preparing supplies for the next day. Suddenly, he heard a knock on the front door and saw a small middle-age man waving.

"We're closed. We'll be open tomorrow morning at eight."

Tino turned back to his work when the man knocked again. He ignored it, but the tapping continued until an annoyed Tino shouted, "We're closed."

The man mouthed something Tino could not understand, tapped again, and gave the come here gesture. Tino approached the door and said again, in a loud voice, "We're closed. Don't you understand?"

The man pulled out his wallet and displayed a gold badge and a laminated card. Tino knew at once that the badge wasn't legit; he'd seen too many real ones. When he came close enough, the badge read, Emeryville Auxiliary Police, and the card identified the man as private investigator Reggie Brand.

Tino cracked the door open. "We're closed. Come back tomorrow and you can talk with Mr. Fischer or Mr. Shands."

"It's you I want to talk with, Tino. Let me in, please."

"I'm not supposed to let anyone in after hours."

"It's okay," said Reggie, "I work for Mrs. Fischer." He pulled an envelope from his threadbare jacket's pocket and removed a one-page document. "This authorizes me to enter the premises."

Tino read the single paragraph signed Ruth C. Fischer, and then he unlocked the door and let Reggie enter. He studied the man. "What's this all about?"

"I'm sure you know that Mr. and Mrs. Fischer are getting a divorce. She's concerned that something peculiar is happening at Horizon Drugs. How long have you worked here, Mr. Ruiz?"

"I've been here about a year and a half."

"Do you enjoy working here?"

This is the soft sell approach, Tino thought. He recognized a manipulation when he saw one. He sneered. "Tell me what you want, Reggie, or get out."

"Take it easy, Tino. I know all about you. It would be smart for us to be on the same side."

"Don't bullshit me, man. I've been bullshitted by the best, and you're not even close."

Reggie smiled. "You're a smart kid. Don't be stupid now. You have a lot going for you. Don't screw it up. You're small potatoes. The last thing you want is to be in the middle of a nasty divorce."

"I still don't know what you want, Reggie," Tino said using the investigator's first name again on purpose.

"I don't want to make trouble for you, kid, but if you force me, I will. I have a few simple questions, and then I'm out of here."

Tino folded his arms across his chest. "I'm waiting."

"Mrs. Fischer is a part owner of Horizon Drugs and she thinks that something's wrong in the operation here. They're making big bucks from this business, and although Mrs. Fischer isn't allergic to money, she's worried. Too much money is coming in. She wants to know why."

That's what this whole thing is about, Tino thought. Maybe that explains a lot about what Brian's been doing. Whatever it is, you have to give the guy credit.

"I can't help you, Reggie. I know they were having big cash flow problems for months, but that's all behind them."

"If you know something, Tino, and you're keeping it to yourself, Henry and Brian can, and probably will, implicate you in whatever they're doing. I don't think they're paying you enough money to take the rap for their activities."

He's right about that. The secrecy, the money, the drug labels…

"Here's my card, Tino," Reggie said handing him his engraved business card. "Think it over. Mrs. Fischer could be the best thing that ever happened to you, son. You may need her on your side. I'll be in touch."

"Don't waste your time," Tino said, showing Reggie out the door while his mind whirled with an old familiar feeling, dread. He hadn't felt this way since his gang days. He didn't like it then. He hated it now.

Chapter Thirty-Seven

I was between afternoon patients when Jack Byrnes had me on the phone. "I want you in for a checkup, Arnie."

"What's going on, Jack?"

"We'll discuss it when I see you."

"I'm pretty busy. I'll call you when I can get away."

"Right. Don't put me off, Arnie. What time are you finished this afternoon?"

"I may not be done until six or maybe..."

"I'll wait for you in my office. See you after six."

Before I could respond, the line went dead.

I wanted to protest, to object, but in truth, I felt the pressure to see someone...to talk about what was happening to me. I trusted Jack, but I feared putting myself in anyone's hands. Dependency and the loss of control was true role reversal. I'd become my most difficult patient.

My office was as busy as usual.

Beverly stuck her head into my office. "Cathleen London is next. She's in your consultation room."

Cathleen was the wife of Marcus London, a Brier Hospital general surgeon. She'd been my patient for about eight years. She was healthy, so her visits were for routine checkups or minor illnesses. Cathleen was a beautiful woman, a runner up to Miss California, twelve years ago. Tall and blonde, with a model's figure, she still turned heads everywhere she went. She wore a knee-length pleated skirt and a purple silk blouse.

People who didn't know Cathy stereotyped her as aloof, self-centered, and unapproachable. In reality, she was the polar opposite. She behaved as if she were unaware of her physical beauty and its effects on others. She was friendly, outgoing, generous, and had an outstanding sense of humor. Like most people who knew her, I enjoyed her as a patient and as a friend.

When I opened the door, it hit me. A subtle floral bouquet on first whiff, but below, a warm, erotic essence swirled in the atmosphere. My mind flew to yesterday morning when Lois embraced me from behind, an easy seduction. I felt my erection, and was thankful that I chose to wear my long white lab coat. My reaction embarrassed me. This was inappropriate, I thought. I was angry that she did this to me. The erotic enlivening had a mind of its own and bewildered me.

"How are you, Cathy?"

When she approached to give me a hug, I nearly ran, but feet frozen, I managed to stick my ass backward thus avoiding an embarrassing collision.

"I'm fine, Arnie, and how are you?"

"I'm fine," I hesitated. "What's that perfume you're wearing?"

"Oh, that's Fiora. I bought it on a lark. It's supposed to have human pheromones…to make me irresistible," she laughed. "Do you like it?"

"Sure, I like it, Cathy, but I think it would be better if you saved it for Marcus."

"Arnie," she cried as her fair skin crimsoned. "I had no idea! I bought it because I liked its bouquet, the rest I thought was hype. I'm so sorry."

My fever defervesced and I reddened to a hue that matched Cathy's blush. I took a deep breath, looked at her, and smiled. We both erupted in laughter.

"Now where were we?"

She held her wrist out to me. "I have this swelling."

Me too, I thought.

I held her hand cautiously, and then saw a small lump. "It's a ganglion cyst. It's nothing. If it gets larger or its cosmetic effect bothers you, we'll remove it."

"That was easy enough," she said preparing to leave. As she approached the door, she turned, smiled seductively, and winked. "And thanks for the uplifting information, Arnie. Marcus will be forever grateful."

Lois met me for lunch at a small Chinese restaurant two blocks from the office. We took a booth and when the waiter approached, I refused the menu. "We'll have the usual, Szechuan prawns."

"How was work this morning, Honey?"

"The usual, but I did have an interesting experience with Cathy London."

"Cathy, I love her. Is she okay?"

"She's fine, but she was wearing a perfume called Fiora that's supposed to contain pheromones. It purports to make a person enchanting to the opposite sex. Do you know it?"

"I've heard the name. I know there's lots of hype about pheromones in perfumes, but it's a marketing ploy and a load of crap."

"You know I love you, sweetheart, and that I'm not interested in another woman, don't you?"

"Yes, I know, but let's face it Arnie, you're also human. What happened?"

"When I stepped in that room, I flashed back to yesterday morning. You remember."

"How could I forget?"

"When I saw Cathy, I remembered our tryst, and smelled that perfume; I was a dog around a female in heat."

Lois laughed. "You didn't hump Cathy, did you?"

"Almost. It was a visceral reaction. I was hot, angry, felt out of control, and I lashed out at Cathy."

"Lashed out. That's not like you, honey."

"I know, but this whole thing makes me think that forces we can't begin to understand, control...no influence us while we remain oblivious to their power."

"If I was a man, I'd have my fantasies about Cathy London, too, pheromones or not. Don't be shocked, but I'd have a passing thought…"

"Very funny! I'd be more amused if this nose of mine wasn't pointing me into a forest of confusion. You don't know what's out in the world, Lois. I'm only beginning to understand."

"Have you heard from Jack?"

"Okay, Lois, let's have it."

"All right, I had lunch with Beth. People don't know anything, but they've noticed that you've changed. Beth and Jack are our friends. Jack wants to help."

"I hope he can. I'm seeing him tonight."

Chapter Thirty-Eight

My anxiety over the upcoming appointment with Jack Byrnes kept me on edge through the day. I wanted help. No, I needed help. Since this supersensitivity began, I'd reviewed the medical literature on olfactory disorders, but found little useful information.

What could Jack do?

What could anyone do?

I walked the two blocks to Brier Hospital. The streets were wet with a late afternoon rain. On this cool evening, the horizon was ablaze in red-tinted cumulus clouds. The rain-exaggerated aromas included roses, succulents, perennials, and California native trees. The scent of vanilla, old wine, lemon, and a thousand other unknown fragrances excited my nose and stirred vivid memories.

I made my way to Jack's office. I raised my hand to the closed door, hesitated a second, and knocked. After thirty seconds, I felt relief, perhaps he couldn't make it. As I turned to leave, Jack opened the door.

"Not so fast, Arnie. I was on the phone. Come on in."

I lifted my head. "Corn Nuts...Ranch flavor. Any left?"

Jack stared at me in confusion, and then he pulled open the desk's center drawer. "Help yourself."

I popped a handful into my mouth, savored the medley of roasted corn, ranch dressing with a hint of soybeans and canola oil. I crunched vigorously while Jack smiled with curiosity.

"Play it anyway you like it, but I'm your friend and I'm here to help any way I can."

"Help me with what?"

"Don't do this, Arnie. Something's wrong. I know it, Beth knows it, and more than anyone else, Lois and your kids know it. Nobody's put their finger on it, but we all know that you're not yourself."

"How could I be myself after what I went through? We tell patients that it takes time to adjust after an illness, especially a life-threatening one."

"What could be so bad that you'd continue to hide what's wrong? I'm your doctor. I'm your friend. Nothing you say leaves this room. Isn't that enough?"

"You had bacon and eggs for breakfast and a French Dip sandwich with iced tea for lunch...Earl Grey, I think."

"How did?...You're spying on me."

"At breakfast?"

Jack stared at me.

"You made love to Beth early this morning. You showered last night, but not again after sex.

And, by the way, how's that itchy rear end of yours?"

Jack's jaw dropped. "Itchy what?"

"You know, the Preparation H you used this morning."

"What the fuck...?"

"You want to know what's wrong with me. That's what's wrong with me."

"I don't understand."

"Jack, the pseudomonas, the Nardil and everything that I told you...they weren't guesses. I knew those things with absolute certainty, just as I know that you're sitting with me now."

Jack shook his head. "Knew it?"

"How can I make you understand? It's not only that my nose has the sensitivity of a bloodhound, I'm responding to things that are way beyond simple smell. Things in the arena of pheromones and who knows what else."

"Arnie, that pheromone business is crap. It's Madison Avenue marketing."

"I don't think so. Scientists have demonstrated the existence of small nerve cells just behind the nostrils that detect airborne molecules we call pheromones."

"That's in animals, Arnie. As far as I know, the studies in humans are iffy at best."

"Maybe in the past, but the last ten years have produced ever more evidence that this system is active in humans. This may explain why women living together long enough will menstruate simultaneously, and why your beard grows faster in the presence of women."

"It's one thing to have a world class nose, and another to blame what's happening to you on a system that may or may not exist."

"Listen, Jack. Each day, I swim in a sea of aromas and chemicals I never experienced before. You...nobody has any idea. My moods, depressive or manic, my sensuality, and my uncharacteristic aggressiveness, says that I'm responding to the unseen, submitting to the influence a sixth sense."

"Sixth sense?" He shook his head. "When did it start?"

"Gradually in the weeks after I came out of the coma."

"What happened?"

"I don't know what happened, Jack. At first, I thought that my heightened perceptive abilities were the euphoria of surviving a near death experience, but soon I knew that this supersensitivity was limited to my nose. It started with increased olfactory acuity. I could detect the slightest of aromas. Then my new talent took off and I became inundated with the molecular milieu of our world."

"That sounds terrific."

"Yes, much of it is pleasant, more than pleasant...use your imagination, food, flowers, women, you name it. Others are unpleasant or disgusting and many more are unfamiliar. Each familiar scent evokes specific memories and the overall quantity of aromas and memories often leave me temporarily unable to respond. It's like having ten people yelling at you at once. That's what people are noticing."

I felt myself turn red with anger and frustration.

"I'm not inattentive. I'm not confused. I'm not disoriented, and yes, I'm not myself. How could I be when I'm living inside an olfactory maelstrom?"

Jack stared at me for a thoughtful moment. "Arnie, I can see the potential for problems, but this is fantastic. Imagine what it can do for you professionally. We know about certain diseases and the odors they produce like diabetes, liver disease and certain metabolic disorders that produce substances that appear in the urine and have a distinctive aroma. We're only beginning to learn about smell and disease."

"I've spent the last month reading the literature and searching the Internet. I think I've seen it all; melanoma and prostate cancer diagnosed by trained dogs sniffing the urine; schizophrenia diagnosed by trained rats, and many others. I can't find a thing about me, Jack. I'm a reportable case, a freak of nature, and that's not half of it."

"It can't all be bad. The whole world has amazing smells that you can experience in ways that I can't possibly understand."

"You're right, of course, but enjoying those fragrances has its limits. I remind myself of Lucille

Ball on the assembly line at the chocolate factory, candies streaming by on the conveyer belt. She enjoys the first few pieces, but the rest are overwhelming. I get that, but there's something more difficult to take."

"What is it, Arnie?"

"You know how when you smell something familiar, it cues memory?"

"Yes."

"Scientists have ample evidence of connections between the brain's olfactory lobes that detect and interpret smell and those parts of the brain where we store memory. I'm living proof of that, Jack. Every familiar aroma elicits one or more associated memories, some pleasant, some disturbing."

"I don't know what to say, Arnie. You know more about this than I, but you need somebody to help you with this thing, to gather resources, to work our way through it, and to provide objectivity. I can do that for you, Buddy."

"Thanks, Jack, but please, I don't want anyone to know about this." I stood, pacing back and forth across the room, shaking my head. "You need to understand that people may be more than a little uncomfortable in dealing with me, knowing that I have this ability. Remember how you felt when I revealed the intimate details of your life just now. I know you can't keep it from Beth, but that's it, nobody else is to know."

"I'll start my own research. I know several Ph.D. physiologists at Stanford. Maybe they can point us in the right direction."

Jack hesitated, smiling a challenge. "Arnie, if you didn't have your nose to the grindstone, maybe your nose wouldn't get out of joint."

I grinned and accepting his dare. "I always find time to stop and smell the roses. But, something fishy is going on."

"Watch out for the stench of evil or you'll have to pay through the nose."

"You hit it right on the nose, Jack. You have a nose for the truth and it's time I woke up and smelled the coffee."

"A rose by any other name might smell as good or stink to high heaven."

"That idea stinks or is a little overripe."

Jack smiled. "It ain't over until the fat lady sings."

I looked at Jack, momentarily confused, and then smirked. "I smell a rat, and I don't like the smell of it."

We looked at each other, shook our heads, and laughed.

"One more thing, Jack. Your sterilizing machine is still on, someone forgot to flush your toilet, and something's dead in your refrigerator."

As the clock approached five the next afternoon, Beverly Ramirez came in holding a chart. "One last patient."

Karen Adams began her apology as I entered the examination room. "I'm so sorry to bother you, Dr. Roth. I know you're busy, but I'm having a problem. Maybe you can help."

She sat on the examining table in a pale blue gown that seemed to swallow her up. At thirty-two, she looked more like someone in her fifties. She was pale, skeletal thin, and had the coarse facial wrinkling of the heavy cigarette smoker. Her brown stained index and middle fingers confirmed that impression.

"What's the problem, Karen?"

"I can't sleep. I've never been what you'd call a great sleeper, but in the last six months I'm lucky if I get two hours a night."

I glanced at the front of Karen's chart.

We organized our patient charts by listing their problems, the so-called Problem Oriented Medical Record. Sleeplessness had appeared before in Karen's chart as number twelve of thirty problems. Reading them again reminded me of my previous impression that Karen's problems had their roots in depression.

"I see you've had that problem before, Karen."

"It's much worse now, Doctor."

"When I look at your chart, Karen, many of your symptoms suggest to me that you're depressed."

"I'm not depressed, Dr. Roth. I'm not laughing all the time, but I'm usually in a fairly good mood. I try not to let things bother me, but even when they do, I soon forget about them."

"We've talked about this before, Karen. This isn't the first time that I thought you might be depressed. Now, I'm more certain. Having trouble sleeping is one of the most common symptoms of depression."

She stared at her feet. "I'm not depressed, Doctor."

We discussed her daily life, her diet, her tobacco use, her alcohol and drug frequency, but I failed to find a smoking gun. Besides asking questions about sex, drugs, alcohol, and unusual cravings like eating starch, dirt, etc., there was one question that too many physicians resisted; asking about spousal abuse.

I girded myself, and began obliquely. "Sometimes when a woman is depressed, we need to look at how things are going on at home, especially between her and her husband."

Her hands trembled and her eyes were glued to the floor. "I told you, I'm not depressed. Harold and me, we get along."

Suddenly, there it was again, that tangy, musty, and repulsive aroma of deception, as distinct to me as the oscillations of the polygraph needle.

I grasped her hands and looked into her eyes. "I can help you, if you let me. I can see to it that he never hurts you again."

Karen collapsed in tears.

Karen's truth, like Bob Dylan's answers, were blowin' in the wind. Literally, in her case, for someone perceptive enough to smell it.

Chapter Thirty-Nine

I phoned Jordan Goodman, the oncologist. "Jordy, I'm concerned about giving the combination of Platinol and Taxol to Beatrice Hodges in the office. It may be too complicated for us."

"I think you're right, Arnie. Let's work together with her and use the Comprehensive Cancer Center for the infusions. We do it daily, so it's routine."

My experience with Platinol, the metal-platinum complex, was limited, and the side effects profile of this potent anticancer drug was horrific.

Irving and Beatrice Hodges sat before me so we could talk about chemotherapy. I obtained informational packets about Platinol and Taxol from the university and the cancer center. They described in graphic detail the drugs, their usefulness, and their long lists of side effects.

I held up the brochures. "The side effects of these medications would have me running for the door, Beatrice."

She gave me the 'that's okay, honey' smile. "But, if that's what it takes to get well, Dr. Roth, then let's get to it."

Was she taking this too casually?

How much of this was denial?

Did she really know what was ahead?

"I'm not trying to scare you off, but these are powerful drugs designed to kill cancer cells, the bad guys. Often, the medication can't tell the difference between the good cells and the bad cells. That's what makes people so sick when we treat them."

Irv held up the information packet and shook its pages. "This scares the hell out of me, Doc. Are you sure it's okay?"

"It's not okay. It's what's available if we're going to try to treat this cancer. I hate it. I hate giving people I care about medication that I know will make them so horribly sick."

"What do you mean, 'if we try'?"

"Some people don't try to treat this form of cancer."

I went over the major side effects of both medications. The Hodges were intelligent, but medically unsophisticated. I doubted they could remember half of what I told them.

Irv stared at me. "Maybe this is too much for her, Doc."

Maybe, I thought.

The courts have made it clear that physicians must receive from every patient an informed consent before procedures or treatments with medication. Consent was a fantasy and a straw man, a clever ploy by aggressive personal injury attorneys. It went like this: first, create unrealistic and largely unobtainable expectations for consent, and then slam those who can't achieve it. Anyone in the business of treating high-risk patients knew that the objective, patients understanding all aspects of complex treatments, was largely impossible.

"Until recently, I thought people in their seventies were old. Not anymore. I see more and more people living into advanced age in good health. I can't decide this for you. Some people, although I often disagree with them, opt out of chemotherapy."

"No way, Irv," Beatrice said, grasping his hands. "I'm tougher than you think, besides, we have too much to live for."

When Irving and Beatrice came to the cancer center for her first infusion, I greeted them as the nurse sat Bea in the recliner. Each combination chemotherapy infusion lasted three hours. The first and most common side effect, nausea, generally occurred during this time and often lasted for a full twenty-four hours.

"I'm going to have the nurse give you medication to minimize the side effects. If you start to feel nauseated, push the call button and the nurse will give you something else."

"Don't worry so much Dr. Roth. I didn't get to this age by being a princess. I'm a tough old bird."

I reached over and grasped Irv's shoulder. "I've called in several prescriptions to Horizon Pharmacy for Bea. They'll help you deal with side effect you might see at home."

Irv sat by Beatrice's side holding her hand. "I'll take care of it, Doc."

Jordy Goodman and I hoped for eight cycles of chemotherapy, but into the second month, Beatrice was so sick with nausea, vomiting, loss of appetite, and weakness, that we had to curtail several scheduled infusions.

"Her kidney function is declining, Arnie," the oncologist said. "We can't give any more Platinol until your kidneys recover. We should continue with the Taxol as she's tolerating it well."

I drove to the Hodges's for a home to check on Bea. I'd asked the visiting nurse to come each day and report on her condition. Each time, the report was the same. "She feels and looks miserable. She's not eating, and rarely makes it out of bed unless forced to the toilet."

Irving Hodges greeted me at the door and led me through the gloomy house to their bedroom. His wrinkled face, with lines usually arcing upward in a smile, had turned downward in grim depression. The air was an acrimonious confusion of vomit, pine disinfectant, spoiled food, and again, that strange tonic water fragrance.

When I entered the darkened room, Beatrice's form lay under the covers. She had pulled up her legs to her chest in the fetal position. Her back faced me as I sat next to her in bed and grasped her shoulder. "Bea, it's Dr. Roth. How are you feeling?"

Irv snorted and grumbled an unintelligible response.

"Let me die...dear God, let me die," came in a whisper from Bea's cracked lips.

"Turn, so I can see you, Bea."

"No, Doctor. Please. I'm too sick. It's too late."

Gently, I grasped her shoulders and turned her to face me. If I didn't know this house and if Irv weren't beside me, I would not believe that the person in this bed was Beatrice Hodges. She was wasted to the bone, especially her head, which showed taut sallow skin stretched over a hairless scalp. Her mottled skin was canvas painted blue-purple, to gray-blue to yellow-green with large bruises. Several thin-skinned areas over pressure points on her hips were red, and one was broken down to form a shallow ulcer. By aroma, our old bacterial friend, pseudomonas had infected the wound.

"Look what you've done to her. She's dying, can't you see that?"

I picked up the bedside phone and dialed East Bay Ambulance.

"I'm taking her to Brier Hospital, Irv."

Chapter Forty

Debbie Wallace sat at the side of the bed while Matt snored softly. The clock's red LEDs showed 3:09 a.m. She'd been a world-class sleeper most of her life and only in the midst of radiation and chemotherapy did she have difficulty in getting a full seven to eight hours. Tonight was the third in a row that she awakened around three. She tried to read in bed despite Matt's grumbling about the light, but she was too tired to concentrate. She got up, did crocheting, and cleaned the house. Although she yawned until her jaws ached, she still could not fall back to sleep.

If this continues, I'll have to give Arnie a call.

Matt's alarm jarred her back into reality at 6:30. She'd finally slept since 4:30 a.m.

"My head's killing me, Matt. I'm not getting enough sleep."

"Maybe it's time to go back to decaf coffee, Babe."

"It's not that. I'm drinking coffee only in the morning."

Debbie got in the shower, luxuriating under the steamy hot water. Her headache lessened, but when she stepped onto the bath mat, it recurred in full force. Suddenly, she felt nauseated and leaned over the sink in preparation for the vomiting that didn't come.

Debbie dressed, moved into the kitchen where the strong aroma of coffee filled the air. She loved the smell of coffee in the morning, but today it made her nausea recur. She grabbed two aspirins and downed them with a small glass of orange juice.

Matt looked up from the morning paper. "What's up today, baby?"

Debbie sat, head down, on the dinette table. "I'm sorry, what did you say?"

"I asked what you're doing today. Maybe I can get home for lunch if you can fit me into your busy schedule," he said smiling.

"Make it a habit, honey," Debbie said, and then rose and rushed to the kitchen sink where she vomited and retched repeatedly. The sink filled with orange juice and undigested aspirins. She sweated and choked each time a new wave of misery crashed into her stomach.

"My God, what's wrong?" shouted Matt. "I'd better call Arnie."

"No, it's okay. I'm feeling a little better now that all that stuff is out of me."

Matt walked Debbie to the table and helped her into a chair. She was pale and covered with a fine sheen of perspiration. He grabbed a washcloth, ran it under the cold water, and placed it on Debbie's forehead.

"My head's killing me Matt, and my vision is a blur. You'd better call Arnie."

As I prepared to leave my office for hospital rounds, the answering service called. "I have Matthew Wallace on the line. He says it's an emergency."

My stomach contracted in dread. "Put him through."

"Arnie, it's Debbie. She woke up with a severe headache this morning and can't stop vomiting. She says her vision is blurred, too."

My God, I thought. Is there no justice in this fucking world?

"Bring her to Brier Emergency. I'll be there shortly."

Modern medicine had many things going for it, but the speed by which you could establish a diagnosis was a two-edged sword. Early diagnosis gave you a leg up on treatment, but it slammed your sails and slashed them to shreds before you had an opportunity to shorten them in preparation for the storm.

Debbie's brain CT scan, completed within thirty minutes of her arrival in the emergency room, showed a single brain mass, a tumor. The odds were overwhelming that this was metastatic breast cancer.

I would give anything to be somewhere else. To be in a different profession. To be a craftsman, an artist, or any job where I didn't have to talk to Debbie and Matt.

I approached the gurney. For the third time, I detected the scent of tonic water emanating from Debbie. What the hell was that? In addition, I noted a tangy, musty, and repulsive emission from Debbie's body — the cancer itself?

Matt was on the other side holding Debbie's hand. They could read me, I was sure, since they brought themselves to attention and looked expectantly into my eyes.

Matt clutched Debbie's hand. "What is it, Arnie?"

My tongue had stuck to the roof of my mouth. I felt my eyes shifting, unable to meet their gazes. I knew what message this behavior delivered, but I was helpless to control it.

"Arnie, what is it?" Debbie cried, holding her head in pain.

"What I'm about to say will shock you. It shocked me, too. Hear me out before you think the worst."

"The worst?" shouted Matt. "What the hell is going on, Arnie?"

"I'm so sorry to tell you this, but it's a brain tumor."

Matt stood. "A brain tumor! Are you crazy?"

Debbie began to sob. "A brain tumor, how can I have a brain tumor? Even I can't be that unlucky."

I reached for her shoulder and rubbed it softly. "The odds are overwhelming that the brain tumor has spread from your breast cancer. We call that metastatic cancer."

"I thought we got rid of that. You, everybody, promised that if I went through that miserable chemotherapy I'd be done with it. You promised!"

We all knew better, but what would you expect from Debbie given her devastating diagnosis.

I pulled a chair to the side of the gurney, sat, and held Debbie's hand. "I can't expect to fully understand what this means to you, but somehow I do. This is what we call an isolated metastasis, a single tumor, and in contrast to widespread metastases, we can treat it."

"Treat it." Debbie said. "What about the rest of it that's spread all over my body. What can you do about that?"

"Don't assume anything. This may be it as far as spread goes. We need to find out, and even if other sites are involved, there's still much that we can do."

"Don't bullshit us, Arnie," Matt said. "You've been straight with us all along. Don't start to lie now."

"I'm not, and I won't. I'm not giving up, and neither should you. We still have a good chance to beat this, and I'll give it everything I have."

"What happened, Arnie?" Debbie asked. "Everyone, including the experts at UC said the chemotherapy would finally kill these cancer cells."

"I don't know, Debbie, and if there's a reason, I'm sure going to find it."

When I returned home that night, Lois greeted me with a warm kiss and an icy glass of

Chardonnay that she placed on the table by my La-Z-Boy recliner. "How was your day?"

I slumped into the soft cushion. "Don't ask."

"Too late now, I already did. What's wrong, you look so glum?"

"It's Debbie Wallace."

"Don't tell me the cancer's back."

"Worse."

"What could be worse?"

"It's spread to her brain."

"My God...she has three girls, doesn't she?"

"Three wonderful girls and an incredible husband, but that's as far as her luck goes. Luck seeks those who need it least and avoids those who depend on it most."

"What's going to happen now?"

"It's a solitary brain metastasis. Hopefully, we can deal with it. This whole thing sucks, babe."

I swivelled the chair to face Lois. "Even today, where pharmaceuticals offer so much promise, it's impossible for us to understand why some patients fail treatment while others do well. It's easy to say, and the statistics confirm, that each medication has a failure rate. Is that why Debbie has a recurrence or could it be something else? Something about her course keeps nagging at me. The whole picture's out of focus. If I can only sharpen the image, maybe I can sense what's really going on."

Chapter Forty-One

After a two-week stay in the Skilled Nursing Facility, Connie Rinaldi was physically ready for discharge, but she wasn't emotionally prepared to return to her own apartment. She agreed to move back in with Tina and Joseph temporarily.

It's a mistake for family, friends, or even a physician, to tell a patient like Connie Rinaldi how lucky she was. Luck was a matter of perspective, and she wouldn't wish such good fortune on her worst enemy. People loved her and were happy that she survived, but none of them was a thirty-seven-year-old single, childless woman with severe advanced chronic bronchitis. None of them would be connected by a tether to an oxygen generator, or to a shoulder sling carrying a portable oxygen tank, her permanent appendage.

Connie sat on Jim McDonald's examining table. She loved Jim, they'd been through so much together, but at times, his boundless optimism pissed her off.

He smiled as her entered the room. "How's it going, Connie?"

"Do you want the truth?"

"No, I want you to lie," Jim said, pulling up his rolling stool to sit with her. "Don't you think I understand what you've been through...what you're going through?"

"I'm sick of the whole damn thing. I'm a prisoner…a lifer, without the chance of parole. Everyone says, I'm depressed, but I say you can't use that term when my life's a living hell. Feeling anything other than depression's not possible. I can't live this way, Jim. I won't live this way."

"What do you want me to do, Connie?"

Tears streamed down her puffy cheeks. "I want you to give my life back to me."

"You're on the list for a combined heart and lung transplant at UC San Francisco and at Stanford."

"Please, Doc, with twenty or thirty heart/lung transplants per year for the whole country, I'm not betting on those odds."

"I know, but you're a good candidate. You're young and otherwise healthy, and you're right here near two world-class transplant centers. That makes a difference."

"What would you do?"

"I'm not you, and I don't know if anyone could answer that question in the abstract. I don't know if I have your courage and strength to get through what you have. Few people do."

Beverly Ramirez was enjoying her big four zero birthday party. Her Richmond home's backyard had a dozen folding tables set and joyously decorated. Red, green, and yellow balloons attached to chairs, branches, and the redwood fence, floated in the breeze. Food overflowed everywhere. Both sides of the family had come to celebrate as kids of all ages played in every available open space, but mostly found reason to streak screaming through the crowds of relatives. The bright midday sun shining from clear blue skies made a perfect party setting.

By four in the afternoon, the families had enough and were trying to corral their children to leave.

Tino Ruiz and Beverly sat under a large oak tree.

"I'm so glad you could come, Tino. We don't see enough of you."

"I enjoyed the party, but I can't believe you're forty."

"You can't believe it. What about you?" She paused and grasped Tino's hand. "How's it going with school and work?"

"School is much easier than I thought. My grades are good and I'm planning to transfer to UC Berkeley next year."

"Wonderful. How's work?"

"Work is work. It's all pretty routine, and I think that Henry and Brian have finally learned to trust at least one Border Bandit. They don't even check their back pockets anymore. How are things at Dr. Roth's office?"

"Pretty much the same. Arnie's back in the groove." Beverly hesitated a moment, and then her face darkened. "Debbie Wallace's cancer recurrence devastated us. I think I told you about her."

"Yes, I remember her. She's the young mother with breast cancer. I also know her because Horizon has provided her chemotherapy drugs. What happened?"

"Debbie's had the worst luck; surgeries, radiation, and chemotherapy, and just when we felt that she was through with the cancer, it recurred and spread to her brain. Everyone's upset. All the expert opinions said that her odds were more than 90 percent for success. I guess that some unfortunates need to make up the 10 percent group. She was doing well. The last few cycles with Taxol were easy for her, with fewer side-effects."

Taxol? Tino's thoughts raced through a disturbing sequence of events: an unanticipated recurrence, fewer side-effects, Brian Shands' furtiveness in the clean room, the drug labels from Mexico, and Horizon Drug's sudden reversal of fortune. His mind resisted the logic of these observations, and a conclusion so evil that it made his gang's worst activities seem like petty theft.

"What's going to happen to her?"

"Arnie will discuss Debbie's case with Dr. Becker from UC San Francisco. We don't know what will happen; more surgery, more chemotherapy, or an alternative form of chemotherapy more appropriate to a woman with advanced breast cancer." She paused and then continued, "This is the toughest part of medicine for me, Tino. I love these people and I have to stand by watching as they fail treatment, get complications, and die. It makes me sick."

I haven't worked so hard to become a part of this, Tino thought. That poor woman, her kids, and everyone's efforts...for what? He stared at Beverly and thought, where did I put Reggie Brand's card.

I dialed Stanley Bank's office at UC San Francisco. "Stan, it's Arnie Roth."

"Arnie, how are you doing? I heard you had a rough time of it."

"I'm doing well, a lot better than Debbie Wallace."

"My God, not another recurrence?"

"Worse, she has a frontal lobe tumor. The only upside is that it's an isolated metastasis. We haven't biopsied it yet, but the odds are overwhelming that it's her breast cancer."

"I agree, and it surprises me. The nature of her malignancy and the combined chemotherapy should have dealt with the tumor, but we all know that treatment isn't 100 percent effective. I need to see her ASAP. We can probably approach the brain with the Gamma Knife and maybe she's a candidate for Herceptin, her tumor was Her2 positive, wasn't it?"

"Yes it was."

Herceptin was a medication that contains specific antibodies that block a protein at the tumor cell surface called Her2. It existed in about 25 percent of women with breast cancer. Since it targeted the cancer cells, it was effective in advanced breast cancer and had few side effects.

The Gamma Knife program began at UC in 1991. It's a form of radiosurgery where they aim multiple beams of radiation at a specific site, in Debbie's case, her brain tumor.

"We're having unbelievable results with the Gamma Knife, especially since we automated the process with our computers," Becker said. "With all that Debbie's been through, the high expectations and the disappointments, making her understand that her chances are still good won't be easy. While she's lost another battle, the war is far from over."

"Be careful with the war metaphors, Stan. Debbie and Matt are smart and determined, but this disease can overwhelm the strongest. Lay it out for them. Tell them the odds, and as I do, emphasize the therapeutic value of an optimistic viewpoint."

"I'll keep you posted, Arnie. After the radiation, we'll begin the first round of Herceptin and outline the protocol for you when she returns to your office."

"I don't know how you do it, Stan. It kills me each time we get a recurrence."

"Cancer is tough business. If I broke down every time a patient died or had a recurrence, I couldn't do my job. I'd love to cure them all, but either way, I'm here to help. It's the best I can do and it's enough for me… it has to be."

Near the end of today's busy afternoon, Beverly came into my office carrying a chart. "Sal

Bruno's back, Arnie. What are you going to do with him?"

"I don't know."

My practice was busy enough without Sal Bruno's intrusion into my schedule. The news about Debbie Wallace and my devastation over Beatrice Hodges left little sympathy for the likes of Sal Bruno.

Bruno was a teamster in his late twenties. He paced my examining room ranting, "What do you mean, no more Vicodin? I'm in pain. What part of pain don't you understand?"

"I've filled that prescription for the last time, Sal. I'll give you anti-inflammatory agents and I'll work with the pain control clinic to help you, but you'll get no more dope from me."

Sal was a large man, hardened by the job—Kojak on steroids. His shiny baldhead and snake and spider tattoos on both arms, sent a message of intimidation, a tool of his trade that he used well. He approached me red-faced, our noses separated by inches. I could smell a citrus scent on his breath, an aroma I recognized. I scanned my increasing inventory of aroma/memory associations and recalled opening an old bottle of Percodan I'd used years ago after a root canal. It had the same distinctive aroma.

"I'm tired of this shit," he yelled. "You didn't mind all the workmen's comp. bucks you took since my injury, did you? I need the Vicodin…I'm in pain."

I wiped the small droplets of spittle off my face and stared back at him. My usual reaction to stress was a sense of the world slowing as my mind remained calm and in control.

"You're hiding something from me, Sal."

"I don't know what you're talking about."

The ammonia-like stench confirmed his lies.

I opened Sal's chart to the summary of his prescriptions. "I gave you forty Vicodan two weeks ago. If you were in so much pain, you should have been out last week. What happened to make things worse?"

"You're the doctor. You tell me. All I know is that I'm in pain and you're giving me shit."

"Yes, Sal, I am giving you a hard time. First, you overused the Vicodan, and second, you're on something else and lying about it."

"You son-of-a-bitch," he shouted as he closed the little gap between us, his face beet red, his fists clenched.

I stepped forward to meet him. "Percodan. You're on Percodan. What's the matter, couldn't you buy or steal more?"

"You've got one hell of a nerve accusing me. You don't know what you're talking about."

"I'd like to help you, Sal, but play it your own way."

He remained silent.

I stood. "We're wasting our time, Sal. Call me when you're ready."

Sal backed onto the chair and sat with his head down. "How did you know?"

"It doesn't matter, does it? You're too deep into this. You can't handle it by yourself."

Sal looked up. His eyes welled. "I'd do whatever you say, Doc."

I picked up the intercom. "Beverly, get me Santa Rosa Rehab. I have a referral."

Chapter Forty-Two

After admitting Beatrice Hodges to Brier Hospital, I began intravenous fluids and medication to control her vomiting.

Irv sat by her side holding her hand.

"Can I stay with her, Doc?"

"Of course, Irv. I'll ask the nurses to bring a cot into Bea's room."

"She looks awful," Irv said, as we stood in the hallway.

"I agree. I'm hoping the chemotherapy caused her dehydration and malnutrition."

"What else could it be?"

Patients often asked questions when they knew or suspected the answers. It was a plea, a hope that their worst fears were unfounded, and that I would come up with another explanation.

"Let's see how she responds to treatment."

Soon it became obvious. My hope that her decline was the consequence of chemotherapy and its side effects had been based on wishful thinking.

By the third day, Beatrice looked 100 percent better. She'd gained eight pounds with correction of dehydration and control of vomiting.

I held Bea's hand. "You look much better this morning. How are you feeling?"

"I'm back from the dead, Dr. Roth, thanks to you. I've never been so sick or felt so hopeless or so alone." She looked at Irving, who sat at her side. She caressed his scruffy unshaven face, and smiled. "Look at him. Clean him up, before you send him back to me."

"Are you eating?"

"My appetite isn't worth a damn. The smell of food sets my stomach off every time."

"Maybe it's the hospital food. You can order anything you want or you can have Irv bring in your favorites."

"I don't think it would help. I'm not hungry."

I examined her carefully. The abdominal fluid, absent on admission due to dehydration, had returned. If that wasn't ominous enough, my stomach twisted when for the first time I could feel her liver. It was firm, enlarged, and irregular, and I knew immediately what the abdominal CAT scan would reveal — a cancer-filled liver.

"I'm ordering a CAT scan of your belly for this morning, Bea. Your liver is a little enlarged."

Irv rose and stared at me. "What does that mean?"

"I won't say anything until I'm sure."

Although I was confident in what the scan would show, I paled when the radiologist flipped the films onto his viewing box. Normal liver substance had a uniform texture, while Bea's showed a dozen or more irregular round densities, the classical picture of cancer's spread to the liver.

"I'm so sorry, Arnie," said the radiologist without explanation.

I discharged Beatrice that afternoon, but met with the Hodges the next day in the office.

"No...No!" Irv cried. "It can't be true. There must be another explanation."

"I'm sorry. The cancer has spread to her liver."

"What can we do? We've got to do something."

Bea reached over to her husband and grasped his hands in hers. "It's okay, baby. It's my time."

Irv lowered his head to their joined hands and sobbed.

Bea looked at me and took a deep breath. "What next, Dr. Roth? I'm frightened of death for sure, but what scares me is the pain and the burden I'll place on Irv."

"Don't worry about me, baby. You've never been a burden and you never will."

"You've heard of hospice?"

Irv's jaw tightened. "She's not going to any nursing home to die. I'll never let that happen."

"Hospice is not a place, Irv, it's a philosophy. It's the best way to care for people in the last stages of their lives. I'm sure we can provide that care in your own home."

"You must find something else. Experimental drugs or treatments," Irv begged. "We can't walk away and let her die."

"I shouldn't put myself or my wife into your situation, but it helps me to help you. I've looked over all the possibilities and discussed them with experts at the university, and I can't find one experimental protocol I'd try for my wife if she was in Bea's situation. They'll only make her miserable and won't help. Hospice will offer her humane and compassionate care. They'll keep her alert, pain-free and she'll live what remains of her life with dignity, surrounded by her loved ones."

Bea tightened her grip on Irving's hands. "It's what I want, Irv. Help me through it. Please help me."

It amazed me that once patients knew they had a fatal illness, the disease surged into ascendency. I knew it was irrational, even mystical. People went for long periods with fatal diseases, but once we made the diagnosis, they died quickly as they physically and emotionally submitted to the inevitable.

So it was with Beatrice Hodges. Three weeks later, with Irv and the family at her bedside, Bea slipped into a coma and never regained consciousness.

Bea's three daughters dressed in black. Irv Hodges wore his charcoal-gray suit. On this warm and bright day at Rose Hill Cemetery in nearby Lafayette, the family sat under a large elm tree. Family mourners filled the front rows. They'd been pleasantly surprised at the large number of vehicles following the black Lincoln hearse through the iron gate at the cemetery's entrance.

The ornate oak casket sat on a platform before the open grave. Each daughter contributed to a moving graveside eulogy, while Irv sat in silence.

Kathy, Arthur's oldest daughter pleaded with her father. "Please Dad, say something for Mom. I know it's hard for you, so do it for us, for the family."

Irv refused to meet his daughter's eyes. He was mortified that he'd let this happen and embarrassed to be alive. Finally, he looked at them. "There's nothing I can say."

After the ceremony, they lowered the coffin. The minister handed Irv the shiny stainless steel shovel, but he refused this as well.

When it was all over, Kathy grasped Irv's left hand, suggesting that it was time to go. She looked into his dispassionate face and saw a single tear streaking from each eye, running over his wrinkled cheeks. In his right hand, a thin gold chain wrapped itself around twice with a gold locket in the center of his palm.

Losing Bea was more than Irv could tolerate. Emotionally, his world ended with the love of his life's death. He became depressed, refusing my offers of support and the exhortations of his family. He ate, slept, did his chores and shopping, but the heart of the man died when Bea took her last breath.

Chapter Forty-Three

I was up most of the night. The ER at Brier Hospital had called at midnight and I went in to admit a patient with pneumonia.

When the coarse buzzing of my alarm clock awakened me at 6:30, I'd only slept two hours. My head ached and my mouth felt like leather. Although awake, my mind remained in park, and then shifted into overdrive as my nose detected maple sausage, fried eggs, coffee, wheat toast, and fresh orange juice. With my mouth watering, I felt energized and leapt out of bed to confront the day ahead.

Lois sat at one end of the kitchen table. On the other, sat two bowls with the soggy remnants of an unidentifiable cereal. The girls had managed to splatter milk and orange juice on the shiny oak table. I heard the door slam as my daughters headed for the Lincoln Navigator at the curb.

"What time did you get in, Arnie?"

"Around 4:30. I admitted Pam Davis with another flare of bronchitis. I knew it was coming and put her on antibiotics, but I acted too late."

"How did you know?"

"When she was in early this week, I could smell the bacterial overgrowth coming from her lungs. She carries bacteria, but this time the stench was pretty powerful."

"How's that proboscis performing?"

"Perfectly...too perfectly. It frightens me sometimes. By the way, your mother was here yesterday. Sometime in the afternoon."

"You're in enough trouble with Nora. Don't compound the felony by sharing your talent for recognizing people by their smell with her. She won't understand. Moreover, she'll be mortified if she thinks you can recognize her that way."

"So mortified that she won't come back?"

"No such luck, sweetie. She'd only shower and drench herself in perfume."

"I have a lot more olfactory data to share with your mom. It could be entertaining."

"The laughs won't be worth it. Trust me." Lois hesitated a moment. "Has Jack come up with anything about evaluating your newfound talent?"

"He's talked with the Chemosensory Perception Lab at the University of Utah in Salt Lake City. Jack's setting up an appointment for me. I think it's a total waste of time."

I read extensively and learned a lot about the unheralded world of smell, a universe described with the limitations of a preschool vocabulary. Perfumes, foods, and the rich aromas of nature won public acclaim, while the rest, 90 percent of the molecules that fill the air, are either unknown or a source of embarrassment and disdain.

"Smell is different from the other senses, Lois. What we see, touch, or hear passes through the thalamus, the back part of the forebrain. Then it goes to the cerebral cortex where we experience those senses. In contrast, smell takes a nonstop path to the cortex. That explains why aromas we know speed to specific brain memory sites and fills our minds with lucid and detailed recollections."

"Every time I smell maple syrup," Lois said, "I find myself back in my Mom's kitchen eating a stack of buttermilk pancakes."

"With my nose, the same aroma often leads to a different memory. The new aromas, the ones that only animals and I can appreciate, fill my world. They're new to me, and elicit no memories. I try to characterize each new aroma by linking it to a known scent or combinations of scents: lemon-skunk, acrid-vanilla, moldy corpse, etc. I add each new aroma to my unending lexicon of smells. Trees, plants, animals of all kinds, industrial byproducts, and a thousand others form a trail of molecules sometimes leading to its origin, while mostly they dissipate rapidly into the atmosphere or are swept away on a passing breeze and remain a mystery."

I drove directly to Brier Hospital, parked, and walked to the Respiratory Care Unit (RCU). As the door to the unit swung open, I gagged on the glut of ghastly odors. I leaned on the wall trying to escape, and then grabbed three pieces of Altoids Peppermint Chewing Gum and rammed them into my mouth. The heavy mint flavor gave me temporary respite by overwhelming the offenders.

When I walked to Pam Davis's bedside, the strong stench of bacterial degradation hit me full force. My mind flashed to my first student rotation in the RCU under the guidance of Harold Haft, a jovial lung specialist. Patients coughed into clear plastic cups and filled them with foul sputum showing nurses and physicians how the lung infection was responding to treatment.

"That's disgusting," I said the first time I saw these collections.

Harold went on to gross me out as he laughed at his own favorite clinical aphorism, "Phlegm, it's my bread and butter."

I popped more Altoids as myriad aromas tried to overwhelm the gum's defensive positions. Soon, they too were expended, and I stood naked and unprotected in a universe reeking of sickening molecules.

I walked up to Barbara Howard, the charge nurse. "What's wrong with the ventilation system?"

She looked at me as if I were crazy. "There's not a thing wrong, Dr. Roth. We went through this yesterday. I had the engineers check the HVAC system. They said that it was functioning perfectly."

"I don't give a damn what they say, this place reeks...it's disgusting. How do they expect anyone to work in a place that smells worse than a morgue?"

Barbara studied me carefully. I knew I had upset her, again. I was upsetting many people lately. My pulse bounded and my hands trembled as I scribbled my orders as quickly as possible, and rushed to escape from this pulmonary purgatory.

Chapter Forty-Four

It was subtle at first, but I noticed the change in people's reactions to me. My staff and others familiar with my talent, suddenly took extraordinary care with their dress and personal hygiene—how could that be bad? Perfumes, scented powders, deodorants, and aftershaves blended in the office milieu. It pleased me at first, but then I understood that my ability became problematic for others—my smeller made them self-conscious. Being with me was like sitting naked or with a mind reader; who could be comfortable with that? We function better in a society where our small secrets remained classified. We were still entitled to private thoughts, weren't we?

As a child, I remembered my mother's allergies. The nasal congestion had her shoving the milk carton or the wrapped leftovers under my father's nose. "Smell this. Is it okay to eat?"

People, especially my office staff, weren't putting things under my nose, but my talent had become the equivalent of installing surveillance cameras in the office. They approached me expectantly, as if I were about to perform an armpit check.

I couldn't do much about my perceptions. I never commented on the scents that flowed over me, except on occasion to compliment a woman on a particularly delightful perfume. In public places, I found myself moving to another location to escape the repulsive stench of those who refused to bathe or change clothes. My sensitive snoot made me aware of my patients' aromas. Some, only I appreciated, while others with medical or dental problem, or a portion of Korean bok choy could offend anybody. Every tactful approach to informing a patient about their smell worked well until they became aware of my true meaning, then it became shock, denial, and aspersions against my manners. It reflected our culture and its sensitivity to issues of smell.

Jack Byrnes and I shared in the care of Sherrie Brown, a dialysis patient.

Sherrie became one of the most intractable patients Jack had seen in the dialysis program. An attractive young woman, Sherrie found clever excuses to skip her treatments and ignore crucial dietary restrictions.

Jack shook his head. "I've tried everything. I've spent too much time, as did nurses and our dietitian, trying to explain to Sherrie that her behavior is compromising her health, if not her life. Nothing worked so far. You give it a shot, Arnie."

I had my office call and set up an appointment.

I didn't know what I could offer, but when I entered the examining room to evaluate her, it reeked of urinous waste chemicals she couldn't eliminate on her own. It had been accumulating in her body and now emanated from her skin and breath.

"I'm always happy to see you, Arnie," she said coyly, smiling in her usual seductive way. She wore a short skirt, a satin tank top, and three-inch heeled sandals. She'd painted her toes pink.

"We need to talk..."

"Don't be mad at me Arnie," she pouted. "This dialysis thing is killing me. I need a kidney transplant yesterday..."

"There's not much I can do about that, except to keep you in good shape until one comes along. That brings me to the reason I've asked you to come today."

"Jack ratted me out, didn't he?"

"Let's not make this thing a father/daughter or teacher/student relationship, Sherrie. I respect you too much for that."

She smiled at that, and then fixed her large brown eyes on me.

Subtlety had no place in this conversation.

"When I came into this room, it smelled like urine. You smell like urine, Sherrie. It's from the wastes you've been accumulating in your body because you're skipping dialysis treatments and not following your diet."

She took a large step backwards, her eyes widened in shock. She covered her mouth and nose with her hands.

I felt like a shit. "I'm sorry, Sherrie, but it's true, and if you continue this way, you may not make it to a transplant."

"Nobody ever told me! Why? I'm mortified! Look at me, Arnie. I'm a pretty woman, I dress well and take time with my hair and makeup...and I smell like urine. People can smell me that way. My God! It's embarrassing...humiliating."

When she cried, I placed my hand on her shoulder. "You're a beautiful woman and it's because I care about you, Sherrie, that I want you to do well. I know that for someone your age, dialysis is a pain in the ass, but we'll get you a transplant as soon as possible. Meanwhile, we can fix this problem with a little extra dialysis. If you make it to your treatments and stick to the diet, this problem will go away in a few days."

Afterward, Sherrie followed her diet and never again missed a dialysis treatment.

At dinner that night, I told Lois, "I'm not looking forward to this trip to Salt Lake City. I have a hard time being a patient, and worse, being a freak of nature."

"We're being overly dramatic today, don't you think, Arnie?"

"Maybe a little, but I doubt that the University of Utah's Chemosensory Laboratory has ever seen the likes of me. I don't see how they can help."

"If we're going to find an accommodation for that spectacular smeller of yours, it's more likely to come from people who do this for a living. It'll cost you a day, no big deal."

I was in a good mood until I picked up the first chart of the day, Missy Cabot. When I turned to Beverly, she gave me her what-can-I-do, look.

In all my years of practice, I'd discharged only two patients: one who falsified a prescription and another who challenged every recommendation and fought with me on each visit. Now, when I considered that Missy might be the third, the thought disturbed me. It was one thing to discharge a hostile patient, it was another to discharge someone so dependant and appreciative, when I was doing so out of frustration. Perhaps someone else can help her, I rationalized.

I opened the examining room door with a "Hi, Missy," and skipped the loaded 'how are you?'

"You've got to help me, Doctor. I can't stand this anymore."

Suddenly, my mind became alert. Something was different with Missy…or was it me? When I placed the blood pressure cuff on her right arm, I sensed it at once, a tangy, orangey aroma. I listened to her slightly irregular pulse beat as I measured her blood pressure and studied her. Her left hand had a fine tremor and her neck showed the linear, elevated red marks of fingernails…a hive-like reaction.

What if, I thought?

"What medications are you taking, Missy?"

"Only what you gave me," she said, bringing out her list. "Cholesterol pills, Xanax at bedtime, estrogen every day, and progesterone five days a month."

"Anything else?"

"Nothing."

"What about vitamins or supplements."

"One-a-Day Women's Vitamins."

"Any unusual coffees, teas, or broths?"

"No. I used to drink Mormon Tea, but they took it off the market. It made me nervous...you remember...it had something in it that the government didn't like."

"Yes. Ephedra. It caused too many problems and the FDA banned it. Did you change teas?"

"Sure. I drink bitter orange tea. It's delicious."

"How much do you drink?"

"Five or six cups a day, but not after four in the afternoon or it keeps me awake."

I excused myself and went to my office computer. The search on bitter orange revealed that it contained synephrine, a close cousin to ephedrine and pseudoephedrine, the active ingredients from the ephedra plant. I shook my head; could her symptoms relate to this tea?

When I returned to the examining room, I turned to Missy. "I want you to stop the bitter orange tea. It may be making you sick."

"Okay, doctor. I'll try."

The next six days brought repeated calls—pleas from Missy that she was so tired, she could barely stay awake. I encouraged her to keep off the tea and her calls gradually abated.

Today was her visit, three weeks later.

Missy smiled when I entered the examining room. I barely recognized her as she looked fifteen years younger. Her voice was strong, she'd changed the bright lipstick to a muted gloss, and her hands were steady.

"You look wonderful, Missy. How are you feeling?"

"The first week was rough. I think I know what addicts go through…what they call withdrawal. The craving I could deal with, but the fatigue and lack of energy, that was a killer. I almost drank some tea when I got tired and needed to do some work."

"Don't you dare, Missy."

"I know, Doctor. I'm a new me and haven't had any chest pain or irregular heartbeats. I knew you would help me, and you did."

I recalled her visits and my conviction that her symptoms were psychiatric and knew that I'd done her a disservice. "I owe you an apology, Missy."

"Whatever for?"

"For not paying enough attention to you. The first lesson you learn in medical school is to listen. I didn't do a good job at that. Moreover, I dismissed your symptoms. You deserved better and I apologize."

Missy smiled. "Aren't you sweet."

I blushed.

"You paid more attention to me than friends, family, and even my husband. I'm not easy, Doctor. I've never been easy. I'm neurotic…that's the word they've used on me. I know that and I'm the one who should be thanking you and your staff."

"Well, I appreciate that, Missy. From now on, I'll pay more attention."

She smiled. "Don't make promises you might not be able to keep."

What could I say?

Chapter Forty-Five

I understood that a major disadvantage of leaving familiar places was losing the one protective mechanism that mitigated against the overwhelming olfactory assaults, sensory exhaustion. People who live next to a pulp plant eventually became oblivious to the pungent stenches, the aromatic byproducts of the manufacturing processes. To a significant extent, I'd reached an uneasy truce with the molecular milieu of home, office, Brier Hospital, and all my familiar haunts. Today when I drove to the Oakland International Airport, I battled a new army of sensory saboteurs.

The hors d'oeuvres was the crowded airport parking lot that stunk of exhaust gases and the fumes from jets landing and taking off. They made me nauseated. The appetizer was the crowded terminal and its human byproducts, the restaurants, the fast food joints, and worst of all, the chemicals they used on the aircraft to obscure the pungent cabin odors. They overwhelmed me.

After we landed in Salt Lake City, I rushed outside to the leper colony of smokers. As an unusual act of courtesy (we were after all in the smoking area), the gentleman beside me lifted his unlit cigarette. "Do you mind if I smoke?"

"Not at all," I said. "I don't smoke, but I love the aroma."

And its ability to crowd out all other smells.

I took a taxi to the clinic, a tan modern two-story building near University Hospital.

"We're expecting you, Dr. Roth," said the receptionist. She led me to a small office and a stack of forms a quarter-inch high. "If you'll take a minute to fill these out, Dr. Whiffler will be right with you."

Dr. Whiffler? I nearly broke out laughing. Some physicians must be fated to their jobs like Dr. Anger, the psychiatrist, Dr. Staggers, the alcohol rehab physician, Dr. Fieler, the gynecologist, and Dr. Frank G. Slaughter, the novelist

Twenty minutes later, after a soft knock on the door, a tall, thin, and balding man who looked about my age entered. He stuck out his hand. "Jerry Whiffler. Nice to meet you."

I can't help but smile again at the name. "Call me Arnie."

He smiled in return then laughed. "Yeah, it's a perfect name for a doc in my business. I think my karma drove me to it."

Jerry took a few minutes to review my history, and then looked up at me. "Tell me all about it."

I went through it all in detail. I described the encephalitis, my awakening, the gradual onset of increased olfactory sensitivity, the aroma-memory associations, the pleasure of this skill, and at times, its repulsiveness.

He directed me into his examining room and performed a physical, emphasizing my nose and throat. "Everything looks fine to me. Let's put your talented nose through its paces."

His nurse brought a wooden box the size of an attaché case containing about fifty small vials. "You've heard of the University of Pennsylvania Smell Identification Test?"

"Yes, I read about it. It's kind of crude for my problem, don't you think?"

He looked at me strangely. "Let's give it a try."

He placed the first vial on the table, but before he could open it, I said, "Vanilla."

"What?"

"That's vanilla."

He reached for a vial in the middle. "Smoke."

I continued the theatrical display of my talent four more times. He looked at me oddly. "This isn't a prank is it?" He looked around the room for hidden cameras. "Sometimes my colleagues get carried away with their practical jokes."

"No joke, Jerry." To drive the point home, I punctuated my performance with, "This morning, you had an onion bagel with lox, cream cheese, and onions, Walla Walla onions, I think. You smoke Amphora Golden Blend Pipe tobacco, like my Dad, but I think you only do that at home. Your wife wears White Shoulders perfume, and your dog is in heat."

"My God," Jerry said. "This is incredible. When can you move to Salt Lake City?"

"Right," I said. "Imagine all that information coming en masse, uncontrollable. I'm a schizophrenic or an autistic child overwhelmed with sensory information. I'm afraid it's going to drive me crazy, and it nearly has on occasion."

I told him about my attempt to protect my sanity by overwhelming my nose with mint and other substances, and my difficulties when traveling to unfamiliar places.

He stared at his notes. "That's sensory exhaustion, not a long term-solution. We might consider desensitizing your olfactory receptors with a local anesthetic, but I'm afraid of permanent damage. We might also consider drugs that work on your brain, like the medicines we use to treat schizophrenia or depression, but that would be all guesswork."

I shook my head. "No thanks. I'll find another other way."

"I won't bullshit you, Arnie. For our work, you're a once in a lifetime discovery. We can study you and write several dozen papers."

"I'm not interested. I have a life, a more complicated life for sure, but a life, a job, a family, and I'm going to do whatever it takes to protect that."

"I have one request, Arnie. I'm going to review your case with my colleagues, here and around the world, for suggestions. I'd love to have you come back after we can obtain an olfactometer to measure how good that nose really is. Can you do that for us? We'll pay for your travel and accommodations."

"First class?"

"Of course," he said taken aback.

"I'm only kidding." I smiled. "I'll think about it."

Irving Hodges sat head down in the middle of his sofa. The drawn drapes left him in the shadows even as sunlight streamed through the front door's stained glass windows.

Irving stared at the portable phone sitting on the coffee table. It rang again for the tenth time in the last two hours. After the fifth call, he'd stopped answering.

The two weeks since Bea's funeral had been intolerable. His daughters, others in the family, and many friends called and visited, but nothing could stem the overwhelming loneliness. He'd attended two different bereavement groups, but found no solace in the misery of others.

Irving rose to answer the doorbell. It was Kathy, his oldest daughter.

She hugged her father. "I was so worried when you didn't answer."

"I'm fine. I'm just tired of the well-intentioned phone calls. I'd rather they leave me alone."

"Daddy, it's not good for you to be alone so much now."

"I know, but, in truth, your mother and I didn't socialize that much. It was mostly us together." He hesitated a moment. "I love you and your sisters, and I know you're trying to help, but I can't be what I wasn't before your mother died."

"Daddy..." she started as Irv stood to leave the room.

"I'll be right back, sweetie."

Kathy heard the bathroom door close. Suddenly from within, came Irv's pitiful cry. "How could you do this to me? How could you leave me, when I need you the most? How can I go on alone, without you?"

She lowered her head and wept.

When Irv returned, his face was expressionless. When he saw Kathy in tears, he embraced his daughter. "It's okay, kitten, I miss her, too."

Kathy reached into her purse, found a tissue and wiped her tears, and blew her nose. "I miss her so much, and I'm worried about you. I can't lose you, too."

"I'm not going anywhere."

"Come to dinner tonight, okay?"

"Sure, just tell me what time."

After Kathy left, Irv walked through the house. He gazed at each picture of his wife and their family. Their photos beamed, the camera's view of their life's events. It was all there from to their wedding picture fifty years ago to the Caribbean cruise. As he passed each object, he'd touch or adjust it, reliving their time together.

Irv thought that he understood death and loss as he and Bea watched their friends and relatives age, become sick, and eventually die. Now, he felt it on a visceral level. The pain, the sense of loss, and the loneliness...maybe they were more than he could bear.

Chapter Forty-Six

Stan Becker's final comment to me about easing a patient's journey toward death with dignity reverberated in my mind. I knew his philosophy reflected reality and while he was attempting kindness, applying it to Debbie Wallace felt profane.

I called Jordan Goodman. "Do you have a few moments to meet with me today, Jordy? I want to talk about Debbie Wallace."

"Sure, Arnie. I'll be at the cancer center all afternoon. Come over any time."

The day was overcast, drizzly, and threatening as I drove the few blocks to meet with Jordy. The air was heavy with the moist air's heightened scents. I parked in the heavily puddled lot and raised my umbrella against the downpour. At the front desk, I nodded to the receptionist. "Dr. Roth for Dr. Goodman, he's expecting me."

"Have a seat, Doctor. I'll page him."

"Dr. Goodman, extension 102," she said into her intercom. A moment later, her phone rang. She listened and said, "Dr. Goodman asked if you'd join him in the treatment pavilion," pointing to the large green swinging door to her right.

I thanked her and headed for the doors. As they parted, a confusion of aromas instantly inundated me. They were the individual aromas of patients, staff, blood, urine, feces, disinfectants,

Desitin, plus an array of perfumes, aftershaves, deodorants and myriad chemicals, many I recognized, the rest remained a mystery. As I moved past the first patient group receiving infusions of God-knows-what, I noted again, as I had several times with Debbie, the unmistakable essence of tonic water.

What was with that tonic water smell again?

Jordy stood behind the central nursing station filling out forms and signing preprinted protocols for chemotherapy.

When I approached, he beckoned me. "Come on over Arnie. I'll be a few minutes more."

I walked behind the raised counter and sat beside him as he finished signing the last of the forms. "Have you been in here before?"

"Sure, I've visited several times to see patients. It's not exactly the kind of place I care to spend too much of my time."

"Me too," he sighed, "but although we try, there's no escaping the reasons why people come to us."

"What kind of chemo are that first group on the right as I entered, receiving?"

"That's our Taxol section. We try to group patients by the treatment they're receiving. It simplifies the logistics."

The Taxol group? I thought.

"Come into my office," he said. "We can talk in private."

The clinic office was cool and utilitarian with a metal desk and chairs. They'd decorated the walls with floral reprints and copies of medical licenses and certificates of physicians who used the facility.

"You don't see patients here, do you, Jordy?"

"God, no. It's just for docs and staff."

"You heard about Debbie Wallace and her brain metastasis."

"That sucks. I thought she'd be one who'd do well after all that she'd been through."

"Me, too." I paused. "Have you notice anything unusual with your Taxol patients lately, Jordy?"

"Unusual?"

"Yes, unusual, like less than expected responses to the drug or a lessening of its side effects."

He stared at me. "What's going on here, Arnie? You know how unpredictable an individual's response may be to a specific drug. Bad things happen. Cancer comes back in a certain percentage of patients in spite of our best efforts."

"Don't bullshit me, Jordy. I know all about the problems with chemotherapy, and you didn't answer my question. Should I repeat it?"

When Jordan Goodman rose from his desk and paced the small room, stopping to fix his eyes on me, I knew that I'd hit a nerve.

"Are you accusing me or the clinic of something, Arnie? Do I need to contact our attorneys?"

"Not on your life, Jordy. I know you. I trust you. You're my friend. If I had cancer, you're the one I'd come to. I know the clinic and many of your people and I'm not accusing any of you, but Jordy, why haven't you answered my question? That's making me nervous."

"I don't know what to think, Arnie. The most difficult part of my job is cancer recurrences, and although we try to maintain distance from our patients, we often fail. I think about treatment failure and cancer's return as part of our limitations in dealing with the disease, but when you asked the question about treatment failures and side-effects, something clicked."

"What is it, Jordy?"

"While I'm not certain that we're seeing more recurrences, I'm sure about one thing," he hesitated.

"You're killing me, Jordy. What is it?"

"We're using more Taxol than ever before and patients are showing fewer side-effects."

My God, I thought. Someone's tampered with the Taxol!

"How is Taxol prepared?"

"It comes in a powdered form. The pharmacist adds sterile water and the drug is then placed in an IV bottle for infusion into our patients."

The tonic water aroma...that had to be it.

"Can you think of any reason why quinine might be added to the Taxol infusions?"

"Quinine? No way. That's crazy!"

"Check it. Send samples of the Taxol to the lab for quinine analysis," I said. "And Jordy, do it now."

Taxol, *Pneumovax* failures, and the QA committee's study of excessive use of EPO use, led to only one conclusion: some son-of-a-bitch is diluting or cutting the active component of these medications.

"Who supplies Taxol to the clinic, Jordy?"

"Horizon Drugs."

Chapter Forty-Seven

"Sam Spade Detectives, Reggie Brand speaking. How can I help you?"

"Reggie, it's Tino Ruiz. We've got to talk."

Reggie's pulse increased. This is it, he thought. "Can you come over?"

"Yes, but I think that Mrs. Fischer should hear this, too."

Reggie didn't want to lose control of the situation. "Let me decide if that's appropriate, Tino."

"Take it or leave it. I could have gone to her first. Be smart. I won't disappoint you."

"Let me put you on hold while I try to reach her," he said as the line went silent.

Two minutes later, Reggie returned. "Let's say we meet here in an hour. Okay?"

"See you then."

"Come in," was Reggie's response to Tino's knock on the frosted glass door.

Tino looked around the dreary office with its cheap furniture and musty smell. Ruth Fischer sat in front of Reggie's desk. She stared at Tino as he approached.

Ruth extended her hand. "Tino, what a surprise. I thought you were one of them."

"Them? Not in this life. To Henry and Brian I'm still a spic. They use me, pretend to trust me, but they never will."

Ruth turned toward Tino and straightened her skirt. "It's no secret, Tino. You know what's been going on."

"I'm sorry," Tino said. "You're a nice lady and you deserve much better than Henry Fischer." He hesitated. "You know all about Henry and Monica Kelly. They didn't even have the decency to try and keep their affair private."

Reggie patted the pile of photos. "We know and we've got the pictures to prove it."

Tino shifted in his chair. "There's a lot of other shit...oh excuse me, Mrs. Fischer..."

"Thanks for the concern, Tino, but I've heard a lot worse. Please call me Ruth."

"Okay, Mrs....I mean Ruth, I've worked at Horizon Drug long enough to know that things are not exactly kosher."

"Reggie's been looking into that for me. We know about the dramatic turnaround and success of the business, and we can't tell why."

"It's bad," Tino said. "Really bad."

"You better tell it, Tino," Reggie said. "I'm sure I've heard it a hundred times."

"Not this one, you haven't." Tino paused. "Let me try to put this in order, and then maybe you'll understand. When I finally realized what they were doing, I called Reggie. I knew something was wrong, but I never knew what. Believe me, if I had known..."

"Tell us," Ruth said.

"First was the secrecy. I thought it was because they didn't trust me, but then I watched Brian working for hours in the locked clean room. He lost it once when I simply knocked on the door looking for something. Suddenly, the business is booming with money coming in hand over fist. Then I found the labels."

"The labels?" Ruth asked.

"One night, I was looking for prescription labels, but I couldn't find any. I thought they might be in the clean room, so I went inside. I found labels all right, but not prescription labels. They had a supply of labels for three drugs, Taxol, *Pneumovax*, and EPO."

"I don't know these drugs," Reggie said.

"I do," said Ruth. "Taxol is for treating cancer; *Pneumovax* is for preventing pneumonia, and EPO boosts the production of red blood cells."

"I still don't get the significance of the labels you found," Reggie said. "Don't you use labels on these medications?"

"These weren't prescription labels. They were counterfeit medication labels, the kind used by the drug manufacturer for their products. Horizon ordered them from a printing company in Mexico."

Reggie scratched his head. "Why would they need these labels?"

Tino looked from Reggie to Ruth and back. "Let me tell you what brought me here. Then you'll understand. You know Debbie Wallace?"

"Of course I know Debbie," Ruth said. "It's tragic what's happened to her."

"When my cousin Beverly Ramirez, Arnie Roth's office manager, told me about Debbie, it hit me."

"What?" said Ruth, getting to her feet.

"Beverly told me about Debbie's breast cancer recurrence, how treatment with Taxol had failed, how the Taxol infusions somehow had fewer side-effects for Debbie...and I knew. Horizon Drugs supplied Debbie's Taxol and when I put it together, I could only think about two possibilities; they weren't giving her Taxol or they'd diluted it to the point that it became worthless."

"Worthless?" Reggie asked.

"Reggie," shouted Tino, "those fucking bastards have been making their fortune over the bodies of cancer patients. They're stealing from them their last chance at life. I've seen terrible things in my life, but this is greed gone wild. This is pure evil."

"Oh my God! Oh my God," Ruth cried as tears streamed down her cheeks.

Reggie grabbed a handful of tissues and handed them to Ruth. It took a few minutes for her to regain control. "Henry...Henry couldn't be a part of this...he couldn't. I know he's no angel, but this?"

Tino felt the weight of her sadness, but if they were going anywhere with this, Ruth had to know. "When I think about it, Ruth, the parties, the Champagne, and all the backslapping, it makes me want to puke. That's your Henry. He's up to his ears in this."

Ruth wiped her tears, pulled her shoulders back, and turned to Reggie. "If they did this with Taxol, who knows what they've done with other drugs. Look at how much money they've made. It has to be more than Taxol. How many people have they injured or killed? How much misery have they brought to the people who trusted Horizon Drugs? We must stop them. Stop them now before they murder or injure more patients."

"Where do we go, Reggie?" asked Tino.

"We go to the District Attorney, to Brier Hospital, and to every doctor and every patient who received medication from Horizon. This is going to be one hell of a mess."

Chapter Forty-Eight

Beverly Ramirez, handed me the phone as I arrived this morning. "It's Dr. Davidson for you, Arnie."

"Ben, what's up?"

"Do you have a few minutes at lunchtime?"

"Sure, Ben, what's it about?"

"I'll tell you when we meet. Come to the medical staff office around noon."

What in hell was this all about? I thought.

I worked through the morning trying to keep focused on my patients' problems. I was chewing five sticks of gum per hour or sucking on the most potent peppermint drops I could find. Nothing helped much.

When Lois when came in to work for a few hours, I found her staring at me.

"What?"

"I don't like all this gum-chewing, Arnie. It doesn't look professional."

"I don't like it either. I'll use more drops, but I need the mints to prevent being overwhelmed with aromas. They're driving me to distraction. So many coming my way; so many memories provoked, sometimes I can't think straight."

"It's not all bad, is it?"

"No, but the peppermint doesn't discriminate between the good and the bad smells, it overwhelms everything. I've come to relish the seductive sensory pleasure. Then I have the power to know things nobody else can. I look forward to the waning effects of the mint so I can resume my exploration of the world, yet I fear it as well. I know one thing, Lois it can't go on this way. It's threatening my sanity."

When I arrived at the medical staff's conference room, Warren Davidson stood outside talking on the phone and gestured that I come in.

Jack sat at the table. He shrugged his shoulders and turned up his palms in a don't ask me, gesture.

"What?..." I began as Warren entered.

"Jack, Arnie," said Warren, "take a seat."

"What's this all about..." I began, but Warren interrupted.

"Take it easy, Arnie, I have a few questions."

I glanced sideways at Jack who shook his head in ignorance of what was to come.

"I've been hearing scuttlebutt about you, Arnie, what's going on?"

"I don't know what you're talking about."

"Don't bullshit me. I'm your friend. I want to help, but I can't if you don't level with me."

I sat in silence.

"Jack, you know Arnie better than any of us. You're his doc. What the hell's happening?"

Jack looked directly at me. He nodded for permission to speak, but I shook my head, no.

Jack returned Warren's stare. "I'm sorry. I don't know what to say."

"We go back a long time. I can't believe you're both withholding something from me." Ben took a deep breath. "Arnie, several people, mostly nurses, have noticed your unusual behavior. They're asking questions. I need answers."

I shook my head. "Maybe I came back to work too soon. Recovery from encephalitis may be more difficult than any of us expected."

"What is it?" pleaded Warren. "I want to help."

"There's nothing I can add, Warren. What are they saying about me?"

"Listen to me, Arnie. You have nothing but friends around Brier. You've changed. You're unfocused and frequently distracted and the nurses are concerned. What about the outbursts, the anger? That's not you, Arnie. Everyone knows it. Nobody's out to get you."

"If you're not charging me with anything, I have nothing more to add." I hesitated. "I want to discuss something else with you, Warren, and it's urgent. Can we talk about it?"

"Jack?" said Warren, "help me out."

I shook no again.

"I'm sorry, Warren. There's nothing more I can say."

"Play it your way, you two," Warren shouted, reddening. "I can't..."

A knock on the door interrupted.

"What is it?" an agitated Warren asked.

"Dr. Davidson, I have an urgent call for you on line one."

"Can't it wait?"

"It's Mrs. Ruth Fischer. I tried to put her off, but she says it's a matter of life and death."

Warren picked up the phone. "Ruth, this isn't a good time..." With the phone fixed to his ear, he listened in silence. "They did what?" Warren shouted, turning crimson. "Ruth do you know what you're saying?"

Warren listened. "The district attorney...wait a minute Ruth, have you thought this through?" he said with alarm. He kept his ear to the phone. "Yes, I'll notify everyone; the pharmacy, the cancer center and everyone who bought any of those drugs from Horizon, and yes, Ruth, I agree with you, I'll contact our attorneys."

Warren turned, replaced the receiver, and stared at Jack and me. "Did either of you know about this?"

"I suspected," I said. "Jordan Goodman and I just put it together, and it's what I wanted to discuss with you."

Jack looked upset. He turns to me. "What's this about, Arnie?"

Warren stared at me. "No more crap now. The police are involved. Tell me everything."

I reached into my pocket and extracted the lab report that came this morning. "Jordy Goodman took samples from Taxol infusions they give at the cancer center. Horizon Pharmacy prepared them." I handed Warren the lab slip. "All samples are adulterated with quinine."

"Those fucking bastards," Jack bellowed standing, and pacing. "I can't believe it." He shook his head and then stared at me. "It all makes sense, Arnie, the cancer recurrences, the failure of *Pneumovax* to prevent pneumonia, and the excessive use of EPO."

Warren held his head. "My wife says that at my core, I'm an idealist, but that the years have left me bitter and defeatist about human nature. She nearly had me convinced that not every puddle on the road hides a deep pothole, then something like this happens and we're in the ditch. It's a cynic's dream come true."

Chapter Forty-Nine

Henry Fischer and Monica Kelly embraced on Horizon Pharmacy's back office couch.

She kissed Henry. "I'm sorry for bringing this whole mess down on you."

"It's not your fault, Monica. My marriage is over. Ruth and I had drifted apart over the years. It was only a matter of time."

"This divorce is going to be messy. If I were you, Henry, I'd bite the bullet, give her whatever she wants. Get it over as quickly as possible. If you let it, the divorce will be expensive, painful, and never-ending."

"At least we'll be together," said Henry.

Monica became silent. She turned her head away from Henry. "I'm not anxious to be part of this legal battle. I had enough of that with my own divorce."

"I don't see that either of us has much choice. I'll do the best I can to make this painless, but Ruth's angry and she's hired a ball-buster attorney who won't be satisfied until she's bled me for all I'm worth."

Monica stood. "Henry, we need to put our relationship on hold."

"What are you talking about?"

"I've accepted a position with Regency Drugs in Reno. Maybe after you and Ruth have settled this, we can get back together."

"You must be out of your mind. After all we've been through together, after…"

Suddenly, loud pounding echoed throughout Horizon pharmacy.

Henry and Monica looked to the door and Brian's alarmed voice. "What the hell."

Four uniformed policemen and a plain-clothes detective rushed through the door. "We have a warrant to search the premises. You're not to touch anything. Sir, please step away from the computer."

A loud knock brought Henry and Monica to the standing position. "Come in," Henry said, barely able to utter the words.

The middle-aged burly detective with a gold shield pinned to his coat entered with two uniformed officers. "We're exercising a search warrant. Please have a seat. Don't move, and do not touch anything."

"What's this all about?" Henry asked.

The detective handed him the warrant. "We're looking at your records and your inventory on Taxol, EPO, and *Pneumovax*."

Suddenly, Henry felt a dull pain in his chest, a pressure building beneath his breastbone and then moving to his jaw and back. He couldn't breathe. His vision blurred and the room spun. He grabbed for the table, as everything turned black.

For Debbie Wallace, the visit to Stanley Becker was déjà vu, all over again, only this time she felt nothing. After the initial shock, after the words brain tumor, metastasis, recurrent cancer, Debbie's mind became an emotional black hole, cold, and devoid of feelings. She sat for hours, immobile, and refused to talk with anyone, even her children.

"She's depressed," Matt said when he called me two days later. "This was a shock to both of us. Debbie's had such strength...I guess I took too much for granted. How much bad news did I think she could take? I assumed she'd snap out of it and we'd move on to do what's needed, but if anything, she's gotten worse."

"Bring her to the office this afternoon, Matt."

When I entered my consultation room, Debbie and Matt sat in the chairs facing my desk. "Give me a moment alone with her, Matt."

Matt squeezed Debbie's hand, and left the room. Debbie held her head down, eyes fixed on her lap. Her face was flat showing no emotion. I moved into the chair beside her and took her hand. She looked up at me, but remained silent. I squeezed her hand, getting nothing in return.

"I know you hear me, Debbie. I won't try to minimize what you've been through. I understand it as well as anyone can who hasn't been through it personally. It kills me to deliver the bad news, but..."

She looked up at me with a sardonic smile. "Bad news? You call a death sentence, bad news?"

Anger was better than nothing, I thought.

"You're right, bad news can't possibly explain how you feel about this disease, but…"

"You are right, Arnie. You don't know a damned thing about how I feel. I keep making the same mistake over and over again. I'll never learn. I made it in spite of everyone's advice to reserve my optimism, for at least a while, but as usual, I don't listen. I'm not going to make that mistake again."

"I never lied to you. I won't lie to you now. You must trust me."

Debbie turned to face me and smiled as she caressed my cheek. "You're a good man, Arnie. I know you want to help, but I'm done. I don't have anything left." Her smile evaporated and she lowered her head into her hands and wept.

"Please listen. I talked with Stanley Becker at UC. We're going to start you on the anticancer drug, Herceptin, we're having remarkable results, and we'll get rid of that brain metastasis simultaneously."

"I'll do what you and Dr. Becker recommend, Arnie, but don't ask me to hope. I don't have it in me."

Chapter Fifty

Monday morning commuters lined up on the two mile straightaway before the Bay Bridge tollbooths. Drivers jockeyed for position like it would make a difference — the triumph of personality over practicality.

Matt looked around as he and Debbie inched along in traffic. "I don't know how people put up with this every day."

Debbie remained silent.

He reached over and squeezed her hand. "Don't be frightened. Arnie said that the term, gamma knife, is misleading."

"I'm not frightened," she replied in a monotone.

"It's a onetime deal, Debbie. Once and it's done. After all you've been through, this will be easy."

Debbie listened to the encouraging words. They were words she'd heard many times before, but this time they came from a distance, muted by her own protective shell. Only the soothing sounds of Matt's words touched her, for she knew, above all else, that he loved her, and remained obsessed with hope.

She smiled tenderly. "It's okay, sweetie, I'll be fine."

As they took the ramp toward the Civic Center, thick morning ground fog draped the car, forcing them to slow. Eventually, they found their way to UC Hospital on Parnassus Heights.

Dr. Becker was waiting for them and together they took the elevator deep into the medical center's bowels. They entered the radiotherapy department where Becker introduced them to Dr. Richard Stark, the director.

"I'll see you later, Debbie," Stanley Becker said, "Don't worry, you're in good hands."

Richard Stark was a friendly outgoing man in his early sixties. His white coat over a green scrub suit carried the film badge, a required device to measure one's cumulative exposure to radiation. They sat at a small round conference room table.

Stark flipped open Debbie's chart. "Whoever called this device a knife, needed his head examined. I can't think of a term more alarming or more flawed than that one. What we do is complicated, but it all boils down to a simple explanation. By using a computer, we can administer focused gamma rays to a specific location, sparing all of the surrounding tissue."

He stood. "Come with me." He walked through heavy metal doors with a large yellow and red sign that read, Danger, Radiation Hazard.

They followed him into a room where indirect lighting revealed a machine that resembled an enormous metallic football helmet. It had an opening in front for a sliding litter. The bleak, pale-green walled modern air-conditioned room sent chills through Debbie's body.

The chills, Debbie knew were not from the room's temperature. "You're not going to slide my head inside that machine, are you?"

"Yes, we are, but first we need to fit you with an aluminum frame that will look like an astronaut's helmet. This will allow us to direct the beams of radiation to the tumor. We'll put you to sleep first. You won't remember any of it."

"How long will it take?" Matt asked.

"We've calculated the dose to 70 minutes. Afterward we'll remove the frame, and keep you overnight for observation. The most common side effect that we see is a mild headache."

Debbie stared at the machine. "One shot is all it takes?"

"That should be it."

Should? Debbie thought.

Debbie remembered the IV's pinch and counting backward from 100. The last number she recalled was 96, then nothing.

In the recovery room, Matt stood at her bedside as she opened her eyes. "Welcome, sweetheart. I'm sure glad you're back with us. How do you feel?"

Debbie reached for Matt's hand, squeezed it. "Tired and groggy. When can we go home?"

"First thing in the morning."

Debbie's mood was somber when she returned to my office later that week. Her affect remained flat, but she looked healthy. I took a deep breath, sampling the room and Debbie. I couldn't detect the tonic water aroma or the tangy, musty stigma of cancer.

"Drs. Becker and Stark called me. They're pleased with your treatment."

"What next?" Debbie said, without emotion.

Matt shook his head. "She won't come out of this depression, Doc. Maybe you should give her something."

"Absolutely not," I replied, looking directly at Debbie. I turned my gaze back to Matt. "She's earned this depression, and if she weren't depressed, I'd be more concerned. I don't use medications for normal emotional responses to life's difficulties."

"What if she doesn't come out of it? Being this way can't be healthy."

"Excuse me," Debbie interrupted us with a slight smile, "I'm still here." She hesitated a moment and then continued, "You haven't answered my question, Dr. Roth. What's next?"

"Today, I'll give you the first dose of Herceptin. That will take ninety minutes. Afterward, we'll infuse it over thirty minutes every three weeks. Most people have either no or minimal symptoms like muscle aches and a little fever. Nothing like chemotherapy."

"How long will she need Herceptin?"

"I don't know," I hesitated. "Maybe forever. We don't know. If we're fussing about it five or ten years from today…"

I turned to Debbie and grasped her hands. "I know what you're feeling. Forever doesn't really mean forever. It means that by then we'll know more or have better drugs. Don't waste your energy worrying about something that might never happen."

It was a beautiful night with the western horizon burning scarlet-orange, so Lois and I decided to take a walk. Early evening has been my favorite time, as the still warm earth radiated aromas of the land into a splendid symphony of smell. My past comments about the pleasure of these aromas seemed oddly out of place now as my nose was overwhelmed with hundreds, maybe thousands of new potent fragrances.

I held Lois's hand as we walked down the street. Holding hands was natural for us.

"It's lovely tonight, Arnie. How are you handling all this input?"

"So many aromas surround me. Many I know while others are foreigners. It's difficult to keep my head on straight."

We walked about three miles, nearing the entrance to our regional park when I spied a street person or what was the PC term for these people today? Homeless? Residentially challenged? Involuntarily leisured? The man pushed a shopping cart crammed with his belongings piled high and extending a foot above the rim.

I smelled him from fifty feet. He had the stink of a body unwashed for a decade, combined with the stench of urine and feces. As we got closer, the fetid putrid smell of decay exploded, especially as he smiled at us through brown rotten teeth and bubbling, bleeding gums.

"Let's cross the street, Lois. That guy's disgusting."

"He's only one of the homeless that live in and around the park. They're harmless."

"Maybe so, but to my nose, his emissions are repulsive."

As we stepped off the sidewalk to cross the street, he approached me and grabbed my arm. "Hey mister, got any spare change?"

I don't know what came over me as my mind exploded with uncontrollable rage.

"Get the fuck away from us," I yelled as I grabbed his upper arm and pushed him backwards. Unstable on his feet, he fell into his cart, toppling it over and spilling its contents over the sidewalk.

I started for the downed man enraged and out of control. My right arm retracted to deliver the first blow when I felt Lois pulling at my arm yelling, "Arnie, it's enough. Leave him alone. You'll kill him."

I started to pull away from Lois's grasp, still infuriated, and when I turned, I met a look that froze me at once. They were the eyes of my wife, the woman who loved me. They reflected her sadness and disappointment at what had become of me.

"This isn't you, Arnie. I barely recognize you."

"I'm sorry, Lois it's…"

"Don't say anything. Take me home."

Chapter Fifty-One

Christy Cooper was a fine arts major at UC Berkeley. She was twenty-two and had spent three months as an exchange student in the southwest China provinces.

Her problems evolved slowly following her return to the states. "I just don't feel well," she told Paul Cass, her fiancé. "I'm tired all the time and my appetite's not worth a damn."

Later, her symptoms became more generalized with profound fatigue, headaches, achy joints and muscles, and chronic diarrhea.

Paul handed her the phone. "Don't be so stubborn, Christy, call your doctor."

Jim McDonald, her internist, was concerned at the outset. Christy's first office visit had occurred when she was thirteen. Her chart contained only routine physicals and an occasional upper respiratory infection or a sprain. She was as solid, stable, and healthy a patient as he had in his practice. Symptoms following a trip to China suggested an unusual infection, possibly a parasitic infestation. X-rays, scans, laboratory tests, stool examinations, and consultations followed.

"I'm sorry, Christy. I don't know what's going on, but more than one physician who knows your case has suggested that this illness may fit into the category of fibromyalgia or chronic fatigue syndrome."

"What does that mean for me?"

"I hate those diagnoses because the criteria for them are too soft. In addition, labeling you with either diagnosis does little in terms of treatment."

"What should I do?"

"I'm going to treat your symptoms, the muscle aches, the diarrhea, etc., and watch closely to see if anything develops."

"I trust you, Dr. McDonald, but this whole thing sucks."

"I agree."

Christy's Google Internet search on fibromyalgia and chronic fatigue syndrome brought tens of thousands of hits. She found useful general descriptions of these illnesses and current thinking regarding cause and treatment. Others reported on hundreds of clinical studies, but the approaches were so divergent, that she concluded that physicians, not knowing what to do, would try anything. The support sites ranged from informative and helpful to extraterrestrial, blaming the air we drink, the water we ingest, as well as Republicans, and aliens. The most disturbing sites were those that questioned the legitimacy of these diagnoses, labeling patients as lazy, neurotic, depressed, or worst of all, as drug seekers.

Friends, family, and especially Paul, were supportive at the beginning. Soon, the novelty of the illness, whatever it was, wore off, and she remained alone with its reality.

Paul rose from the sofa. "Let's go out for pizza tonight."

"I'm too tired, sweetheart, and I'm not hungry."

"You can't stay cooped up in your apartment. We haven't been out in months. Can't you try?"

"I can't. I'm beat."

Paul reddened with anger.

Christy knew he'd been understanding since she became ill, but she could tell he was running out of patience.

"You've given up, Christy. You sit around like a slug." He paled as the words came out. "Even Dr. McDonald said that for the sake of your body and your psyche, you needed to get out, to do things."

Why am I not surprised? she thought.

"You think I like being this way, Paul? I remember what our lives were like. Look at me, now. I don't blame you for being upset, but don't attack me for an illness that's not my fault."

He hugged her. "I'm sorry. I know it's been difficult. I should be more understanding, more supportive, and yes, less selfish. Your illness had posed a character question for me, and I don't like the answer. It's not rational, but I keep thinking that if you'd only get off your ass and do something..."

I'll never be happy, Christy Cooper thought, as she strolled into the first aisle of Berkeley's Andronico's Market on Telegraph Avenue. She watched couples and families shopping together, enjoying each other's company, and acting as if they didn't have a care in the world. While Christy suspected this was pure illusion (hell everyone thought that she and Paul were happy) she couldn't resist the fantasy.

She and Paul had been separated for three months, and the promised adjustment to her single status had yet to occur.

Paul called last night as she watched the evening news. After the perfunctory questions about work, he struck home with the loaded question. "And how are you feeling, Christy?"

"Don't ask me that question unless you really want to know."

The phone remained silent, but for his breathing. "I love you, Christy, and I'm worried."

"Look, Paul, I love you too, but it's not enough. This thing, whatever it is, is killing me, and it's destroyed what we had together."

Aisle one at Andronico's was a walk through a virtual jungle of fruits and vegetables. The left side of the aisle had every variety of vegetable, while the right was reminiscent of the Farmer's Market in Los Angeles, where every fruit looked as if it were on steroids. Juicing machines squeezed oranges and grapefruits and the air was ripe with their scents. Christy bought a quart of orange juice, and opted for two dozen beautiful ruby-red grapefruits for eating and squeezing later.

When she returned home, she stored the groceries before bringing out her Sunkist commercial juicer. She squeezed eighteen grapefruits into a ceramic pitcher. She covered the top of the pitcher with plastic wrap and replaced it in her refrigerator. Later that night, before going to bed, she poured a large glass of cold grapefruit juice, enjoying its rich flavor and the tang of the fresh squeezed citrus.

Two days later, she was so weak that she couldn't get out of bed.

She dialed Paul's number.

"It's Christy. Something's terribly wrong with me," she said in a whisper. "You must help me...I'm so frightened."

"I'll be right over. I'm calling Dr. McDonald to let him know I'm bringing you to Brier Hospital."

Jim McDonald met them in the ER just before noon.

Christy looked pale, and although she was slow to respond, her answers showed that her mind was intact. She had scaly lesions on her arms and hands, her scalp showed patches of hair loss, and her neurological exam revealed areas of loss of sensitivity to touch and diminution of reflexes.

Jim ordered a blood count, a screening laboratory panel, drug screen of blood and urine, and a brain CT scan. All were normal. Jim asked

Jack Byrnes to consult, and afterwards they sat together.

"I don't know what's going on," Jack said. "None of this fits with fibromyalgia or chronic fatigue syndrome and whatever it is, it's progressive. I'm worried…I hate to worry."

"Me too," said Jim. "What do you suggest?"

"If we can't find something soon, maybe we should consider sending her to UC medical center or Stanford. Maybe they've seen this, whatever it is." Jack paused for a moment. "I do have one suggestion. It's going to sound odd to you, but we've got nothing to lose."

"What is it?"

"Let's ask Arnie Roth to come by to see her."

"Arnie Roth. He's merely a family practitioner. What can he offer?"

"Arnie's helped me before with unusual or odd medical problems. Maybe he can help her."

That afternoon, Jack placed the call. "Arnie, it's Jack. I'd like you to see a patient for me."

An internist, and particularly a subspecialist like Jack Byrnes asking for help from a family practitioner was a stop-the-presses moment.

"Come on, Jack. What's the joke?"

"This is an odd case, Arnie, and you're an odd fellow. Maybe you can pick up the scent of something."

"Very funny. When I finish here, I'll come over."

Jack held Christy's chart. "Thanks for coming, Arnie."

I walked into the ER. The place was a madhouse. The usual disharmonious confusion of scents inundated me at once. I slowed for a moment as I entered as if forcing my way through a heavy aroma curtain. I knew Jim McDonald well and considered him a friend and a colleague, yet he stared at me strangely.

Jack reviewed Christy's history, the progression of her illness, and the extensive and negative diagnostic testing.

I looked at Jack. He smiled back at me, and I knew why he called.

"I'll do the best I can," I said.

When I entered Christy's room, the strong smell of garlic hit me at once. I turned to Jack. "Have you tested her for arsenic or pesticides?"

Jim stared at me. "What are you talking about?"

"Arsenic's on the toxicology screen and it's negative," said Jack. "Nothing here suggests pesticides."

I walked to Christy's bedside. "My name is Arnie Roth. Your doctors asked me to see if I can help."

"Nice to meet you, Dr. Roth," she said slowly.

"I understand that you were recently in China. Did you bring back any souvenirs?"

"I bought clothes, several paintings, and some statuary."

"Anything else?"

"A ceramic pitcher."

"Tell me about the pitcher."

"It's a beautiful piece with an intense floral motif and Chinese characters. I bought it in Guizhou Province in China. I use it to hold my freshly squeezed grapefruit."

I felt suddenly warm all over and a little dizzy. I turned to Jack and Jim. I tried, but couldn't control the smile bursting from within. "It's chronic selenium toxicity."

Jim stood upright. "Selenium toxicity! Where in the world does that come from?"

I looked at Jack. He smiled and nodded.

"Let's put it together," I said. "A healthy woman returns from China with an illness that defies our best diagnostic testing and it gets worse before our eyes. You may not detect it, but my nose, which is extraordinarily sensitive these days, recognizes the strong aroma of garlic exuding from her lungs. In the absence of arsenic or pesticides, it must be selenium. It's leaching out of that ceramic pitcher because the grapefruit juice is so acidic."

Jack took a deep breath. "I'll send someone over for the pitcher and we'll analyze it and the juice."

Jim turned to me. "What's this all about? That was amazing."

"I don't want to talk about it, Jim. Let's leave it at this, I'm real sensitive to aromas, and it allows me to help my patients. Please don't let this get around, Jim. Please."

"What next, Jack?" Jim asked.

"Let's confirm the diagnosis, and then I'll call the poison control center. I don't think that they have any specific form of treatment except to avoid selenium. I think she's going to do well when her body rids itself of this toxin."

Christy felt better within a week. By the sixth week, she was overjoyed to be virtually back to normal.

Christy felt vindicated. She wasn't neurotic, depressed, or a malingerer, but she was having a difficult time dealing with those who thought she was, or couldn't stick by her. Was she asking too much—expecting too much of those who professed to care for her? She understood, but could she forgive? Could she forget?

Chapter Fifty-Two

The police ambulance screeched to a halt at Brier Emergency. The EMTs whisked Henry Fischer through the sliding glass doors into the treatment room's intense fluorescent lights.

"When we got there," the EMT said, "the detective described Fischer grabbing his chest seconds before he collapsed. His monitor tracings in the ambulance looked like a heart attack to us."

The EMTs removed the handcuffs as they transferred Henry to the hospital gurney. Afterward, the uniformed officer who'd accompanied them, reached for Henry's wrists to reapply the cuffs and heard, "Leave them off."

"And who the hell are you?" the policeman said, turning toward the bulldog-faced Sharon Brickman, the chief of cardiology.

"I'm Dr. Brickman. And I won't have this man in handcuffs while we're trying to treat him."

"I'm sorry, Doctor, but he's in custody. Policy requires me to keep him cuffed."

"What's your name, officer?" Sharon barked.

"Patrolman Kelly."

"Well, Kelly, first, the man's unconscious, second, if you get in my way and anything bad happens to my patient, I'm holding you and the Berkeley P.D. legally responsible. Get on the radio and see how well that sits with your bosses."

Within thirty minutes, Sharon read the EKGs, studied the blood tests, and performed an emergency echocardiogram. Her conclusion: Henry was in the midst of a massive myocardial infarction, a severe heart attack.

Sharon put his chart down. "Does he have any relatives here?"

"His wife just arrived, I'll bring her in," said the ER nurse.

Ruth trembled as she entered the room. "How is he, Doctor?"

"He's having a major heart attack. We need your permission to get him to the cath. lab immediately for an angioplasty."

"We're in the middle of a bitter divorce, am I the right person for this?"

"Right or wrong, I don't give a damn. If we don't get to him, and soon, the discussion will become academic."

In spite of all that had happened, Henry was still the father of her children and her bitterness didn't encompass his death. "Where do I sign?"

The procedure went well. Once inside the blocked coronary artery, Sharon extracted the clot. Then she passed a thin flexible wire through the narrowed segment and opened it up with a balloon catheter. In moments, the signs of heart muscle injury disappeared.

When Henry Fischer awakened in the CCU, he tried to scratch his nose, but found his right wrist handcuffed to the bed rail.

Panicked, he screamed, "Where am I? What am I doing here?"

Henry pulled on the handcuffs, rattling the bed as the nurse entered. "Calm down Mr. Fischer. You're in Brier Hospital's coronary care unit."

"What am I doing here? Why am I handcuffed?"

"My name is Sherrie Blake, and I'm your nurse. You had a heart attack, but you're doing well. The doctors had to do an emergency angioplasty to open a major vessel to your heart."

Henry's head swam. He vaguely remembered the police, the pain in his chest, but nothing more.

He pulled on his right wrist against the cuff. "Take this thing off me."

"No can do, Mr. Fischer. You're under arrest and the police insist on the cuffs."

"Under arrest?"

Sherrie handed Henry the San Francisco Chronicle, folded open to page two, and he read:

Berkeley,

Berkeley Police yesterday raided Horizon Pharmacy suspected of misbranding and adulteration of a cancer treatment drug. Henry Fischer, the president of Horizon, and Brian Shands, his assistant, were charged with a felony for diluting prescriptions for Taxol, an anticancer drug.

District Attorney Kevin Walters said that these men will face additional charges stemming from the alleged dilution of several other medications, including the Pneumovax vaccination for pneumonia.

Henry Fischer has been hospitalized at Brier coronary care unit with a heart attack. Brian Shands remains in custody awaiting arraignment.

"This is crazy," Henry said. "I want these cuffs off now."

Sherrie walked to the door and stepped into the hall. She turned to the officer. "The bastard wants the cuffs off."

The patrolman smiled. "Is that the way you talk about your patients?"

"You know what he did."

"Alleged, Sherrie. Alleged." He entered Henry's room. "I'm Officer Blair. Can I help you, sir?"

"Take these cuffs off."

"I'm sorry, sir, but I'm not authorized to remove them. The DA has instructed me to give you your Miranda warning, sir. You have the right to remain silent…"

"I want to see my attorney," Henry said.

Lilly Shands spoke into the intercom's hand piece as she sat in the booth looking at Brian through the Plexiglas window. He wore an orange jail jumpsuit and hadn't shaved since they arrested him. "I don't understand what's happening, Brian."

"It's all a mistake, Lilly. I'll be out on bail tomorrow."

"The newspapers and the television have been saying terrible things about what you and Henry did. People stare at me on the street. Tell me what you did."

"We did what all pharmacists do, what all business people do, we tried to maximize our profits, but only in a completely ethical way."

"They're saying that you and Henry were responsible for people dying. That can't be true."

"That's the DA enjoying his fifteen minutes of fame and boosting his prospects for reelection."

"What's going to happen to us if you go to jail?"

"I'm not going to jail, and anyway, I've provided for your needs."

"I'm frightened."

"Bring me my gray pin-striped suit. I'll need it in the next few days when they release me."

She paused a moment and looked into Brian's eyes. "When you get out, I want us to go to a marriage counselor. Things haven't been right between us for at least a year. I can feel it. I know you're drifting away." She held her face and cried.

Oh Christ! Brian thought. On top of everything, I have her too. She's such a pain in the ass.

"Whatever you want," Brian said with a thin smile limited to his lips.

Henry Fischer remained in the hospital for nine days then they transferred him to jail.

Two days later, Henry Fischer and Brian Shands stood before Judge Horace Miller for arraignment. Sylvia Collins, Horizon's business attorney, asked for their release on their own recognizance.

Kevin Martin, the DA, stood. "These are men of means, your honor, and they face serious charges and long sentences if convicted. I request five million dollars each for bail, and that they surrender their passports."

"That's ridiculous, your honor," Collins said. "These men are pillars of the community. They have deep roots in Berkeley, and pose no flight risk."

Judge Miller looked sideways at the defendants. "Three million each, and the defendants are to surrender their passports."

"You're not looking well, Henry," Brian said as they left the courthouse and walked into the nearby park. In a remote area, away from the crowds, they stopped and sat on a stone bench.

"You wouldn't look so great either, if you'd just had a heart attack, not that you give a shit."

"Give me a break, Henry. We were never friends. This was a business arrangement. We used each other, nothing more."

"You really fucked up both of our lives. I told you we should stop. I begged you after Ruth threw me out, but you were too greedy, too sure of yourself. You wouldn't listen."

Brian smiled. "With your heart, Henry, I wouldn't get too excited. You're a fool. When I finish ratting you out, they'll be more than happy to make a deal with me."

"I'm a fool? You're living in a dream world. Deals, ratting me out...that ain't gonna happen. They have us cold, I know it, and if you'd take a minute to think about it, you'd know it, too. You did everything, diluting the drugs, substituting the medication, and falsifying the labels. Your hands are all over this thing."

"I won't walk, but when I tell them that you were the mastermind, that you threatened and coerced me, and they look at the bucks that you made, they'll believe me and will make a deal to get at you."

Henry stood and studied Brian, and with a sardonic smile. "Too many people knew what you were doing, Brian. I knew, Tino Ruiz knew about the long hours in the clean room and the labels, and your own meticulous records of drug purchases and drug billings. The discrepancies are damning. I don't think Monica can help us."

"One more thing, Henry, if you're so naive as to believe that there's a chance in hell that Monica's going out on a limb for you, you're more stupid than I thought."

Henry remained silent.

Brian shook his head, staring into the distance. "I'm not going to jail, Henry. No way."

Henry rose, started away, stopped, and turned to face Brian. "Dream on Brian, and by the way, you're not looking so terrific yourself."

Chapter Fifty-Three

Jordan Goodman sat with me having our morning coffees. "Arnie, my phone's ringing off the hook. Everyone who received Taxol in our program is in full panic mode. Even those who are doing well and are beyond the period of recurrence are sure that their cancer is back. Those who failed treatment and the families of those who died are out for blood. They're enraged that those sons-of-bitches at Horizon Pharmacy destroyed their last hope."

"It's inconceivable," I said, my mind whirling, overwhelmed again with sensory input. "Henry Fischer and Brian Shands are sociopaths willing to sacrifice innocent lives to make a buck."

"You read the paper, Arnie. These felony charges are a joke. I'm calling the DA to demand that he charge those bastards with murder or manslaughter."

My first call came from Matthew Wallace.

"When I read the paper, Dr. Roth, I broke down in tears. These bastards brought misery, destroyed Debbie's hope, and perhaps stole her very life. I'm not a violent man, but Arnie, if I had the chance…"

"I couldn't agree with you more, but let's focus our energies on Debbie, and what's best for her. How did she respond to the news?"

"She didn't, Arnie. She sat there, saying nothing."

The second call was from Irving Hodges.

"Is it true, Dr. Roth?" came the subdued question.

"I'm afraid so, Irv. The entire medical community is in an uproar that this could happen here. They won't get away with it, I promise."

"Will that bring my Beatrice back to me, Doctor?"

That night I sat at the side of the bed. The alarm clock displayed three a.m.

Lois turned over. "What's the matter, Arnie?"

I looked into her eyes. "It's reaching the point of distraction. The aromas haunt me everywhere I go. I can't think straight. Memories constantly flood my mind, and my dreams are nightmares of harsh visual and olfactory hallucinations. During the day, I'm barely functional."

"Call Jack or call the Utah program. You must let them know how far this has progressed."

"I'll think about it. Maybe I'll call Jack in the morning."

It had finally happened, I thought, as I stood outside the ICU the next morning, overwhelmed by unseen forces. I was trembling, panting, and retreating from what? In fear of what? Sweat dripped over my face and soaked my neck and shirt.

My forebodings of the night before were becoming reality. I was obsessed and more distracted by the avalanche of aromas and memories. I had no way of escaping. I tried everything: staying in familiar places, chewing gum, and sucking on mints. I even placed *Vicks VapoRub* under my nose. I first used that trick when attending autopsies in medical school. It worked then, but not now — nothing worked.

I managed to get into the fifth floor dictating room and closed the door behind. I sat with my head down on the table. The dual assaults on my olfactory system and my psyche continued with the profusion of aromas permeating the hospital: disinfectants, from alcohol to iodines; antibiotics; perfumes and lotions from floral to spicy; human waste; blood, fresh and decayed; perspiration, pure and foul, with or without deodorants; bacterial and fungal decay; foods of all types and conditions from fresh to putrid; coffee, from rich and aromatic to burnt, and uncountable others, some recognizable, others unknown.

I picked up the phone and dialed home. When Lois answered, I said, "It's too much for me, Lo. I can't think straight. I can't take this anymore."

"Where are you?"

"I'm at Brier."

"Where at Brier?"

"The fifth floor dictating room."

"Can you come home?"

"What?"

"Can you leave and drive home?"

"Leave what?"

"The hospital and come home," she tried again.

"I barely made it here. I can't drive. I can't concentrate on anything. It's too much...It's too much."

"I'm calling Jack Byrnes. Stay put. Don't move."

"Lois, I'm losing my mind. I can't control the memories, the images, and the confusion of aromas."

"Stay put. I'm putting you on hold, but I'll be right back. Don't hang up, baby."

The line clicked. I stared at the phone, and then put the handset on the table. I was living the sensory equivalent of James Joyce's stream of consciousness. It was the chaos of a brain mired in a cloudburst, a downpour of olfactory-memory confusion. My brain felt as if it were drowning. Images and thoughts flashed through my mind, frenzied breaking waves and no life preserver in sight.

I was afraid to breathe as the room air lingered at the threshold of my nose. I held my breath, a moment's respite, before my body forced the issue and my nasal cavity filled with the vivid, compelling molecules that demanded my attention to the exclusion of all else, an olfactory kaleidoscope of multicolored fireworks filling the night sky. Every recognizable molecule now evoked a memory, while the unidentifiable and the unknown played games with my brain as it struggled to make sense of the overwhelming molecular quagmire.

I heard the distant resounding voice yelling my name. "Arnie…Arnie, it's Jack." I couldn't focus enough to respond. I felt someone or something pulling at my arm and shoulder. All of it, the aromas, the memories, the sounds, the touch, and a blinding white light took over as my brain, to protect itself, switched into shutdown mode. My mind raised its protective barriers and the sensory input finally faded into oblivion, sinking into the abyss of my unconscious mind.

Jack approached the transcription room. Arnie was sitting, head down, and frozen and immobile. Lois' voice sounded through the handset.
"Arnie…Arnie…pick up. It's Lois, pick up."
Jack grabbed the handset. "Lois?"
"Yes. Jack. Where's Arnie?"
"He's here. Hang on."
Jack shook him. "Arnie, are you all right?"
Arnie's head remained on the table, his eyes open, but unseeing. Jack pulled him into a sitting position. Arnie's passive movement was that of adjusting the position of a manikin. He remained frozen in position, expressionless, silent.
"You'd better get down here ASAP, Lois. Arnie's unresponsive."
"Unresponsive!" shouted Lois. "I don't understand. Where will he be?"

"I'm admitting him to the psych ward. Ross Cohen, the psychiatrist, will be in to see him as soon as possible."

Chapter Fifty-Four

Following the *San Francisco Chronicle's* article about Horizon Drugs, Jim McDonald, like all who did business with Henry Fischer and Brian Shands, was frantic about the effects on his own patients.

Edith Keller, Brier's infectious disease specialist, had formulated an approach to the pneumonia vaccine patients and distributed it to the staff.

"Get me a list," McDonald told his nurse, "of everyone who received *Pneumovax* in the last two years. We must determine if they're protected, or will need re-vaccination."

As Jim prepared to see his first patient of the day, his intercom buzzed. "I have Joseph Rinaldi on the line. He'd like a word with you."

My God, he thought.

Connie...*Pneumovax*...pneumonia!

Jim picked up the phone. "Joe. What's up?"

"You read the Chronicle article about Horizon?"

"Yes."

"Is it true?"

"I'm afraid so. It's the most despicable thing I've ever heard in all my years of practice. I can't tell you how angry I am."

"You're angry," he hesitated, preparing for the eruption he'd been suppressing, "I'm about to explode that this could happen...that it happened to Connie. They nearly killed her. Look what's left of our daughter's life. I could murder those bastards."

"I couldn't agree with you more, but I must focus on Connie and my other patients and what's best for them now."

"Is there anything we can do to see to it that they pay?"

"It's with the DA now. I'm sure they'll get what they deserve."

"I mean, can we sue them for what they did to Connie?"

I don't any part of this, thought Jim.

"I'm not an attorney, but we know that justice is not always just."

"What does that mean?" he said, raising his voice.

"I don't want to get into this with you, Joe. We're on the same side. We'll have to wait and see what the DA does."

"That's not enough. They nearly murdered her. Shouldn't they have to pay?"

"Find a way of making peace with this, Joe. Focus on your family, on Connie. I'll do what I can, believe me."

"But," he persisted, "it's clear, isn't it? They nearly killed Connie."

Shit, Jim McDonald thought, he may be relentless, but he's right.

"Don't shoot the messenger, Joe. Their attorneys are going to spin this to the defendant's advantage. They're going to say that Connie had severe bronchitis to begin with. That illness predisposed her to respiratory infections, and that we can't prove that the adulterated vaccine had anything to do with her pneumonia. It makes me more cynical than I am, that they'd go so far, and more infuriated that it's a strategy that might work in court."

Jack Byrnes had Warren Davidson, the chief of medicine, on the phone. "Can you get over to a meeting at noon to discuss the Horizon Pharmacy situation?"

"No problem."

"I reserved the medical staff office conference room." Jack hesitated a moment and then said, "I admitted Arnie Roth to the psych unit this morning."

"You what?"

"I had no choice. He's catatonic. Depressed. This olfactory thing has been overwhelming."

"My God," said Warren. "Who's going to see him?"

"Ross Cohen."

"Good, he's the best. Can Arnie have visitors?"

"Not yet. I'll see you at noon."

Cindy Hines carried a tray of sandwiches into the QA meeting room. Edith Keller had come early and was sitting at the table reading the *Oakland Tribune*. She looked up at Cindy "It's all over the news. Henry Fischer and Brian Shands; why am I not surprised?"

"I can't help thinking that those bastards had a part in what happened to Mike," Cindy said. "I hate the 'what ifs' of life, but what if Mike responded well to the EPO? What if his healing improved? What if we'd had a chance to deal with his depression? Would he be here today?"

Edith shook her head. "Those bastards never gave him a chance."

"It's unbelievable," Cindy said.

Edith shook her head slowly. "No, it's not. It's the logical extension of what's happening in our culture overall, and with health care providers in particular."

"You've come a long way from Ames, Iowa, Edith. You've become a cynic."

"Maybe, but I understand greed. It doesn't know geographic boundaries, but naively, I expected more from a place like Berkeley. I expected more from people who call themselves medical professionals."

Cindy held Edith's hand. "Judges can be corrupt, priests can be pedophiles, cops can be killers, and medical people can be incompetent and evil. Let's not blame the institution, let's put the blame where it belongs, on sociopaths like Henry Fischer and Brian Shands."

Warren Davidson and Jack Byrnes entered the meeting room.

Jack picked up his sandwich. "Let me have a quick bite, and we'll get started."

"Whatever we think of these men now," Warren said, "I can't believe that anyone thought they'd stoop to such a level. It's astonishing. It's like Lily Tomlin said: no matter how cynical you get, it's impossible to keep up."

Jack took his last bite, downed his coffee. "That's the reason we're here today. It all makes sense now."

"Of course," said Edith, "the excessive use of EPO and the failure of the *Pneumovax* immunization to protect patients. All of it stems from the same problem."

Warren turned to Jack. "Bring me up to speed."

Jack told Warren about the QA study on excessive EPO usage, and the chart review revealing the deaths of patients from pneumonia — deaths that should not have occurred in patients previously vaccinated.

Warren reddened. "Those bastards messed with the EPO and the pneumonia vaccine, in addition to the Taxol."

"The EPO dilution meant that the docs had to prescribe more for the same effect," Edith said, "but diluting or failing to give an effective dose of *Pneumovax*, can leave our chronically ill and aged patients vulnerable to infection. We must deal with that right away. It's probably simplest to reimmunize them and hope that patients won't suffer any adverse effects."

"I'll notify the district attorney," Jack said. "They will need to pursue that side of the investigation as well." Jack hesitated. "Can we do that, Ben, considering that this is confidential QA information?"

"Fuck it!" Warren said. "This is too important. I'll call the DA myself if you like."

Kevin Walters, a moderate conservative, had inexplicably been elected District Attorney in ultra liberal Berkeley where, for once, the highly politicized electorate went for competence rather than ideology. Nevertheless, both sides of the political spectrum discovered ways of constantly scrutinizing and disparaging the DA's actions.

His sizable city hall conference room walls had the flags of the United States and the State of California. Governor Jerry Brown's face smiled from a large gold-framed portrait. The victims and families and their attorneys packed the room, all trying to talk at once.

Walters raised his arms in an attempt to silence the crowd. "If you'll stop yelling for a moment, I'll try to answer your questions."

"How come you're not charging these animals with murder or manslaughter?" said a middle age woman sitting in the front row.

An elderly woman with the PETA (People for the Ethical Treatment of Animals) logo on her sweater rose. "Don't you dare use the term animal about these murderers. No animal is capable of such evil."

"First of all," Kevin said, "we're not finished charging these defendants. Today, we received indications that Mr. Fischer and Mr. Shands were altering, misbranding, or diluting two other drugs. We're investigating and will amend the charges as needed."

"You didn't answer her question," said a well-dressed man holding a legal yellow pad standing at the rear.

"I'm not going to tell you now what additional charges we may file after we fully understand what these defendants have done. We need a chance to review the case law on the subject. I see several attorneys in the room, and I'm sure they'll agree." He paused and continued, "and please don't think me cruel, but it won't be easy to prove that someone who is already sick with a fatal disease was murdered by the actions of these defendants."

"They killed my Betty," said an elderly man, clearly distraught. "She had one chance, her chemotherapy. They robbed her of that opportunity."

"I know how you feel," Kevin said. "If it was one of my family, I'd like nothing better than to string up the bastards, but I'm an officer of the court, and a servant of the people, and I can do only what the law allows. I promise to do my best to add other charges when and if the evidence supports them, and I think we can win in court."

The room burst again into shouting as Kevin rapped on the table. "That's all I have to say today. I'm sure your attorneys will inform you of the other venues where you can seek justice, such as the civil courts. Thank you," he said as he left the room.

When Kevin returned to his office, his secretary stood and apologized. "I couldn't keep him out. He just barged in."

When he entered his office, Byron Potts, the Republican Party Chairman, sat behind Kevin's desk.

Another stupid power play, Kevin thought.

Kevin walked to the side of his desk and waited.

Byron smiled then stood and moved into a chair before Kevin's desk. "You got yourself a big headache here, Kev."

Byron Potts, now in his early sixties, had been the party chairman in Alameda County for years. Byron was a study in contrasts. While personally disheveled and sucking on an unlit, soggy cigar, he wore a beautiful Armani suit. Byron, brought his chrome monogrammed Zippo lighter to the end of his cigar. "You won't mind if I light up."

"I certainly mind, and so do the people of Berkeley."

Byron frowned, the put the lighter away. "Kevin, whatever you do, you better not fuck up this case. You're about the only thing going for us in this liberal wasteland."

"You've got balls to come here now about this case. I know what's at stake politically, but I'm an officer of the court, not the judge, jury, and executioner."

"If you plea this out, we're going to look bad. We're the tough law-and-order party."

"Would you rather have me overcharge and lose in court because we can't make our case?"

"Hell, yes, I would. I'd rather have the public blame the liberal courts and the gutless Berkeley jurors than take it out on us."

"Find me one case where I can prove that the actions of these defendants directly caused the death or injury of someone, and I'll take this to the limit. I'll charge them with manslaughter. If you can't, then get the hell off my back."

Chapter Fifty-Five

How cliché, I thought as I watched my life flashing by in black and white like the pages of a newspaper streaming across a microfiche viewer. The images were recognizable even at this speed, but moved too rapidly to focus on any one. Images and aromas of a life: Mom and Dad around the breakfast table with bacon sizzling in the frying pan and fresh-grilled buttermilk biscuits stacked high on a plate; the feeling of security as I lay under the warm bed covers with a cold, the vaporizer spewing billows of steam and tincture of benzoin; the locker room filled with the jibes, taunts, and the smell of high school athletes; my first touch of Lois's skin and the soft scent of Shalimar; Amy's birth, her new-baby smell, and thousands of other images.

I embraced each event, each sensation, basking in each delightful memory, clutching each one, and refusing to relinquish them even as a distant voice called my name.

"Arnie...Arnie, come back to me," Lois cried as she sat by his side holding his hands. Tears rolled down her cheeks.

The hallmarks of being human weren't strictly anatomical, for the best renderings of Madam Tussaud's Museum, although perfect in every detail, remained inanimate, and lacked life's force. The shallow respirations and the occasional blink of wide-open unseeing eyes said that Arnie lived, but in truth, he had begun to look more like a wax figure.

Ross Cohen sat with Arnie's chart writing admission orders. "I'm not sure that he hears you, Lois."

Lois and Jack had laid the whole thing out for Ross.

"We were a wreck during Arnie's prolonged coma from the encephalitis, and were overjoyed when he awakened," Lois said. "In spite of mild residual damage, Arnie seemed to appreciate and celebrate life more than ever."

"He had muscular weakness," Jack said, "as you might expect after lying in bed for so long, but he had coordination problems as well, that suggested brain injury. We carefully tested him for intellectual and memory deficits, but found none."

Lois continued. "Within weeks after awakening, Arnie said that all his senses seemed more acute than normal, but soon it was clear that this was limited to his nose. We had a grand time with it. His sniffer was amazing. He sensed things only animals could appreciate, an entire world unknown to humans, but gradually it overwhelmed him. Arnie was a rock, but soon he became easily upset, distracted by the torrents of smells, and plagued by the memories elicited by each one."

"I arranged for Arnie's evaluation at the University of Utah's sensory perception program," Jack said. "They had never seen anything like

Arnie's ability. They wanted to study him, but had no suggestions regarding therapy."

Lois looked at Ross. "He struggled at home and at work. We were helpless as we watched Arnie's gift degenerate into an overwhelming burden."

"It's going to take a while to sort this out," Ross said. "At first blush, it looks like an acute depressive breakdown. Did either of you note a psychotic component to Arnie's complaints?"

Jack shook his head. "No, no overt hallucinations, but there's no way we could evaluate any of the sensory data that only Arnie could appreciate."

"None of this is in the textbooks," Ross said. "I'll pick the brains of my best colleagues, but meanwhile, we should start Arnie on antidepressants."

"How long does it take to see the effect of this medication?" Lois asked.

"Two to three weeks."

"That's too long for him to remain this way. You must do something."

"We're out of alternatives right now. It's still early. Maybe he'll snap out of this himself. If we need to, we'll feed Arnie by tube."

Jack held Lois's hands. "We need to give this time."

Lois looked into Ross's eyes. "What if the medication doesn't work?"

"We'll deal with that if we must. If all else fails, we can consider shock therapy."

"Oh, my God," Lois shouted. "Oh, my God!"

When Lois arrived home after another day with Arnie, her sister Sally and the girls were watching television.

Sally rose to embrace Lois. "How is he?"

"The same."

"How long can this go on?"

"I don't know. It takes time for antidepressants to work."

When the program hit a commercial break, Amy ran to Lois and hugged her waist. "Hi Mommy. I missed you."

"Hi, sweetie. Did you have a good time with Aunt Sally?"

"She's fun." She paused and then looked into her mother's eyes. "Where's Daddy?"

"Daddy's in the hospital. He's sick."

"Can I see him? I drew him a picture."

"Not now, honey, but soon."

Rebecca's gaze remained fixed on the television. She was determined to ignore Lois. Lois walked to the sofa and sat beside her older daughter. "Can you give me a kiss hello?"

Rebecca stared ahead, refusing to meet her mother's eyes.

Lois caressed Rebecca's hair. "What's wrong, sweetheart?"

Rebecca recoiled at the touch and turned her head further away from her mother.

Lois was tired and emotionally drained. "I'm upset too, Rebecca. I love Daddy and miss him so I understand what you're feeling."

"No, you don't. He's going to die, isn't he? He promised me he'd never leave me again...he promised."

Rebecca burst into tears.

"Daddy's sick, but he's not going to die. Don't think that."

"I'm so scared."

"Me too, baby. It's going to take a while, but the doctors think he'll be fine."

Rebecca grabbed a tissue, blew her nose. "Why can't I see Daddy? I'll stay only for a minute. I won't disturb anything. I need to see him...to know he's okay."

My God, thought Lois. I can't let them see him this way — catatonic — unresponsive. They'll never understand and they'll never forget.

"Daddy's in a special hospital where he can't have visitors, but when he's a little better, you can see him."

Rebecca held Lois as tears again streamed from her eyes. Amy, equally upset cried, "I want my Daddy."

Chapter Fifty-Six

Henry Fischer sat on the sofa in Teddy's living room. He looked down to avoid his father's disappointment and his sister Joanie's contempt.

How did I get myself into this?

"How could you do this to our family?" asked a distraught Theodore Fischer.

"Dad, he manages to pull the wool over your eyes," said Joanie. "Henry could do no wrong. Look at him now."

His father shook his head. "I don't understand how you could have done this. All those patients. They depended on that medication; depended on us, our integrity…a trust we nurtured over a lifetime."

"We faced bankruptcy," Henry said. "We were going to lose everything. All our investors, all our employees…I couldn't let that happen. Brian convinced me that we could dilute the medication without harming anyone."

"Now, it's all Brian's fault," Joanie said. "Even you must have had a hard time swallowing that. You disgust me."

Henry stared at his father. "I'm going to need your help, Teddy."

"Help! Go to hell," Joanie screamed as she jumped up and left the room.

The old man paled. "How can we help when we're about to lose everything we have?"

Henry tried repeatedly to reach Monica Kelly in Reno. He left messages at her work and on her answering machine at home. She never returned his calls.

Finally, using a false name to her secretary, he got her on the phone. "Why aren't you answering my calls, Monica?"

"Don't you get it? I knew you could be ruthless, but this, Henry, this is beyond the pale. Don't call again. I don't want anything to do with you," she said as the phone clicked.

Henry shed the last vestige of his dignity when he picked up the phone, and called Ruth. "It's me," he said, expecting the worst.

"What is it, Henry?"

"I want to talk with you."

"You sure made a mess of everything."

"Can I come over? We need to talk."

"Not here. I'll meet you at the Claremont Hotel bar."

"Thanks. I'll see you in about twenty minutes."

Ruth watched Henry drive his new Lexis through the gates of the Claremont Spa and Hotel, a landmark of the San Francisco Bay area. She waited for him to park, and then enter the lobby before she drove in.

When Ruth stepped into the bar, they had seated Henry at one of the many tables facing southeast. The spectacular view encompassed a panorama of the bay and the city skyline.

As she approached, Henry placed his drink on the table and stood. He looked like he intended to offer her a kiss, so she sat immediately to avoid an uncomfortable moment.

"It's so good to see you, Ruth. You're looking well."

He looks dreadful, she thought. Pale, thinner than I remember, but where's the remorse? Does he give a damn about all those he harmed?

"What can I get you?" the cocktail waitress asked.

"A Cosmopolitan, please," Ruth said.

Lois turned to Henry. "You don't look well. I suppose with your heart problems, and everything else, it's what we might expect."

"I need your help, Ruth," he said in a near whisper. "If I can't mount a proper defense, I'm going to jail."

"From what I hear, Henry, you are going to jail. I doubt if O.J. Simpson's lawyers could get you out of this."

"I know. After all I've done to you and the family, I don't have the right to ask for help, but I don't have a choice. I have to raise enough money to retain a first class attorney. Can you help?"

"At one time, that request would have had me laughing and enjoying your downfall, but now, in truth, I don't feel anything."

"Please, Ruth, I'm begging."

"Don't," she said, stiffening. "I'm willing to help by giving you your fair share of what we have left, but my accountant, and my attorneys have advised me that the expected flood of civil litigation could leave us with little or nothing. I must protect myself and our children first."

"Please, Ruth. I need your help."

"Maybe Monica Kelly can help you," she said, getting up to leave. "Ask her."

Chapter Fifty-Seven

Henry Fischer's criminal attorney, Harrison Pollard, was a senior partner at Greenly, Baxter, and Pollard, one of the premier law firms in the east bay. As Henry sat in their Emeryville offices at the foot of the San Francisco Bay Bridge, Harrison said, "Don't be naive, Henry, Brian Shands is going to fuck you over at the first opportunity."

"I have no illusions about Brian, but don't we have a mutuality of interests here?"

"Yes, Henry, but only if he thinks he can't get away with blaming the whole thing on you. I'm betting, and so should you, that's exactly what he has in mind."

"I'm not saying that I'm not responsible, but this was Brian's idea from start to finish. He assured me that we could do this without hurting anyone."

"Oh please, Henry, that's a load of shit. I'm your attorney and I'd choke trying to put that to a jury. I don't buy it, and neither will they."

"What can we do?"

"Brian's attorney is Karl Hirsch. I've worked with Karl. He's tough, but reasonable. If I can convince him that we're all better off sticking together, maybe we can help each other in court."

Henry hesitated. Keeping things from his attorney was plain stupid — I've been stupid enough, he thought.

"When Ruth tossed me out, and I knew we were due for a contentious divorce, I told Brian I wanted to stop the whole damned thing. He wouldn't hear of it and threatened me."

"Threatened you. What did he say?"

"He said that this was all my idea, that I'd fire him if he didn't go along. He said that I coerced him and that I made a lion's share of the profits. Finally, he said that if I fucked with him, I'd wind up in jail."

"That's great," Pollard said, "just great."

Across town, in downtown Berkeley, Brian Shands was meeting with Karl Hirsch, the former Berkeley DA, and now a criminal defense attorney.

"If you try to blame this all on Henry Fischer, it will only damage your credibility with the jury."

Brian shook his head. "Any other approach will only make things worse."

"I can't see any way of defending you, Brian. You did it. Henry Fischer and Tino Ruiz will testify to this, and then they have the diluted drugs as evidence. In addition, it's doubtful that we can get any of this evidence excluded on technical grounds."

"What are you saying?"

"I think we should make the best deal we can."

"Deal. You want me to agree to a prison sentence?"

"Brian, get real will you. True or not, the jury is going to believe that giving cancer patients inadequate chemotherapy is equivalent to murder or manslaughter. They're going to call both of you monsters in white coats. Trust me, you don't want your future in their hands."

No way am I'm going to jail, Brian thought.

Brian drove to three banks, each time withdrawing several thousand dollars. He looked repeatedly at his rear view mirror to see if anyone was trailing him, but he failed to notice the 1992 Toyota Corolla following several cars behind.

Brian's wife and daughter wouldn't be back for several hours, so he rushed home, packed an overnight bag, and departed for the airport. He left the car in short-term parking, knowing he need not concern himself with the steep fees, and walked to the American Airlines counter where he bought a round-trip coach ticket to New York (a one way ticket drew too much attention in the post 9/11 world). As he waited to board, he looked around continuously. He took no notice of the elderly man standing on the other side of the concourse.

Irving Hodges watched. He'd anticipated Brian's action and had been following him for several days. He tried repeatedly to reach the DA's office, but each time they put him on hold listening to elevator music. By the time the irate Irving Hodges reached Kevin Martin, the plane had departed.

"That bastard, Brian Shands is on a plane to New York. Don't let him get away."

"Who is this?"

"It's Irving Hodges. He killed my wife. Get him."

"Do you know the flight number?"

"Yes, American 417."

"I'll take care of it, Mr. Hodges. Don't worry."

Brian slept soundly for most of his flight. He felt relaxed as he finished a third martini and the captain announced their arrival at New York's JFK. He had enough cash for several days in the city and contacts to obtain a new identity and a passport. Then he'd fly to Grand Cayman Island to claim the bulk of his estate.

As he walked down the arrival ramp, he was shocked to see a large dark-suited man with heavy black shoes holding a sign with big letters reading, 'Welcome, Brian Shands'. He turned immediately to his right and ran into another large man who snapped handcuffs on him in one swift movement.

"Welcome to New York, Mr. Shands. You arrived in time for your flight back to San Francisco."

Standing between the two officers, Brian heard one laughing to the other. "Who said cops ain't got no sense of humor?"

Chapter Fifty-Eight

Lois visited Arnie every day, but saw no change. Arnie, whether in bed or in a chair, stared ahead through vacant eyes that rarely blinked.

Merely entering the locked psychiatric ward was more than she could bear. She walked into the day room with the TV blaring and scanned the otherworldly inhabitants. Something about mental illness made people uncomfortable. In spite of her intelligence, Lois, like others, felt a strong desire to escape, as if psychiatric problems were contagious.

"Why can't we see Daddy?" Rebecca had asked that morning.

"We've been over this. Daddy's too sick now. The doctors said you can visit soon."

Jack had inserted a feeding tube for fluids, nutrition, and for the administration of antidepressants.

"Jack, I can't go on," Lois said. "I can't stand to see him this way."

"There's nothing else we can do for now. He's only been on antidepressants for ten days. It's too soon to expect any therapeutic effect."

"I think he turned to me this morning when I gave him a hug, but his eyes were blank. He said nothing, but he's in there somewhere, I know it."

Jack placed his hand on her shoulder. "I won't lie to you, Lois. Ross is concerned, and so am

I. This much withdrawal, this much catatonia, sometimes requires more drastic action."

"You mean shock therapy?"

"Yes."

"Shocking the brain feels wrong, Jack. It feels like a barbaric act of our dark medical past. Arnie had several patients who did remarkably well with their treatments, but frying his brain with electricity?"

"Lois, that's all wrong. They only use a tiny amount of current, only enough to provoke the brain into convulsions. Often, the results are miraculous."

"Please, Jack, you know the procedure has its problems afterward, especially memory loss."

"That depends on the number of convulsions it takes, but you're right. I hope it doesn't come to that, but it's a small price to pay to get him back."

When Lois arrived the next day, Arnie was in bed with his legs elevated, wearing white compression stockings.

Lois turned to his nurse. "What's happening?"

"Dr. Byrnes became concerned with swelling in Dr. Roth's legs, so we're using TEDS stockings to prevent clotting in his veins."

"Does he have any clotting?"

"Not that we know."

Lois sat by Arnie's side, reading. She looked over from time to time, but his eyes remained fixed on the ceiling. Lois must have nodded off, because when she startled herself awake, Arnie's was panting heavily and his lips were blue. She pushed the call button, and after two minutes without an answer, she rushed to the nursing station where she saw only the ward clerk.

"Get the nurse, stat. Something's happening to my husband," Lois shouted, "and page Dr. Byrnes now."

By the time the nurse arrived, Arnie's breathing had become gasps. He struggled to breathe with his chest and neck muscles straining to assist. His lips were now a bluish-purple.

"Get him on oxygen," Lois yelled.

When the nurse returned and placed nasal prongs for oxygen delivery, Arnie's breathing eased slightly.

Suddenly, he coughed and choked. Bloody foamy fluid dripped from his mouth. His color worsened.

Jack entered, took one look at Arnie, listened to his chest, examined his legs. "He's having pulmonary emboli, blood clots to the lung. I need him in ICU right now."

Jack picked up the phone, dialed ICU. "Get bed one ready. I'm bringing a patient with acute pulmonary emboli. Call Sharon Brickman. Tell her to get up here stat."

Lois grasped Jack's arm. "Tell me what's happening?"

They transferred Arnie to a gurney, attached his oxygen lines, and wheeled him out of the room toward the elevator.

"Come along, Lois," Jack said. As they hurried along with the gurney. "Lying in bed and sitting in a chair without movement, caused blood clot formation in Arnie's leg. Part of the clot came loose and traveled to his lungs."

The elevator doors slid opened and they pushed the gurney inside. Jack, Lois, and two nurses stood around Arnie watching him gasp and choke. Blood sprayed over the white sheets each time he coughed. His lips and nail beds were deeply purple and his neck veins were tense from high pressure. Jack shuffled his feet into position like a sprinter in the starting blocks waiting for the elevator doors to open.

Finally, when they reached the sixth floor, Jack gave the gurney a violent push thrusting it down the hallway, and through the ICU doors held open by the ward clerk.

They lifted Arnie by grabbing the gurney sheet and swinging him in one movement into bed one.

Sharon Brickman suddenly appeared next to Jack.

"It's a big one, Sharon. He's going down quickly. Look at those neck veins. His heart can't take the load. We've got to get that clot out of his lungs; extract it or dissolve it, right away, or he's had it!"

Chapter Fifty-Nine

This is a nightmare, Lois thought as she and Beth Byrnes, Arnie's nurse, sat at the bedside. Lois held Arnie's cool hands. His fingers had dusky colored nail beds and his lips were still purple-blue, showing the lack of oxygen in the circulating blood.

Jack Byrnes and Sharon Brickman stood before the x-ray viewing box looking at Arnie's films.

"I don't know which way to go, Sharon," Jack said as he grabbed an IV infusion bottle sitting on the bedside table containing about 8 ounces of a straw-colored fluid, Activase, a powerful clot dissolver.

"It'll take me thirty minutes to get ready," Sharon said, "then I'm pretty sure we can remove the clot with a catheter passed into his lung."

"I don't know if we have thirty minutes, and I'm not crazy about your 'pretty sure' part of that comment."

"Jack," Beth cried. "His BP's falling and his breathing's getting worse. We're going to wind up coding and intubating him any second."

Jack quickly examined Arnie, and then turned to Beth. "Push the Code Blue button, get the intubation tray, and start infusing the Activase."

"Jack!" Lois cried.

"Have someone take her outside, Beth. She can't watch this."

"Jack. Please let me stay."

"No, Lois. If you want to help Arnie, don't give me something else to worry about. Leave now. Beth will let you know what's happening."

Lois bent over Arnie, kissed his icy-cold lips, turned, and backed slowly from the ICU.

Jack slipped his hands into sterile gloves, grabbed the endotracheal tube, and after visualizing Arnie's vocal cords over the arched stainless laryngoscope blade, passed the tube into a trachea choked with bloody foam. They inflated the tube's balloon cuff to fix it in place and breathed for Arnie with an Ambu Bag attached to an oxygen line.

Jack squeezed the bag between his strong hands to inflate Arnie's lungs. "This is requiring too much pressure. His lungs must be stiff."

Jack passed a plastic suction tube into Arnie's lungs and pulled out large bloody clots. During the intubation, the room filled with the Code Blue team and other physicians who were nearby.

"Set up the ventilator," Jack said to the respiratory tech. "Get an arterial blood gas and a portable chest x-ray stat."

Twenty minutes later, they let Lois return to Arnie's bedside. A sense of calm had replaced the frenzied scene of a few minutes ago. Arnie lay immobile in bed with fresh sheets, the bloody ones stuffed in the soiled linen basket. The nurses encased his wrists and ankles in leather restraints and tied them to the bed frame.

Lois looked expectantly at Jack. "He's not so blue now. Tell me what's happening."

Arnie's blood showed as brown stains on Jack's green scrub suit. Perspiration soaked the area around his neck, back, and underarms.

"His breathing's much easier and his blood gasses are better. I gave him a sizable dose of Activase that should dissolve the blood clots everywhere, especially in his lungs."

"What if they don't dissolve? What if the clots come back?"

"The chance that another big clot will go to the lungs is remote. If smaller ones recur, we might have to tie off a vein or put a filter into the large vein in his abdomen. We have lots of things we can think about, and now, thank God that he's stable, we can deal with them in relative calm."

"I'm frightened to ask, Jack, but what's next?"

"The next few days will be critical. If he has no further clots to his lungs, he should heal quickly and we can get the tube out. Later he may need to take anticoagulants so he won't form clots again."

"What about his depression?"

"Right now, if we can get to the point when we can focus on Arnie's depression that will be a major victory."

Chapter Sixty

Henry Fischer had aged ten years in two months. The court's concern for his heart had kept him out of jail. He'd lost twenty pounds from his already lean body. His hair had turned white, and his flat affect reflected a total emotional meltdown.

"Pull yourself together, Henry," said Harrison Pollard, his attorney. "No way are we letting this case go to trial. The sooner we make a deal to settle these charges, the better it will be for everybody."

"That's not the outcome I'm paying you for."

Harrison laughed, "If we can't settle this soon, you won't have enough money left to defend a DUI charge, especially if the public forces the DA to pursue murder or manslaughter charges, to say nothing of all the civil litigation you face."

"Murder...manslaughter. I don't see any way he can prove that we injured anyone. Those people had fatal diseases."

"The EPO cases involve issues of fraud and misbranding, but the dilution of the pneumonia vaccine presents additional problems. If even one patient who got your bogus *Pneumovax* developed bacterial pneumonia and died, I think they can make a case for manslaughter, maybe murder two."

"Whose side are you on?"

"Don't put me on your side," Harrison said, standing. He turned to face his client. "I'm representing you although what you two did makes me sick. Feel free to fire me." He paused. "Nevertheless, I suggest you heed my advice before it's too late."

"Whatever you say," Henry said in defeat.

Harrison Pollard sat with Karl Hirsch, Brian Shands' attorney outside the DA's offices.

"Brian's no fool," Karl said. "He wants the best deal he can get. What about Henry?"

"Henry's terrified of murder or manslaughter charges. He's fully on board with the negotiation. How do you read Kevin Martin?"

"He wants this to go away quickly, as much or more than we do. The murder/manslaughter charges are problematic for him. He knows that whatever we do here or in court won't satisfy the public."

"Come in, gentlemen," Kevin said as he opened the door to his office.

Kevin pointed to the two stuffed leather chairs in front of his large oak desk. "Have a seat."

After Kevin returned to his high-backed desk chair, he sat and tilted back. "What can I do for you gentlemen?"

"As if you didn't know," Karl said. "I sat behind that desk longer than you have, Kev."

"Then you'll understand what I'm up against, Karl. Emotions are running high. If the public had its way, your boys would be hanging from the gallows right now."

"Look, Kevin," Harrison said, "they're both ready to plead this out, so let's put it to bed."

Kevin looked at each attorney. "If I'm to have any future in this business, I must go for big time jail sentences, especially if I can't make murder or manslaughter work. They're going to be old men when they get out."

"How old?"

"When you add up the charges, the number of patients involved, and the state and federal violations, I expect that they'll serve thirty years each."

Harrison Pollard paled. "Thirty years?"

"That's it, gentlemen, thirty years. Take it or leave it."

"I'll take it," Karl said. "It's what they earned, and between you and me, it's a better deal than they deserve."

"I'll present it to Henry," Harrison said. "I'll make it clear that he'd better grab the deal while it's on the table."

At his press conference two days later, Kevin Martin announced the terms of the plea agreement to an overflowing conference room: "Both defendants have agreed to a thirty-year sentence for multiple offences regarding the misbranding, adulteration, and the dilution of several medications. By statute each defendant will pay a fine of $25,000 each..."

The room filled with groans, gasps, and boo's. The crowd surged toward the front, held back by a group of uniformed officers.

"...if you'll allow me to continue," Kevin shouted. "In restitution, Mr. Shands will pay an additional fine of $ 2.4 million, and Mr. Fischer will pay $8.3 million."

"You're letting them get away with murder," shouted a woman from the back of the room.

"They're killers. How could you agree to such a sentence?" said a man in the second row.

"I'm sorry," Kevin said. "I can only file charges when I think we can sustain them in court. This conference is over."

As Kevin departed through a line of protecting policemen, he heard, "You won't get away with this."

"Don't bother filing for reelection."

"How much payoff money did you take?"

"How do you sleep at night?"

That wasn't too bad, Kevin Martin thought.

When the last of the crowd left through the conference room's rear doors, one elderly man, Irving Hodges, remained seated, his mind whirling with this newest insult.

Kevin Martin knew that the plea agreement with Henry Fischer and Brian Shands would not end his problem. Maybe he should have pursued the manslaughter charges and let the jury take the heat if they failed to convict. If I were fifteen years younger...

Kevin heard a soft knock on his outer door. His secretary must be away from her desk. He opened the door to a well-dressed man in his late 70s or 80s.

"I'm sorry to bother you, Mr. Walters," said Irving Hodges, in a soft voice, "but your secretary wasn't here. Can I have a moment of your time?"

Kevin retreated into his office, his usual respectful reaction when dealing with people of advanced age. "Of course. Please have a seat. What can I do for you?"

"My name is Irving Hodges, I'm the husband…I was the husband of Beatrice Hodges. Does that name ring a bell?"

"Of course, Mr. Hodges, and thanks to you, Brian Shands is in jail where he belongs."

"I was talking about Beatrice, my wife."

"Yes, she was one more unfortunate victim of the Horizon Pharmacy scandal. I'm so sorry for your loss."

"Excuse me, sir, but to talk of Beatrice as an unfortunate victim demeans her and horribly distorts the disgusting actions of Fischer and Shands."

"I'm sorry, sir. A bad choice of words."

"If you knew what this did to me, did to all the others who put their lives in the hands of these men, you couldn't let them off so lightly."

How can I make him understand? Kevin thought.

"I'll assume you don't know me, but if you ask around you'll find that I'm considered a tough district attorney. While I'm not a victim, I share your outrage at the despicable actions of these defendants, and like you, I want them punished to the maximum of what the law allows. That's the problem."

"Please, sir. Beatrice would be alive today, as would many others, if they'd received the proper medication. Depriving patients of lifesaving drugs is tantamount to murder."

"My folks are about your age. If this happened to one of them, I'd want revenge, too, but we live in a country of laws, imperfect laws that don't always provide a true measure of justice."

"Some true measure of justice," Irv said, "what an idea. Was this plea bargain the best you could get? Prison and fines?"

"Thirty years is a lifetime for men their ages."

"How long will they actually serve? Will they enjoy the taste of food, the delights of reading, music, movies, and the company of friends and relatives?"

"I'm sorry. It's not fair or just, but I did the best I could."

"I'm sorry too," Irv said his dark brown eyes boring into Kevin's, "but it's not enough, not nearly enough."

Chapter Sixty-One

It's not déjà vu, thought Lois Roth, as she sat by Arnie's bedside. It's happening again. She was reliving the trauma of those ICU days before Arnie awakened from encephalitis.

Beth Byrnes came over and placed her hand on Lois's shoulder. "How are you doing?"

Lois grasped Beth's hand. "It's worse this time. The ventilator, the depression, the clots...I think we may lose him."

"Don't do this to yourself. We're optimistic, and you should be, too."

Lois watched as the ventilator's yellow light glowed before each breath. She knew this was Arnie's breathing center triggering the ventilator, a good sign. Arnie's chest expanded and contracted. The clear plastic hose that connected to the ET tube still showed bloody mucous, but the heavy bleeding and the clots had disappeared.

Jack came to the bedside. "His tests show much better levels of oxygen in his blood and his chest x-ray this morning is clearing."

Jack removed the leather restraints so he could examine Arnie. He listened to his heart, lungs, and felt his extremities without comment. He then did a neurological evaluation that also was normal except that he was unable to awaken him.

After he completed his examination, Beth reapplied the restraints.

Lois stared at Beth. "Is that necessary? It looks horrible."

"It's absolutely necessary. If he should awaken and grab at the ET tube in his airway or his IV lines, he could do a lot of damage."

"I can't find anything wrong in Arnie's nervous system," Jack said, "except of course, that he won't wake up. I don't know what to make of that. Maybe he's still catatonic. I'm ordering an EEG to measure his brain waves. Maybe that'll clarify the situation."

"Are you still treating his depression?" Lois asked.

"No. His case is complicated enough as is."

Lois grasped Arnie's hand. "Has Ross Cohen been in to see him?"

"Not yet. I'll call him today to see what he thinks about the depression and where we go from here."

Lois stared at Jack. "You're not still thinking about shock therapy, are you?"

"I can't rule it out."

For the next two days, Arnie's condition remained stable. Everything except his mental status had improved.

Jack returned Arnie's chart with new orders to the rack. "I'm going to repeat his chest x-ray and blood gasses this afternoon. If they're as good as I expect, I'm going to remove the breathing tube."

I'm swimming through warm tropical waters. The rays of bright sunlight slant through the water at a thirty-degree angle illuminating the overabundance of marine life. As I move across the coral's surface, small brightly colored fish scatter away. I look up to see the twinkling of the small surface waves forty feet above, enchanted to be a part of a world so few ever experience.

Suddenly, I try to inhale. Nothing! Panicked, I look up for salvation. I kick hard for the surface, but something's holding my leg. I struggle to escape, my mind in the full flight of terror. Unable to hold my breath a second more, I inhale the salty water, hoping it won't take too long.

Lois was asleep in the chair next to Arnie. When the bed's rattle awakened her, she raised her head. Arnie was struggling to sit upright. The muscle fibers of his arms were taut as he fought against the restraints to reach for his breathing tube.

"No, Arnie," Lois screamed as she grabbed at his arms to prevent him from removing the ET tube.

In an instant, two pairs of arms joined Lois trying to restrain Arnie's powerful arms.

Arnie's eyes bulged and watered with tears as he fought. His face puffed out red as he tried to speak and pointed repeatedly to the tube in his throat. His strength was enormous.

"Get me Valium stat," shouted Jack as he released the pressure on the ET tube's cuff in preparation for its withdrawal.

Suddenly, Arnie's right arm came free and moved with lightning speed to the ET tube as Jack shouted, "No Arnie! Don't do it! I'll have it out in a second."

A moment later the bloody airway tube lay on the bed as Arnie coughed repeatedly.

"Get him on an oxygen mask stat, and bring me an intubation tray right away. We may need to reinsert the tube."

Arnie continued to cough and gasp, but his color remained good. He pulled at the restraint on his left arm and across his chest. "Let me go, God damn it. Let me go."

Jack reached across the bed and released the restraints.

Arnie coughed vigorously, sat upright, and expectorated a glob of blood-tinged mucous. "What are you guys trying to do, kill me?"

Chapter Sixty-Two

Matt Wallace understood the depth of Debbie's depression—how could he not? He believed that with time and good news, she'd come around.

For a few days after the radiotherapy, Debbie suffered headaches and mild dizziness. The infusions of Herceptin were, in Debbie's words, a walk in the park compared to her experience with chemotherapy.

Matt watched Debbie pretend to be normal, but she didn't fool the kids or him.

Heather, their oldest, noticed. "What wrong with Mommy? She never smiles anymore."

In Arnie's absence, Jordan Goodman had again taken over Debbie's care. "This depression has gone on long enough," he said. "I want you to see someone."

"A shrink?" she asked.

"We have good psychiatrists in town. They can help you through this."

"Can they make me forget that I have breast cancer?"

Jordan hesitated at the challenge. "Sometimes you're lucky, sometimes you're not. There's not a damn thing either of us can do about that, but mostly people make their own luck."

She reddened. "Sure, like getting cancer. Like getting quinine instead of Taxol. Like getting a brain tumor."

"I'm not telling you to be happy or to forget what's happened. I'm only outlining what's best for your future, Debbie."

"Future? I just want to live long enough to testify against Henry Fischer and Brian Shands. I want to see those bastards rot in jail."

"We're all doing what we can to assure that, but you have better reasons to live, Debbie."

"You don't understand…I can't take it anymore. I'm burned out. Hope has become just another useless four-letter-word."

"Please, Debbie," Matt cried, "you must try. If not for you or me, do it for the kids. They need their mother. They need you."

"Have I refused anything?" she asked, still in a monotone. "I did that disgusting chemotherapy, the Gamma Knife, and I'm doing Herceptin, and I guess I'll get shrunk, too. What more can I do?"

"I'm sending you to see Ross Cohen," Goodman said. "He's the best. I'm sure he'll begin with counseling. Commit to it, Debbie. If that doesn't work, he'll prescribe antidepressants."

"Okay," she said. "Anything else?"

How terrible my timing is, thought Jordan. "It's time for a follow-up CT scan of your brain."

"I can't wait."

I'm glad I'm not a writer, Debbie thought, as her body slid into the CT machine, because more than any original phrase, the cliché, 'moment of truth' fits how I feel.

Jordan Goodman peered over the complex machine and its computer screens through the thick glass window looking at Debbie.

After the machine went into repose, he stuck his head around the corner. "I'll join you in a second."

"Let's run through it," Jordan said to the CT radiology tech.

After Jordan watched the slices of Debbie's brain pass across the screen, he said, "Can you print them out and put them next to her first scan."

"Sure, Doc."

Jordan looked at each frame on the fluorescent view box, comparing each to Debbie's previous films.

"I'll get a radiologist for you, Dr. Goodman."

"It's okay," Jordan said, "I can wait for an official reading."

Debbie remained on the sliding litter outside the scanner and looked expectantly at Dr. Goodman as he entered the room.

He smiled broadly and grasped her hands. "It's gone."

Debbie wept.

Chapter Sixty-Three

I felt sore all over, as if I'd just finished fifteen rounds with Mike Tyson. Everything ached.

I raised myself in bed to survey the damage. I was bruised from head to toe. Deep purple-blue discoloration covered my extremities, chest, and abdomen. I had incisions in both groins sutured with ugly black thread, as they'd paid no attention to esthetic considerations. IV puncture marks decorated both arms. My face was sticky with the remnants of the tape that held the ET tube in place.

"You guys really beat the crap out of me."

Jack grinned. "And we'd do it again…got to get our kicks somehow."

"What happened?"

"You want all the gory details?"

"Give me the Cliff Notes version."

"What's the last thing you remember?"

"I remember sitting in the fifth floor transcription room, and then nothing except dreams…nightmares really."

"My best guess, buddy, is that you finally succumbed to olfactory overload. Like a schizophrenic, overwhelmed with the flood of chaotic sensory data, your mind couldn't absorb or react to it all, so it retreated into a catatonic state."

"Catatonic?"

"Don't you remember any of it? The hospitalization, the tube feedings, the meds, and all our attempts to shake you out of it?"

"Nothing. Just bad dreams, dark places, and bad smells."

"How's your smeller now?"

I sniffed deeply. "I can't smell a thing. I hope that's not permanent, although I'm not looking forward to resuming my olfactory nightmares."

"It's probably a combination of factors that may have injured the olfactory epithelium. It takes about sixty days to regenerate new tissue. We'll know then."

I looked down at my body again. "Catatonia doesn't explain why I'm black and blue."

"While you were on the psych ward, you developed a leg clot which broke off as a pulmonary embolus."

"How bad was it?"

"You don't want to know."

"Yes, I do."

"It was bad. You had a large clot blocking the pulmonary artery and putting a strain on your heart. It looked like we were going to lose you. Sharon was getting ready to try to pull the clot out when you went into shock. I gave you Activase, and it worked."

"So that's why I'm multicolored. Where's Lois?"

"She went to the ladies room. She was here all the time, Arnie. It was hell for her. She's an extraordinary woman. I don't know how you got so lucky."

"Me neither. Where do things stand now?"

Before Jack could answer, Lois returned. She'd brushed her hair and reapplied her makeup.

I grasped her hand. "You look sensational, babe."

"You're not exactly beautiful, Arnie, but you never looked so good to me. You scared the hell out of all of us."

"It's my way of getting attention."

Lois smiled. "I can think of easier ways of getting my attention, sweetie. I can't wait to get you home."

"Jack was about to lay out his plans for me."

"The worst is obviously over. You'll need a few days to a week of nutritional and physical rehab. We'll repeat the chest x-ray and scan your legs for clots."

"What about anticoagulants?"

"I'm not sure, but it would be the smart thing to do for a few months."

After Jack left, Lois sat on the bed at my side. She held my hands, leaned forward, and kissed me on the lips.

"How are the kids?"

"They're terrific, and can't wait to see their Daddy."

"I look so bad, Lo. I want to see the girls, but my appearance will only upset them."

"The unknown is worse for the kids. They need to see you. Give each a smile and a big hug, and tell them you'll be home soon. That's all it will take."

"What's happening with the practice?"

"It's fine, Arnie, don't worry."

"What's happening in the world?"

"The usual, but you'll be pleased to hear that Henry Fischer and Brian Shands are facing major charges. They probably won't risk a court trial."

"If it goes to trial, I want to be well enough to testify. Those sons-of-bitches ought to rot in hell."

"That sounds like the old Arnie. Welcome back."

Jim McDonald's was on the phone with his wife when his nurse barged into his office and shoved the note under his nose. The phone's for you, Jim. It's the Stanford heart/lung transplant program!

"Honey. I gotta go." He pushed the blinking button. "Dr. McDonald, can I help you?"

"Jim, it's Barry Harter from Stanford. Are you sitting down?"

Jim's pulse increased. "Sitting, standing or lying on the floor, let's have it."

"You know I told you that it would be years before we got the heart and the lungs for Connie Rinaldi, well…"

"I'm going to kill you, Barry."

"Our next patient was in flight from Dallas for these organs, when he had a stroke. We need to get these organs transplanted into someone else in the next six hours or they won't be of use to anyone. Connie's the only one who's close enough. Is she okay for the transplant?"

"Okay, she's more than okay. I can't believe it."

"Believe it, buddy, and get her down here ASAP."

Jim called Connie's number. The phone rang six times before the answering machine picked up. Shit, he thought, as he left a hurried message.

"Keep trying all the numbers for the Rinaldis," he shouted to his nurse. "I'm driving over to Connie's."

He drove through the North Berkeley streets ignoring the many Do Not Enter street signs and pulled in front of the Rinaldi home, a 1950s ivy-covered brick structure. He ran to the front door, pushed the button repeatedly, and banged loudly on the door.

Goddamn it!

Jim ran up the alley between the homes to the wooden backyard gate and let himself in.

He sighed in relief when he saw Connie sitting in the sun, her oxygen tank at her side, and her new puppy on her lap.

"Dr. McDonald! What's wrong?"

"For once, Connie, not a damned thing."

Chapter Sixty-Four

The area around the Superior Court of California, County of Alameda courthouse on Washington Street in downtown Oakland was a media circus. Onlookers and demonstrators of every stripe crowded the sidewalks. Media trucks lined the nearby streets, microwave transmitters elevated to the ready position. Kevin Martin, turned to his deputy, Patricia Davis as they drove around the corner and into the restricted parking lot. "Look at that crowd."

"We're not going to make anyone happy today, boss," she said. "Let's hope we get through this quickly."

"How do I look?" asked Kevin as they entered the elevator. He straightened his tie and checked his image on the mirrored walls.

"That new suit looks like it was made for you."

"Gotta look good for the cameras."

When the elevator door opened on the fifth floor corridor, they walked onto a sea of humanity. As they approached the entrance to Judge Horace Miller's courtroom, the police formed a protective lane allowing them to pass.

The courtroom was packed.

Henry Fischer and Brian Shands sat with their attorneys at the defense table. Henry's Brooks

Brother's suit sagged on his skinny frame. He appeared pale and withdrawn.

Brian was in fine spirits in his perfectly tailored Armani suit. He smiled and joked with Karl Hirsch, his attorney, who looked at his client with disbelief.

The worn oak flooring creaked with each step as Kevin and Patricia walked to the prosecution table. The walls were bare, and with the absence of any acoustic absorbing material, the room echoed with the crowd's noise.

"All rise," said the bailiff, as the judge entered. "The Superior Court of California for the County of Alameda is now in session, the Honorable Judge Horace Miller presiding. Be seated."

Horace Miller was seventy and nearing retirement. He had the world-weary look of someone who's seen too much of life's darker side. His reputation among those who appeared before him was smart, tough, and fair.

"I understand that the people have reached an agreement with these defendants."

"Yes, your honor," said Kevin Martin, handing the bailiff a sheet of paper for the judge.

Judge Miller read the document shaking his head and staring at the defendants and at Kevin Martin.

"I see," Judge Miller said, "that the defendants have agreed to the following: each will serve thirty years with the California Department of

Corrections and pay a fine of $25,000 for tampering, misbranding, adulteration, and dilution of prescription medication, and overbilling of same. In addition, Henry Fischer will pay $8.3 million and Brian Shands will pay $2.4 million in restitution damages. Is that correct?"

"Yes, your honor said each defense attorney."

Judge Miller stared at Kevin Martin. "And this is agreeable to the people?"

Kevin gazed at the floor. "Yes, your honor."

The judge shifted in his seat, leaned forward glaring at the defense table. "I find this plea agreement an affront to the community."

The courtroom exploded in applause.

"I'll have order in this court," shouted the judged as he gavelled the court into silence. "I'll see counsel in chambers," he said as he rose and walked through the door behind the bench.

Brian grabbed Karl Hirsch's arm. "What the hell's going on? We had a deal."

Karl pulled his arm away. "Don't touch me, you son-of-a-bitch."

Both defense attorneys, Kevin Martin and Patricia Davis followed.

The judge removed his robe, and as his bottom hit the chair behind his large antique oak desk, Karl Hirsch shouted, "We had a deal, your honor."

Judge Miller stared at the DA. "This plea bargain stinks. How can you be a part of this Kevin?"

"With all due respect, your honor," Harrison Pollard said, "the defendants in this case entered into this agreement in good faith. The court should think twice before interfering."

"Your honor," Kevin Martin said, "due to the emotion engendered in the public's mind by the acts of these defendants, the people were under extreme pressure to overcharge..."

Miller smirked. "Nobody would accuse you of over overcharging in this case."
He turned to the defense attorneys. "Are you gentlemen saying that the court will have overstepped its bounds if it rejects this plea arrangement?"

"Of course not, your honor," Harrison Pollard said, "but we have a system that works. Agreements like this are part of streamlining the process."

The judge placed a thick book on his desk. "Let me read you from the People v Grove, a case from the Michigan Supreme Court. I find their words to be directly on point: A trial judge is authorized to reject the entire plea agreement when it includes either a sentence agreement or a sentence recommendation. To determine otherwise would transfer the trial judge's sentencing discretion to the prosecutor in cases in which the plea reduction results in a substantial reduction in the potential range of sentences. A rule compelling a judge to accept a defendant's plea would reduce the judge's role to one of rubber-stamping the plea, regardless of the level of imposition on the judge's sentencing discretion. The authority to impose sentences is vested exclusively in the trial courts."

Judge Miller turned again to the District Attorney. "My court will not rubber stamp any such agreements. You chose, for your own reasons, not to charge these defendants with manslaughter, although by my reading of the facts of the case, these charges could be substantiated."

Karl Hirsch stared back at the judge. "Respectfully, your honor, those comments are totally inappropriate. We all have our roles in these matters, sir and you shouldn't usurp the DA's role in charging these defendants."

"The court, as does the District Attorney," the judge said, "has its responsibility to the people as well."

The room became suddenly silent as all eyes moved to Kevin Martin.

"Your honor, the actions of these defendants are highly offensive to the people, but we cannot bring charges that we can't sustain. At this point, since those who died had fatal cancers, the people are unable to link the actions of the defendants to anyone's premature death beyond a reasonable doubt. The moment we can do that, we'll proceed with additional indictments for murder."

"I've heard enough," Judge Miller said rising from his seat and donning his robe. "Let's return to court."

"All rise," cried the bailiff, as the judge resumed his position.

"Before I reveal my decision on this plea arrangement, I warn the spectators that I will not tolerate any disruptions. Is that clear?"

He paused for effect and then continued. "The court has flexibility in whether or not it accepts the sentence agreement, however, the court is not the district attorney, nor can it substitute its authority for that of the district attorney. The court would have heard charges of murder or manslaughter in these cases if the DA had so charged them, but since Mr. Martin, in his judgment, chose not to pursue these charges, there's nothing that the court can do. If at any point in the future, the DA feels that the people can sustain the charges of murder, he's free to file these when appropriate."

That son-of-a-bitch is crucifying me, Kevin Martin thought.

"Will the defendants rise," the judge said.

"I've been on the bench for thirty-two years. Before that I was a District Attorney and an attorney for the defense. In all that time, I cannot recall being so disgusted or angry over the actions of any criminal defendants. I've sentenced murderers, rapists, child molesters, and while all those criminals deserved what they got, you two have reached a new low in human depravity.

"For money, to materially improve your lives, you were willing to place the lives of others at risk. Whether or not you had a hand in killing them is a matter for another place and another time, but there's no question in my mind that these patients put their trust in your integrity and professionalism as pharmacists, and yes in your humanity.

"You betrayed that trust in the most egregious way. If this court had the power, I'd sentence you to life in prison for each patient you betrayed. Unfortunately, I have no such power, so I hereby sentence you both to the terms of the plea arrangement previously submitted to the court. Take the defendants into custody."

Judge Miller rose, and then headed back to his chambers.

"Court adjourned."

Four policemen escorted the newly convicted prisoners to the atrium at the rear entrance. A police van sat with its door open awaiting the newly convicted. The crowds anticipating this move, pushed their way into the gated yard, and surrounded the van.

"Make a lane for us," an officer said, as he and another officer dragged Henry and Brian toward the van.

Just inside the gate stood an elderly man wearing a charcoal gray suit and a black felt hat. His hand was in his pocket as he approached the handcuffed prisoners. Nobody noticed as the man pulled the .38 police special. It was the image of that infamous day in Dallas, when Jack Ruby, wearing a dark suit and a felt hat held the pistol in his outstretched arm and shot Lee Harvey Oswald.

Suddenly, the blast of the revolver froze the crowd as Brian Shands grasped at the gushing hole in his chest, exactly at the spot of the 'X' on the man's law enforcement paper target. Brian's face was fixed in shock — his smirk finally gone.

As Brian sagged to the floor, the police rushed the man as he raised the gun to his temple and pulled the trigger, just as the first policeman reached him and crashed into his arm.

Irving Hodges stared through his tears at the tree branches overhanging the atrium as strong hands turned him to his stomach and applied handcuffs. The small gold chain and locket remained tightly clenched in his fist.

At last, Irv thought, we have a true measure of justice.

Chapter Sixty-Five

I remained at Brier for a week, and then Jack came in one morning with a bright smile. "Time's up, Arnie. You're out of here. I want you on anticoagulants for three months so no contact sports and watch yourself shaving."

A week later, I sat with Lois after dinner. She held my hand. "How was dinner?"

"I know you worked hard, but..."

"It'll come back, I know it."

"I had this overwhelming sense of freedom when Jack sprung me from the hospital. Food's one thing, but I've lost so much more. The complications from my oversensitive nose are nothing compared to losing that talent. In all ways, the world's lifeless, drab, and boring."

Lois smiled. "Boring. That's a hell of thing to say to your wife."

I leaned over and kissed her cheek. "Bad choice of words. It's not you or the kids or really anything extrinsic to me. I'm at odds with the world, with nature. My perceptions of everything have changed. It's not only the obvious, the effects on food and drink, or even the loss of a major warning system, it's an absolute disconnect on a most primitive level with people, loved ones, and the environment."

Lois held my hand. "Jack says, be patient. It may take a few months."

I hugged Lois, placing my face into her neck. "I can't smell you. I loved the way you smell."

"I love your aroma too, babe. It'll come back. Think positive."

"The medical dictionary calls it anosmia. If you're born with it, you never can understand that world. For ordinary people losing the sense of smell is a profound disability, but for me, it's worse. An injury to a hand is painful and difficult for anybody, but it's cataclysmic for a concert pianist."

I constantly challenged my disability by opening a container of freshly ground coffee — nothing. Perfume — nothing. Spirits of ammonia, caused an involuntary reflex withdrawal, but I smelled nothing.

I returned to work and remained busy enough to keep myself distracted from obsessing about my nose.

I hugged Debbie Wallace when she returned to my office to resume her care and the ongoing Herceptin treatments. "You look terrific, Debbie, how are you feeling?"

"I'm feeling so much better. Once Dr. Goodman said that the CT scan showed no tumor, everything changed. I don't know if I'm fooling myself again, but I feel so good. I'm optimistic, and I don't care why."

"You've earned it…enjoy. We'll continue the Herceptin about every three weeks. We'll do regular checkups and periodic blood tests and x-rays, but I somehow know that you're going to do well."

"How much longer will I need the Herceptin?"

"Until we know more about this drug and this disease, we'll continue it indefinitely. I know the infusions are a constant reminder of things you'd like to forget, but it's a small price to pay."

Debbie rose and gave me a kiss on the cheek. "It's happy to see you back again, Arnie. You've had more than your fair share of health problems, too."

"Tell me about it. There's nothing good about any of it, except for the insight into my patients' experiences." I hesitated a moment. "That Horizon Drug fiasco…I feel I should apologize for that whole thing. We trusted them. We knew them as colleagues and friends and they did this…It's beyond belief."

"We're suing in civil court, but I doubt if we'll see dime one…too many plaintiffs and too little money."

"Have you heard about Irving Hodges? His wife Beatrice was my patient."

"I'd like to pin a medal on the man. I'd never vote to convict him. By the letter of the law, he's guilty, but he's paid enough. I'd call it justifiable homicide or diminished capacity or whatever it takes to keep him out of jail."

"If the DA brings this to court, he won't get a conviction. Let's hope Kevin Martin puts his plea bargaining skill to better use this time."

Two weeks from Irving's scheduled trial date, he complained of stomach and back pain. The jail transferred him to the Highland County Hospital for evaluation. Like most serious diseases, the diagnosis came quickly. Irv had terminal pancreatic cancer.

As in the past, I marveled at the association between depression and fatal diseases in surviving spouses.

I entered the jail ward to visit with Irv. His broad smile and bright gray eyes greeted me as he lay in bed. He groaned with pain as he tried to sit up to shake my hand.

"Thanks for coming, Dr. Roth. Sorry to have to entertain you in these surroundings."

"It's wonderful to see you too, Irv. I wish it were under different circumstances."

"I've lived a long time, Doc. Bea's gone, and I did what had to be done."

I hadn't seen Irv so relaxed, so confident, or so at ease with himself and with the world since their last visit before Beatrice first became ill.

"I feel like I need to say something," I paused. "Something about that whole disgusting matter with Horizon Drugs, Henry Fischer, and Brian Shands."

"What can I say, Doc? You can't live as long as I have and not know that evil exists in this world.

Thank God, Bea and I had so many rich, rewarding, and satisfying years together. In retrospect, I think I let Brian off too easily. I'd have visited him in jail purely for the enjoyment of watching him suffer, but that arrogant bastard thought that somehow he'd beat the rap. I couldn't allow myself that possibility. Henry Fischer, for as long as he lives, and I'm hoping it will be a long time, will pay, at least in part, for what he did."

"I can't get over the feeling that somehow we should have known what they were doing. If we'd discovered it earlier, we could have spared lives and saved so many from the misery of their diseases and its treatments."

"You couldn't have known, Doc. Nobody could have known. We can't live in this world without placing trust in people and institutions. We trust that the pilot won't be drunk in the cockpit, that the policeman or the fireman won't leave town when we need them, that our clergymen won't break their faith with us, and that our health care providers want us to get well, whatever it takes."

As he paused, his eyes filled with tears. "That's the way Beatrice and I felt about you, Arnie. Our faith had never been better placed."

I tried to respond, but couldn't speak. Finally, I grasped Arthur's hand. "Doctors have many patients. We're indifferent to some, have a real antipathy to a few, and have real love and affection for the special ones. I'll never forget you and Beatrice and the gift you gave to me by allowing me to be your physician."

Thank God it was Friday, I thought, after one of our busiest weeks in the office. We were done, and I was off call for the weekend. After we finished for the day, Beverley sat before my desk with her legs up on the other chair.

"We love having you back, Arnie."

"It's great to be back, Bev."

"You're more like your old self, and yet you're not. Are you okay?"

"I'm not where I want to be, but I'm getting there. How's Tino?"

"He's doing well. His depositions provided the evidence the DA needed for the case against Horizon Drugs, and they cleared him of any wrongdoing. He's going to UC Berkeley next semester. I couldn't be more proud of him."

"You were right about Tino, Bev. All he needed was a chance."

"Like the one you gave me, Arnie. I'll never forget it. I may not have been a wetback, but I was surely wet behind the ears when you gave me this job."

"Besides marrying Lois, hiring you is the smartest thing I ever did, and next to Lois, our pairing is the longest and most successful relationship I've ever had with a woman."

"Thanks, Arnie, but that's only because we're not married. If we were, I would have killed you long ago." She hesitated a moment, and then, like a question you ask yourself, she said, "What is this all about? What does it mean?"

"You're getting philosophical in your old age, Bev. To paraphrase Van Gogh, we are adventurers not by choice, but by fate. Life keeps lying to us, giving us the illusion of control, laughing as it foils our careful planning. In the end, mastering our fate may be more important than controlling it."

Epilogue

Two months later, my nose began its comeback. Like throwing the light switch on a fifteen-watt bulb, I went to bed in the shadows and awaken in dawn's dim light. The intense red LEDs showed 6:23 a.m. As Lois's head rested on my shoulder in semiconsciousness, I awaited the buzzing of our alarm. Suddenly, they were here — the first few molecules of coffee.

I sat up in bed, rudely casting Lois' head off my shoulder. "Thanks a lot buddy," she said. "I'll remember that."

"Lois," I said, "Coffee...I smell coffee."

The aroma I recognized was like the taste of a coffee candy, coffee flavor for sure, but nothing like full-bodied Cappuccino or the aroma of freshly ground beans.

Every evening, Lois set the automatic coffee maker to go on minutes before we were due to rise. Before my loss of smell, Lois said that it was the coffee aroma that helped drag her out of bed each morning. Since I could smell nothing, she'd skipped her usual comments about the coffee aroma each morning, although, in the corner of my eye, I had caught her several times, as she moved her nose surreptitiously through an arc of the morning's ambiance.

"Incredible," she said. "I'm so happy for you."

Each morning my nose was better than the day before.

"I'm like a kid in the candy shop," I said to Lois. "Viscerally, it's like regaining lost sight or hearing."

"You're not going to drive us or you crazy again, are you?"

"Only, good crazy."

Gradually, I approached the levels of sensitivity that I had before my breakdown.

"My nose is back in full form, Lois. I'm worried about being overwhelmed again, but somehow I've learned to compartmentalize it to protect my sanity — the best of all worlds, I hope."

"I can't wait to tell Jack and Beth."

"Except for them, let's keep this to ourselves, Lois. There's too much downside to people knowing about my talent. We've seen it before in their reactions. I won't go public, but if they promise me anonymity, I'll spend time with the nose people in Utah."

Subtly, I employed my powerful proboscis in caring for patients. I took special care to attribute my diagnostic successes to something other than my olfactory apparatus. Often this was a stretch. At these times, Jack looked at me with a knowing smile, but said nothing. I didn't know how long I could keep up the charade.

I volunteered twice a month at the local free clinic. Treating sexually transmitted diseases, body lice, and prescribing contraceptives wasn't all that interesting, but it was a good cause, they needed physicians, and I felt obliged to contribute.

I finished with my thirteenth patient of the evening. I needed a box of gloves for the treatment room, so I waited outside the combined examining and storeroom. A thin teenage girl with multiple tattoos and piercing left the room with her mother. I recognized them immediately, Ellen Kelley and her daughter Brenda, my patients. The older woman carried a sample packet of birth control pills and a prescription.

"Ellen, Brenda," I said, "how are you guys doing? It surprises me to see you here."

Ellen reddened as she approached me saying, "I…we were embarrassed…"

"Please, Ellen, don't be. I've seen and heard it all. I prescribe contraception all the time and in circumstances like this, it's better for all of us if I know what's going on."

"I'm sorry," she said, looking at her feet.

"Don't be. I'm here to help, not to judge. Come see me when you're comfortable or when you need a refill."

"I will," she said taking Brenda's hand as they cued up at the end of the long line in front of the pharmacy window.

When I entered the examining room that Ellen had just left, among the multitude of aromas, people, perfumes, soaps, disinfectants, deodorants, etc., one hit me immediately. It was the now unmistakable tangy, musty slightly repellent aroma of breast cancer.

I looked down the hallway at Ellen and Brenda still lined up at the pharmacy, and I knew.

I'm not getting into this again, I thought. Nobody knows. I'd like to keep it that way—yet...

I grabbed a Post-It from the office desk and printed the note.

I walked into the queue before the pharmacy window, jostling those in line. "Excuse me, please." When I reached the window, I said, "Is Dr. Cass inside?"

"No," the pharmacy tech replied. "He just left."

As I returned through the line, I managed to stick the Post-It onto the side of Ellen's purse.

I watched at a distance from my office doorway. When they arrived at the window, Ellen placed her bag on the counter and noticed the yellow Post-It. She read it impassively at first, and then her eyes widened. She scanned the room, drew her hand to her face, and then folded the note into her handbag. I watched in fear that what I had done wasn't enough. I stepped back into the office. I couldn't let this go. Suddenly, there was a soft tap on the door.

"Come in."

Ellen entered and walked back toward me. "Can I see you in the office tomorrow, Dr. Roth? I need you to examine my breast. I think something's wrong."

How long could I continue this way? I didn't know. Since fate gave me this fantastic talent with so much potential to help my patients, putting it aside wasn't an option, but neither was my exposure in the tabloids or in the *Guinness Book of World Records*. I sensed that the unseen molecules of my world would write my future, a script that the critics would review with complimentary olfactory adjectives.

"Arnie," Lois said, "can you take Archie to the office with you today? The pest control people are coming in to spray the house."

"Sure, no problem. He'll be my company during the commute."

The Golden Retriever wagged his tail, sniffed at the air vents and when I opened the window, he plunged his nose into the unseen paradise of aromas. The office staff greeted him like a long lost relative. Afterward, I placed him in the small lounge with a bowl of water and a few of his favorite toys.

At 11:30, I approached the examining room nearest the lounge. Archie stood and wagged his tail for me. "A few minutes boy, then we'll go for a walk."

When I opened the examining room door, the rancid stench hit me. I shook my head, and then turned to Archie. "Why don't you see this patient, boy?"

Printed in Great Britain
by Amazon.co.uk, Ltd.,
Marston Gate.